Fakes, Fraud and Deception

an FFSG novel

Bill Dughaille

Contents

The Week

Tuesday: Deep in the doghouse

Someone had once commented, with the sudden clarity of insight that results from a fine repast, little thinking, a liberal libation of the fruits of Bacchus, and an inspiring shaft of understanding light, almost Damascene-like in its brightness, that the town of Wellbury was, without doubt, the very last refuge of the lunch hour.

Wise heads had nodded slowly, silently and sagely at this remarkable and powerful insight into the cultural and social identity of the small and happy – if not to say, self-satisfied – town.

Though with Wellburians you could never be sure whether they were nodding assent or just nodding off.

The comment had been made in response to an article in the local Herald comparing Wellburian luncheon habits vis-à-vis those of London, where apparently lunch had almost entirely disappeared as an event, and existed only in ancient and scarcely believable mythology of the "when I was a lad" tales of old people, old people who had long gone ga-ga and had now taken up residence in worlds of their own imaginations. According to the report – and the Wellbury Herald naturally never lied nor exaggerated – those poor London folk were reduced to the extent where most, if not all, took lunch as a manufactured sandwich while still slaving over their computer keyboards. If they had time for the sandwich in the first place.

Imagine! A single, solitary sandwich! And no doubt made with all those funny, foreign breads with birdseed in them.

Poor things. Poor, poor, little things.

The good citizens of Wellbury had taken the "last refuge" comment as a compliment. It was a town where independent shops could still display a sign "Closed for lunch" almost as a boast.

Though there was the occasional new arrival who had to be inducted into the concept of this way of life. Jim Pettigrew, a fine and respected widower from somewhere defined loosely as "up North", who had retired in order to follow his life-long ambition to run a transport caff, had to be taken aside to have a minor point explained to him, namely that transport caffs and other enterprises catering to the peckish were not expected, themselves, to close for the luncheon hour.

"Hour", needless to say, being an extremely flexible concept rather than an accurate measure of the passing of time.

Above all, Wellburians' reaction to the idea, returning to the subject of Londoners' oppression in the culinary stakes, was that people who came out with remarks such as "lunch is for wimps", were, to put it politely – and politeness was probably the most prized of attributes for Wellburians – a bunch of total and utter prats. It was one of the few things Wellburians could agree about. Even their prejudices were open to dispute.

'Typical Frog,' Desk Sergeant Eric Johns said in the police canteen, polishing off a meal of roast potatoes, roast beef, gravy and Yorkshire pud, 'sleazy as they come. Can't trust them further than you can spit the Eiffel Tower.'

'I don't think he's sleazy,' Detective Constable Gertie Gregson said, ploughing through her own lunch of chips, eggs, sausages and peas in order to get to the waiting apple-pie and steaming custard next to the main course. 'I think he's rather sexy, really. In a cute sort of a way.'

'Sexy? Sexy?' queried an aghast Eric Johns at this suggestion of heresy. 'You must be joking. Back me up on this one, Frank. There's no such thing as a good Frog. By definition. They're arrogant, unreliable, double-dealing, back-stabbing, greasy little .... Frogs!'

A tired Detective Sergeant Frank Summers finished off a tub of yoghurt with little enthusiasm, scraping mindlessly at the bottom with his spoon as if it were something he had to do or otherwise fall asleep. A measure of his tiredness was that he was consuming lunch as a solitary yoghurt, braving the wrath of Agnetha in the canteen kitchen, who would take deep and grievous offence at this slight, implied or otherwise, of her cooking. Fortunately for him she was currently absorbed by the work of producing the delicacies – or, considering the types of luncheon nourishment which she deemed necessary to sustain what she thought of as her young girls and boys through the day, solidities – which made the canteen's productions a focal point of any visit to Wellbury police station for those fortunate enough to have an excuse to be there.

They were so good that some people even tried to get arrested in time for the lunch hour.

'Brigitte Bardot is French,' Frank noted in response to Eric Johns' appeal for support. 'And this yoghurt is apparently original Greek yoghurt but made in Swindon, according to this label.'

'Who's Brigitte Bardot?' asked Gertie with mild interest, her concentration focused on a chip that was attempting to make good an escape westwards away from a pool of tomato sauce.

'She used to be a French film goddess,' Frank said, trying not to yawn. 'Back in the Sixties or Seventies, if I remember correctly. Eric probably had her poster on his wall as a teenager. I think she's an animal rights campaigner these days.'

'Oh, Brigitte Bardot, oh la-la,' Eric sighed, suddenly lost in memory lane, so much so that an almost unimaginable event took place: his fork slowed temporarily on its pre-ordained and unstoppable track to his impatiently waiting mouth. 'Now you're talking! You know, these so-called actresses these days, they couldn't hold a candle to her. Ah, yes, she had sex appeal, real sex appeal. These modern things are just skinny clothes-horses.' He finished the operation of transferring food to his mouth, and chewed while pausing to reflect on the contradiction between his earlier statement of the undesirability of the French in general with his views on Ms Bardot in particular. 'Ah, well, French women, that's different of course,' he pointed out, swallowing. 'They've got style. Panache. Va-va-voom.'

'And English women don't?' asked Gertie aggressively. 'I'll bet you haven't told your wife that. She'd give you va-va-voom. I certainly would. I'd give you va-va-voom right up your –'

'What you have to remember,' Frank interrupted diplomatically, pulling a cup of coffee towards him, 'is that Guillaume Matisse, as he calls himself, is a con man of the highest order. People will always find him attractive. He wouldn't be any good at his job if that weren't the case.'

Guillaume Matisse – probably not his real name, nor the many others he had apparently used – was at that moment sitting safely in a cell in the imposing Victorian edifice that was Wellbury police station, the same building that housed the canteen in which the three sat currently appeasing the

4

gods of the appetite glands. Frank had been the one who had effected the arrest that had seen M Matisse take up involuntary residence within the police station. It had been purely by chance that Frank had recognised him from an Interpol photograph on a wanted poster that he had borrowed from Eric Johns' desk in reception, the back and front of which, depending on which surface was uppermost at the time, he had needed to use to write down his shopping list.

Frank Summers' shopping habits could be termed eclectic – by Frank Summers, at any rate – though the correct word was more likely to be "erratic". He invariably forgot what he needed to stock up on, often resulting in such situations as having three bottles of tomato sauce in the cupboard with nothing to pour the contents over. At times he would have a pasta collection to be proud of, as long as you did not check the use-by dates. He could have ten different types of breakfast cereal, without the milk to pour over them. And the really stupid thing, as he acknowledged to himself, was that he hardly ever ate breakfast cereal.

And if he ever had, he had now definitely given up the stuff for good, with reason.

But he knew, deep down, that he was normally – often – not unusually – could be – if he concentrated properly – pretty efficient when he wanted to be. He had thus decided to discipline himself to keep a list of requirements, noting each down as they came to mind. This resolution was immediately mediated by his forgetting the rather basic requirement of some material to keep the list on, such as a piece of paper or a portable computer, and it was the jogging of his memory that had prompted him, as he passed through the station reception, to purloin the Interpol poster from Eric Johns' desk, which would have unforeseen consequences for all of them.

From the details on the poster several and various police forces wished to interview M Matisse about a number of frauds involving rich art collectors and his claim to be the grandson of the famous painter. The French Sûreté, the Italian Carabinieri and even Scotland Yard, to name a few, had voiced a wish to have a quiet chat with M Matisse, or, perhaps, in the case of the first two, quite a voluble one. Only slightly behind them were the Spanish, the Dutch, the Belgians, the Norwegians and, strangely, the Nigerians. No doubt, as soon as they found out, the Americans would be clamouring to be on the list as well, if only to see their name there.

And they'd want to be at the top, no doubt, as usual.

It was just M Matisse's bad and Frank's good luck that they had been simultaneously in the bakery section of the supermarket at the time that Frank had taken out his shopping list and spotted the remarkable similarity between the photograph in his hand and the man pondering on the choice of breads, cakes and other assorted delicacies available in front of him. The similarity was remarkable in its preciseness; no grey or fuzzy image this, not taken with a telephoto lens on a dark night, nor a picture of someone taken several years previously from a great distance in the rain, it could have been a professional photograph taken only minutes beforehand. And what really stood out were the raucous pink tie and pink carnation the little man was wearing. It was an affront to Frank Summers' first rule of fashion: if anyone was going to wear a radioactive tie with matching carnation it should be him. Acting on this indisputable evidence, without a thought for his own safety nor the arduous paperwork this could generate, Frank had promptly made an arrest.

Well, perhaps promptly wasn't entirely accurate, not if one were going to be pedantic.

Personally Frank was becoming increasingly unsure of how much good luck it had been for his own self, for several reasons, none of which he wished to linger over. Firstly he was supposed to be off duty the previous day, the Monday, when it had happened. He had taken night duty over the weekend to avoid Inspector Frieda Garold who had yet to forgive him for inviting her new secretary, Tricia Leigh, over to his flat for a few drinks a week or so ago. He had issued the invitation to the young Tricia only because it had been his birthday and he fancied some company, everyone else being apparently unavailable. He had been ordered to stay housebound because of a motorcycling accident, which order he had obeyed apart from a necessary trip to the police station in the afternoon. Unbeknownst to him, while he was on his visit to the station Frieda, Gertie and his soi-disant girlfriend Doctor Susan Pleadle had arranged a surprise birthday party at his flat, and did not appreciate the appearance of the young Tricia scattering declarations of her affection for him. That, from what he could glean from their less than favourable reaction, was somehow supposed to be reserved for them.

He just wished someone could have mentioned the fact beforehand.

His life at the moment, it seemed, was constrained by Frieda's, Gertie's and Susan's opprobrium. He felt like a dead duck in a gilded cage.

Added to that was not only the tiredness induced by night duty over the weekend, but tiredness due to some rather disturbing dreams he had been having recently, the type you don't mention to anyone, not even your nearest and dearest, who would, should you do so, hurriedly start browsing the Yellow Pages for the name of a good psychoanalyst. Quite possibly they would start at the straitjackets section, if there was one.

On top of all that was the fact that, while the Chief Constable and the male officers had congratulated him on his fine arrest of M Matisse, the female officers, including Gertie, felt sorry for the smiling, apologetic, silver-haired and moustached, five-foot-two little rogue with the charming French accent and an air of almost winsome absentmindedness. After all, defrauding wealthy art collectors who could afford it and should have known better wasn't that big a crime, was it?

And he was sweet, wasn't he? Cute, really. Charming. Charmant. French men, aaahhh ...

Even he himself, Frank, had to admit, would not have bothered had he known what crimes M Matisse stood accused of. Not having wasted valuable time in minor details such as reading the information on the wanted poster – or shopping list, as he had thought of it – he had presumed the man was a dangerous international criminal, a drug dealer or murderer, possibly even a wanted war criminal, someone whose incarceration could only increase the safety of innocent civilians and citizens going about their daily lives. An arts con man whose primary victims were extremely wealthy – and consequently unlikely to be naive and innocent – was not worth giving up a fresh-baked baguette for, especially not on a day off.

And – to add to all the other "ands" and "on-top-ofs" and "by-the-ways" which were combining to make his current existence less than salubrious – the incident had meant that he had forgotten to do his shopping, so the Monday evening meal had been a choice between either a take-away or baked beans on toast, except that he had run out of both bread and baked beans, rendering the choice somewhat simple, if not to say entirely academic. In the end it had been a curry, not one he had enjoyed to any great extent, but one that had liked him so much it had responded to this unrequited love by staying with him, still lingering at lunchtime, reminding him of its presence and prompting his decision to stick to good English food, like the wholesome Greek yoghurt made in Swindon.

That tasted bloody awful as well. His taste buds yearned for Agnetha's creations. His stomach responded, "just you dare, sunshine, I haven't forgiven you for last night yet".

'Go to the cinema often, do you, Sarge?' Gertie asked Eric Johns casually, interrupting Frank's mental internal rumblings.

'Not these days, love,' Eric Johns replied as he wiped the last spot of gravy from his plate with a slice of bread. 'They don't make movies the way they used to. Not like the blockbusters we used to have. In my day you had proper screens, not these titchy little things they have these days. And cinemas that could seat thousands. These days it's all computerised, you can't believe any of it. Actors just don't know how to act anymore, they rely on special effects and such rubbish.'

'I wish I could have seen that,' Gertie said, giving what Frank recognised as a mock sigh. 'It must be so nice to be old enough to remember the good old days.'

Frank hid a wry smile. Eric Johns looked somewhat discombobulated. He had a feeling that he had been insulted, but wasn't quite sure how.

'Anyway, Matisse. He's a typical Frog, can't trust them,' he concluded, deciding that what he didn't understand was best ignored in favour of a prejudice he did. 'Still, we've always beaten the French. Trafalgar, Waterloo, all the rest.'

'Ten-sixty-six,' Frank noted.

'Precisely,' said Sergeant Eric Johns with a mild burp. 'Stuffed them, didn't we? Never could play football, the Frogs.'

Frank was sitting at his desk that afternoon trying not to doze off, or, more accurately, trying to disguise the fact that he was dozing off, when Eric Johns appeared in the doorway, a clipboard in his hands, a weary look on his face.

'The Frog wants to see you,' Eric said with a hint of distaste.

Frank looked at him through bleary eyes, running this statement through his mind. Rather than attempt any kind of work – which at this stage of the afternoon and in his condition would have been counter-productive, if not downright destructive – he had been reviewing the dreams he had been having recently. They were the sort where you found yourself running through Kowloon central market wearing sandals on your feet and full uniform elsewhere – including helmet – carrying a parakeet in a cage in one hand and trying to push a wheelbarrow with the other, while the parakeet screeched at you "Where's ye boots, laddie, where's ye boots?". And all the time your subconscious was telling you that this is ridiculous, you wouldn't recognise Kowloon central market – if there was one – if someone showed you a picture of it with the words "Kowloon Central Market" three inches high, never mind the fact that you probably couldn't tell the difference between a parakeet and a parrot, if parakeets could speak in the first place.

And what was that stupid wheelbarrow all about?

Those dreams were tiring and silly. His recent ones were worse because the same dream had occurred three days running, the sort of thing that would prompt any normal person to wonder if someone wasn't trying to send them a message. In it a young girl of about ten wearing a tutu and ballet shoes was dancing in front of him, a river below her, excitedly saying "Look, Daddy! I can dance on water! Look, Daddy, I can dance on water! Look, Daddy, look!"

Now he knew he did not have a daughter, nor any child at all, of that he was certain.

Pretty certain.

So why was this child calling him Daddy? And why did she think she could dance on water? And what was he supposed to do? Was she in danger? Was she actually talking to someone else behind him? And why did the dream re-occur?

He noticed Eric Johns waiting for a reaction to his earlier statement. He shrugged the thoughts of dreams away. A result of bad eating habits and excessive brain activity, probably related to the earth's magnetic field and falling asleep during the day while watching B-movies on television. Something like that. There were closer, more real problems to worry about.

'Not my case, Eric, you know that,' he said. 'Tell the Inspector, she's looking after it.'

By being off duty at the time Frank had managed to avoid taking responsibility for the case. Frieda, scenting a high profile arrest which could do her career no harm, had eagerly taken it on. Frank's natural aversion to getting involved with anything which might involve expending energy on something in which he had no interest in was combined with a growing irritation with Frieda which he had allowed, against his normal approach to life, to grow into an itch that just had to be scratched, and often.

Such as now.

So what if he had asked Tricia around for a few drinks? His social life was not Frieda's concern.

Anyway, he had not intended it as some sort of prelude to seduction. He just wanted company, and he liked the young Tricia.

And even if it had been the prelude to seduction, which it wasn't, that was none of Frieda's business, even if he were Frieda's Sergeant and Tricia were her secretary.

Frieda was being totally unreasonable. Under the circumstances. Almost as if she had some sort of stake in his social life. Anyone would think she was his mother. Or wife. Or something.

They were just colleagues, right?

Right?

That's okay, then.

Eric's weary look had a touch of wariness added as he watched Frank cogitating on what he knew not of, but hoped was not what he suspected. He had not missed Frank's use of "the Inspector" rather than one of Frieda's nicknames, "Frigid" or the recently more often used "Fabulous". The entire station was aware of a looming confrontation between the two and when something finally ignited the explosion there would be a rush for the doors with the less swift being trampled without mercy. There were some occasions when you just couldn't stop to help others. Not even the band on the Titanic would have carried on playing for this one. Or, if they had, it would have been very quickly and while they were running as fast as they could in the general direction of anywhere else.

'I think he wants to speak to you personally, Frank,' Eric said with an unusual hint of delicacy. 'I don't think it's official – can't be, anyway, not without his lawyer.'

'Well, okay, just for a few minutes then,' grumbled Frank, standing up and stretching, covering a yawn. 'Just so long as he doesn't say anything I might have to repeat to Wonderwoman.'

'Cheers, Frank,' Eric said in relief. 'I'd better get on with this stocktake. Don't let Matisse run away, he's probably listed in here somewhere.'

Wellbury police station was having its annual stocktake, though "annual" could have been construed a misnomer, as it had quite happily missed the previous fourteen years. On discovering this Frieda had taken on the duty of organising a thorough job. It hadn't endeared her to any of the others in the station. Wandering around with clipboards counting chairs and desks was not a popular pastime.

'Slimy French Frog, one, occupation of cell for the purposes of,' Eric continued his theme, grimacing.

'Could be worse, Eric,' Frank said cheerfully. 'Remember the paperclips.'

Some years before – a story often recounted at such times by the older hands – an ambitious but misguided Detective Sergeant had been given the job of organising the annual

13

stocktake. He had also been thorough, though not in a way Frieda might have approved of. On his own initiative he had included in his list of things to count, and account for, such items as paperclips. When, shortly afterwards, this overly industrious officer had been posted to some other unsuspecting station, the collection envelope for his farewell gift was found to contain three one-pence pieces and two hundred and fifty two paperclips.

They had been carefully counted.

Eric Johns rolled his eyes at the memory.

'At least things couldn't get any worse than that,' he said.

'Oh, I don't know,' Frank replied, an evil grin on his tired face. 'I reckon I could come up with something special if I was put in charge of the stocktake. I rather fancy the idea.'

Eric Johns looked at him.

'You would, too, wouldn't you, you sod.'

Eric Johns had been on the receiving end of Frank's sense of humour a few times, the evil side of that sense of humour. At the time he had accepted that it was deservedly so, an understandable act of revenge, however unpleasant it had been. Since then he had learnt to respect Frank Summers, but in his current mood Frank reminded him of the adage of the Devil finding work for idle hands. If that keen brain was not occupied with honest police work it would soon find dishonest mischief to keep it amused.

'Cheer up, Eric, Frigid is hardly likely to give me a chance like that,' Frank assured him. 'My next assignment will probably be lollipop man at the local primary school.'

'Makes me feel sorry for the kiddies,' Eric commented before leaving.

Frank thought about that, smiling as he wandered down towards the cells and a word with M Matisse. Lollipop man. It did suggest a few ways of making the lives of the good, honest citizens of Wellbury a little more interesting. At least the kiddies would have a good laugh.

Down in the cells his mood was further lightened by the sight of a short Guillaume Matisse standing quietly next to the thin plastic mattress on top of a bunk with constituted his bed, a sad, appealing smile on his face, his bright tie neatly in place, his pink carnation in a mug of water which he must have conned some helpful constable into supplying. It was the apologetic smile of someone Frank would never have trusted in a thousand years.

Like, yes, trust, not until snowflakes took up house-hunting in hell.

'You wished to speak to me, M Matisse?' he asked, keeping a distance and checking that his wallet was safe.

'Yes, Sergeant Summers,' Matisse said with a soft, slightly rumbling French accent, 'I wished to convey my apologies for any injury I may have unintentionally caused you. I did not realise at the time that you were a police officer. I would have proffered apologies earlier, but I fully expected to be interviewed by you, at which time I could have utilised the opportunity to declare my sincere regret. I now understand, however, that you will not be doing so.'

'No, M Matisse, not my case. You have the dubious pleasure of Inspector Garold to look forward to. As far as injuries go, nothing permanent. But I would point out that I did identify myself as a police officer.'

Guillaume Matisse sighed deeply and long, and shrugged

airily. It was a performance that would have revived Eric Johns' memories of the good old days.

'Unfortunately I suffer a little from the deafness,' Matisse said. 'I was concerned you might be an assassin sent by my political enemies.'

Frank had no doubt that M Matisse's deafness was a handy and occasional event.

'Political enemies?' he asked out of a curiosity he knew he should not indulge in. Say thank-you, goodbye, au revoir, and get out before he became involved. But this little fraudster? Political enemies? Frank could not resist a desire to hear how the man translated his victims into "political enemies". The logical sleight of hand that humans use to conjure up justifications for their actions and perception of reality had long had a fascination for him. While he had no time for the extremes of the practice – political sophistry and wilful ignorance – he could not resist the attraction of other forms, ranging from the need to make sense of an obviously insensible world to M Matisse's simple requirement – to lie his way out of a police cell.

'Ah, mais non, mais oui, but this is all political, do you not see?' Matisse exclaimed, throwing up his hands exaggeratedly. 'Allow me to explain, I beg of you. Over the years I have acquired a few paintings from time to time, nothing of much value, mainly copies or fakes, but all I can afford. Then some wealthy personage decides he wishes to purchase one or two, perhaps three, maybe four, he believes they are the real thing, as you say. I attempt to dissuade him, I point out that these are probably not genuine, no, more than that, they are undoubtedly by some lesser painter, fakes even. I plead with him, beg him to reconsider, I go, almost, on my knees, but he will not have it. In the end I have to give in, these are powerful men with persuasive arguments. Then, once the transaction I have so bitterly fought against is concluded, he discovers that what I have said is true. He wishes his money back, and he wishes the revenge. Such people are more angry when they find themselves in the wrongs and have already been told they are in the wrongs. And wealthy peoples have high political friends in political high places. I am forced to flee for my life, even though I am innocent, entirely innocent. It is, how you say, an outrage?'

Frank smiled. It was one of the oldest cons in the book and one of the most difficult, but still played well to the greed of the acquisitive and the gullible. Let the mark know that you own something which you believe is worthless, but at the same time subtly get them to believe that object is actually priceless. The mark will chase himself in circles pretending to agree with you that it's worthless, while doing his or her utmost to obtain whatever object it was, the price going up with each reluctant and apologetic refusal.

And the conman could shrug his shoulders afterwards and say "Well, what did I tell you?", and walk away counting the banknotes. A jury would be killing themselves laughing as they acquitted the garrulous little Frenchman.

Unless, of course, his target was wealthy and well connected and could call upon both official and unofficial sources to recover their bruised pride. In which case it was time to relocate to somewhere quieter. Somewhere like Wellbury. Unfortunately for Matisse Wellbury was not such a sleepy old provincial town as he had thought.

'So what was the latest non-genuine treasure that you reluctantly parted with?' Frank asked, intrigued against his better judgement.

'Ah! That is just it! I have not sold it, and it is not even a copy or a fake! Not even a copy of a fake, or a fake of a copy, or even a fake of a fake!'

Frank tried to re-arrange the words into some semblance of English and logic, but failed. He tried a mental translation with the little French he knew, but that just made it worse.

'I don't understand,' he said finally.

Matisse took a deep and dramatic breath before continuing.

'You have heard of Degas, of course, Sergeant Summers? Quite one of the best of the modern painters, a man whose work is sadly undervalued in these godless times of sham and duplicity, where a cow cut in half is considered art, or a bed or a shed, or a bed in a shed or a shed in a bed. Très imbécile! Très, très imbécile!'

'I've heard of him,' Frank admitted, ignoring the outburst, although he agreed with the sentiments. To his mind Matisse was a con man. Had he thought that Frank considered unmade beds the cutting edge of art he would have praised them to the skies. Shortly thereafter trying to sell him one, with his own personalised design of dirty laundry.

Plus the offer of discounted dry-cleaning of said linen ware, no doubt.

'Matisse painted a work entitled Red Studio,' the Frenchman continued excitedly, 'said to be based on Degas' La Coiffure, a famous and extremely valuable work of art. I was browsing some stalls in your Camden Lock in London when I came across a work almost exactly a copy of Matisse's Red Studio, entitled The Blue Studio – where Matisse had used red this painting had blue. It had the signature of Matisse. Obviously a student prank or joke, but very well done, yes, extremely well done, I might say. I purchased it, not to sell, but on a whim. Unfortunately this news spread, and some collectors came to believe that it really is a missing work of Matisse, looted by the Germans during World War Two, and only recently rediscovered. They think that, since my name happens to be Matisse, I am somehow related to the great Matisse, and this is how I come to own this painting. Ma foi! Where is the logic in that? It is madness! There is not a trace of such a work anywhere, no history, no written records, yet there are people out there willing to pay a great deal of money to get their hands on it. Or prepared to use other methods.'

Interesting, thought Frank. He starts off with Degas, but the story really concerns Matisse. An enthusiast giving too many details, or a con artist muddying pools by swamping the target with too much information?

'And you thought I was one of them?' he asked, playing the game. 'One of those prepared to use other methods? That's why you tried to make a run for it?'

Matisse nodded and hung his head in shame.

'This is it precisely, Sergeant Summers. I can only beg your forgiveness, humbly beg your forgiveness.'

'Nothing to do with the fact that you're wanted by the police forces of about fourteen different countries?'

'Que? Par blieu, c'est impossible! Why should this be? I have committed no crime. You make the mistake, Sergeant Summers, or someone 'ere has made the mistake. They search for a different man, perhaps.' He seemed to think about this. 'Yes, that is what it is, there can be no doubt. It is the case of the mistaken identity, n'est ce pas?'

Frank concealed a smile. "Mistaken" had come out as "misteeken". Give him a pork-pie hat and raincoat and Matisse could have left the cells posing as Inspector Clouseau. With his patter he could well end up running the entire station. Something of that ilk was decidedly possible in Wellbury. Wellburians would bring chairs out into the streets to sit and enjoy the fun.

'The Interpol poster had your photograph on it,' he pointed out reasonably. Matisse smiled sadly.

'Another mistake, no doubt. Polices forces and posters makers are not infallible, Sergeant, n'est ce pas? The posters maker, he gets the photographs, he drops the box, perhaps, something gets, how you say, mixed up? Soon, you will speak to Scotland Yard, and the mistake will be uncovered, non?'

Frank resisted the urge to reply "non" in disagreement.

'And then I make it up to you, yes, Sergeant Summers? I buy for you the dinner, non? As apology for my mistake. None of the hard feelings, as you English say. A true English dinner with lots of the rosbif and gravy, non?'

'No need, M Matisse, these things happen,' Frank said, deciding that he had heard enough. It was time to be elsewhere. 'I presume you're being properly looked after?' he added out of politeness.

'Indeed, Sergeant, very well, apart from not being allowed to smoke. As a Frenchman I am addicted to the Gaulloise, of course. I don't suppose ... ?'

'I'll see what I can do,' Frank promised.

He left with a smile. There was no way Matisse was a smoker, that was obvious from the lack of nicotine stains. He looked more like someone who would turn green at a puff from a

Gaulloise. It was all part of the illusion. All Matisse lacked was a beret and strings of onions hanging around his shoulders to complete the image.

Stereotypes, he thought shaking his head in sad acceptance as he walked back to his office, stereotypes of the other. Hardly a week went by without a story in the media about someone who had been conned by another pretending to be a wealthy Arab sheik, Russian oil baron, American billionaire, Peruvian midget sitting on a goldmine. The good people of Hartlepool, it was said, had once hanged a shipwrecked monkey in the days when Britain had been faced with the threat of invasion by Napoleon and his triumphant armies. The Hartlepudlians had believed it to be a Frenchman, since they had never seen a Frenchman before, nor, presumably, a monkey. These days people might be able to tell the difference between a man and a monkey, but that was about as far as it went. Newspaper journalists regularly posed as rich foreigners and supposedly sensible people fell for it almost every time.

He decided he would see if he could get Eric Johns to allow him to pass a pack of Gaulloise to Matisse, maybe even a carton. Matisse would be forced to keep up the pretence and physically smoke them. In the confined cell, with little outlet for the smoke, it would be nauseating. And Matisse's lawyer could hardly object to them allowing Matisse to enjoy his "addiction".

On second thoughts he decided against it. Matisse was a first-class con man and much as Frank would have liked a spot of mental jousting with him, giving him cigarettes to smoke in his cell would be against regulations. Apart from that it wasn't his case, and he was damned if he was going to get involved. Frieda could handle this one herself.

Besides which, he could smell trouble coming. Something was wrong, something didn't fit. Like an old sailor sniffing the air, he could sense a storm brewing. He didn't know where it would come from, but he fully intended to be somewhere else when it arrived. He wasn't going to get involved in this one.

'You're going to tell me that Inspector Garold has been called away on urgent business and no longer wishes to see me?' Frank enquired of Frieda's young secretary, Tricia, that afternoon, having been ordered to present himself at Frieda's eyrie at five o'clock precisely. 'I can go home and have a relaxing evening then. I'll just toddle off, shall I?'

'I'm afraid not, Frank,' Tricia said, smiling.

When he had first met her she had appeared as a plain, if not dull, young girl with drab blonde hair and overly thick glasses, her only outstanding features being enthusiasm and a twinkling cheekiness in her eyes. Since starting to work for Frieda she had totally transformed her appearance. She had adopted much of Frieda's power-dressing approach, though where Frieda, with raven hair, preferred navy-blue, Tricia, whose hair had been somehow metamorphosed into a golden halo, went more for red. Despite this, her desk was almost ringed with soft, furry, cuddly toys, a suggestion that the little girl in her was not far away. To the surprise of those who considered Frieda a martinet of the first order, she had made no attempt to suggest to Tricia that the secretary's desk of a professional police inspector was not the place for such things.

Tricia had been the reason for his latest fall in Frieda's estimate. Frieda had issued a stern order to Frank that young

Tricia was out of bounds.

The itch was back. He began scratching again.

He had tried to ignore it as folly, he pointed out to himself, but it irked him that Frieda thought she could tell him what he could and could not do in his private life. That's what happened when you developed a relationship with a senior officer, he thought, however platonic. Put your trust in a superior and sooner or later they would betray you. Put not your trust in princes or superior officers, as the bible had it, or something similar.

'I suppose I'll have to go in, then,' he said grimly, not moving.

'I suppose you will,' agreed Tricia. 'But before that, your tie needs straightening.'

She stood up, came around her desk, straightened Frank's perfectly straight tie, dusted his pristine jacket shoulders off and gave him a brief kiss on the cheek.

'Good luck, Frank, don't get into any trouble,' she said, and returned to her desk, smiling.

I think I just have, he thought.

He squared his shoulders as much as he could after the unexpected kiss, knocked on Frieda's door and entered her den.

Frieda was standing looking out her window, hands behind her back.

I wish she wouldn't do that, thought Frank, closing the door behind him. She always wore pencil skirts with a slit up the back, revealing legs that invariably gave him thoughts he shouldn't have.

They were very, very nice legs. And he liked very, very nice legs.

'Ah, Frank,' she said, turning around. 'Take a seat. There's something we need to discuss about M Matisse.'

She went to her desk as Frank took a seat. She sat down, picked up a pencil, tapped it on her desk top a few times while looking at him. She wasn't wearing her schoolmistress glasses, which was a good sign. But there was a thin smile playing around her lipsticked lips which was a very, very bad sign. It was the one she used when Frank Summers was not about to have a good time. It was the sort of smile the villain gave James Bond knowing that Mr Bond stood on a trapdoor beneath which swam several hungry sharks with bad attitudes, empty stomachs and very sharp teeth.

The difference in the analogy was that Frieda was part-writing this script, and wouldn't make the casual mistake that Mr Bond's opponent would. And Frank was severely lacking anything of the compressed-submarine or hidden-helicopter type of device concealed in his watch or lapel carnation that Mr Bond would have had in which to make good his escape.

'The Sûreté are sending over an officer to interview our Guillaume Matisse,' Frieda continued. 'A Capitaine Jean Tromperie. I've always thought French names sound so charming, don't you?'

She repeated the word "Jean", smiling, rolling it around her mouth like a rather tasty piece of Belgian chocolate.

'Absolutely,' agreed Frank, smiling back. 'Especially as tromperie is the French word for deception. I wonder how appropriate it will turn out to be.'

Frieda's smile froze.

'I'm glad to see you haven't lost your sense of humour,

Detective Sergeant Summers,' she said, the words grinding out in a way that suggested that "glad" was not being used in the accepted sense. 'No doubt it will comfort you as you go about arranging the paperwork just in case we have to hand M Matisse over to the French.'

'Paperwork?' asked Frank weakly. If he had an option between paperwork and being burnt at the stake he'd be happy to supply the matches. The firewood also. And the stake. Paperwork was something that someone else gave you and you filed away and ignored. You didn't go around creating the stuff yourself. That was against human nature.

'Precisely. Paperwork. It's essential that we get every comma and full stop in the right position. We don't want to ruin such an outstanding and well publicised arrest by allowing M Matisse to get off on a technicality, do we?'

Frieda was baiting him by referring to an "outstanding and well publicised" arrest. Someone had taken a picture of the moment. After a short chase, which had included the collision of two shopping-trolleys, the involvement of a burst packet of soap powder and his accidentally slipping on a fresh, loosely rolling organic cucumber, Frank had managed to grab hold of his man. Someone had photographed him holding on to Matisse's jacket tail for dear life while Matisse hit him slowly and repeatedly over the head with a box of Golden Frosties. Frank had only been grateful that it hadn't been a bag of organic muesli. That could have hurt a lot more.

The combination of having his photograph taken, something he hated intensely, and its subsequent appearance on local television and in the newspapers had not endeared him to the media. Fellow officers had, however, thoroughly enjoyed it. He seemed to achieve new nicknames every month, one of which had been "Psycho". The latest was "Cereal Psycho". It had just added to the other slings and arrows of outrageous fortune being sent his way at that particular time. He would far rather have been considered a wit than a twit. Being photographed while a small elderly Frenchman assaulted him with a box of alleged breakfast food did not help things. His only consolation, as far as the name of the cereal went, was that it hadn't been a box of Sugar Puffs. Either word could be used to supply a never-ending list of suggestions smacking, to the supplier if not the recipient, of the best of ribaldry.

'Oh, and the house M Matisse had rented was broken into last night,' Frieda continued. 'A team has checked it out, but I'd like you to take another look tomorrow.'

'Matisse isn't my case,' Frank pointed out.

'You don't get to choose your cases, Sergeant,' she snapped. 'You do as I tell you to.'

Frank did not reply. While he didn't share Frieda's abhorrence for swearing he did try to keep it within reasonable limits, and the only words that sprang to mind at that moment weren't within those limits. The phrase "take a running jump at yourself" was interspersed with other words which started with the letter F. He very rarely allowed other people to wind him up, but Frieda was doing an incredibly good job. He wasn't sure he would be able to restrain himself from saying something they both might regret.

'I expect the paperwork to be in order by Wednesday at the latest, Sergeant Summers. Capitaine Tromperie will be arriving tomorrow morning. Someone will have to look after him until you have the documents ready, just in case they're needed. Show him the sights of Wellbury, that sort of thing.'

'And that someone wouldn't be yourself, by any chance, would it, Inspector?' asked Frank through gritted teeth.

Frieda buffed her hair modestly with her right hand, the pencil rolling casually in her left.

'I think it only right a charming French Capitaine should be accorded the company of someone of similar rank,' she said. 'And it will give me a chance to improve my French. I've been meaning to do that for some time.'

Translation: you're deeply in the doghouse, Summers, and I'm going to flirt with a Frenchman.

Frank began to agree with Eric Johns. The French shouldn't be allowed to leave their miserable, stinking little country. Garlic-soaked, cheese-eating surrender-monkeys. Matisse was typical of the lot of them, the greasy, smarmy little Frog. This Tromperie would be just as bad no doubt. He'd probably ooze charm and flattery. No doubt the first thing he'd do would be to kiss Frieda's hand, the oleaginous, greasy, Gaullois-smoking, effeminate, French Frog. He felt like thumping him already.

"Hey, whoa, Frank," said one of his mental voices, hiding carefully out of sight at the back of his brain, "this isn't like you. What happened to the Enlightenment and rationality?"

Frank suggested the voice leave. The second word was "off". The first wasn't.

'Anything else, Inspector?' he asked grimly.

'No, I don't think so, Sergeant.'

He stood up to go.

'Oh, one last thing, Sergeant. Susan, Gertie and I are having a girls' night out this evening. I suggest you spend it practising your scales.'

The three of them had bought him an electric piano for his birthday, the same night Tricia had turned up. Her meaning was clear. Be a good boy, behave yourself, and we might let you off in about a zillion years.

What he should have picked up on, but missed as was his wont in personal relationships, was her use of their first names. If she had really meant the use of his rank to put him down, it would have been "Doctor Pleadle and Constable Gregson". The cosiness of "Susan" and "Gertie" should have sounded alarm bells in his mind. Unfortunately his personal mental bell-ringer was hiding behind the voice he had told to "off" and had no intention of making the slightest noise which might attract Frank's angry attention.

'I was planning on doing just that,' he said instead, walking to the door. 'The theme tune from The Great Escape, as it happens.'

The door slammed closed behind him. The pencil in Frieda's hands snapped. She threw the two pieces at the door and put her head into her hands.

Eric Johns would have been somewhat surprised and not a little perturbed had he known her thoughts. What she really wanted to do was put Frank in charge of this blasted stocktake. The problem with a stocktake was that different people had different motivations. The person carrying the clipboard wanted to get it over with as fast as possible. So long as they could tick the box that said Wellbury police station had n number of chairs they were happy, whether or not a closer check might reveal that those counted in interview room two looked suspiciously like they had been in interview room one thirty seconds before. Likewise the average constable was driven by the avoidance of someone discovering something missing, for which they, the average constable, would be held accountable, and might have to do so financially.

Would undoubtedly have to do so financially.

Frieda wasn't interested in numbers of chairs. She wanted to know what operational kit they had and whether it was functional. It was no good knowing, for example, that there were twenty riot shields in the armoury if only two were serviceable. She also had no interest in playing the blame game. There were many ways to disguise reasons for equipment being unserviceable or just plain missing. When push came to shove, and you had to send out officers with equipment that could save their lives, there was no excuse for not knowing the condition of that equipment. It was an approach Frank would understand. Instead they were playing silly buggers, acting like little children having a spat, not speaking to each other more than was absolutely necessary.

The armoury was a case in point. Wellbury police force was too small to have its own armed-response unit, but it did have an armoury. Of sorts. It did even, apart from assorted boxes and refuse chucked into the solid room as if it were a junk room, contain firearms. Of a fashion.

Frieda did not like the idea of her officers being armed. It went totally against her concept of what the modern British police force should be. As she often pointed out when gathered with others of her rank, the death of a police officer in Britain was a front-page news event precisely because it was so rare, and because the public empathised with the police. Send officers out armed and that empathy would be lost.

But if they were going to have firearms available should the necessity of their use arise – which, in Wellbury was a rather ridiculous notion – she was going to make damn sure that those firearms were in working order.

She had had her own Victor Meldrew reaction when she had read the list of firearms available should they be needed. The word "varied" did not even get near to describing the collection. She had seen less variety in a packet of liquorice allsorts. Apart from other items, two World War Two or possibly World War One Lee Enfield 303 rifles, with ammunition, had been religiously ticked off for well over forty years. Ignoring the possibility of any officer trained with modern firearms having sufficient knowledge of those antiques not to pose a danger to his or her own colleagues – never mind the public – the ammunition was so old that the only thing to do with it was dump it in the sea and hope it didn't go bang on the way, and hard luck to any fish that mistook it for being of edible form.

She had called on the services of an armourer from one of the larger, neighbouring divisions, and he was doing his best to rectify the deficiencies. Most of the time he spent in dumb silence. It was the discovery of tear-gas grenades with a use-by date of twenty years previously that had confirmed him in a diet of black coffee, and an urge to get this job over as soon as possible before he disturbed something which had lain peacefully for generations, something that reacted angrily, such as by making a very loud noise and spreading him across the thick walls of the armoury like so much strawberry jam.

Her rival Inspector Percy Hanson might have understood, but he was far too fly to get involved in a stocktake. His Sergeant, Pete Phillips, could possibly have been relied on had the requirement been explained very slowly and carefully to him, but he was on leave. Frank was the one person she could count on to understand and share her concerns. He was bright, efficient and firearms-trained. He knew what was important and what inconsequential. His biggest failing was his inability to restrain his sense of humour. He had taken the requisite exams and should himself be of inspector rank, and would have been, had not some anonymous person noted in his personnel file that he "perhaps lacked the expected respect for those of senior rank".

But, however suited he might have been to the task, he was now firmly in the doghouse, and she would no more ask of him a favour than she would howl at the moon.

She could make it an order, but he would know that it was because she needed him, and that she was not about to do. If he thought she was going to show the slightest sign of weakness he had another thought coming.

Grow up, a voice in her head told her, stop being childish.

I am not being childish, she replied. Wellbury police force have not been issued with firearms since 1940. Centuries will elapse before that is required again, if ever. By that time I will have the armoury in tip-top condition and the relevant officers properly trained. Frank Summers does not come into it.

The irritable tapping of her fingers on her desk belied these thoughts. She might, by virtue of her gender, never have been a boy scout, but she firmly believed in the motto "be prepared". Her job, as Detective Inspector, responsible for the well-being of her officers amongst other things, meant that she could take no risks as far as the known was concerned, and the known included making sure that equipment and kit was in working order. Anything else was sheer negligence, and she was not about to be accused of that.

But she'd bloody do it without Frank bloody Summers. For the moment at least.

The same, brave, foolhardy voice in her mind suggested she look up the word "petulance" in her dictionary, it wouldn't be far away from that other word she was so fond of, "professionalism".

It was rewarded with a mental six-inch stiletto heel through its head.

Unbeknownst to her Frank was very up to date with progress in the armoury. He was a sociable person who understood that the armourer would have felt somewhat of an outsider and had taken him a cup of tea on the first day John Stevens, the armourer, had commenced work. Sociability aside, Frank found that the varied contents of the armoury provided fascinating clues to the history of Wellbury police force.

Added to this was the fact that Frank Summers loved firearms. In previous postings he had done all the courses he could. Firmly disliking the basic purpose of firearms, the first course had been taken merely for the same reason he had taken any course available at that time: to keep him out of sight of superior officers. On the course he discovered a fascination for the mechanics and engineering of the weapons, and a love of shooting, which he found himself to be extremely good at. So long as the thing in his sights was just a paper target, he was quite happy.

But it was over a year since he had last shot, and, apart from the enjoyment, he needed to keep his training up to date. Having an acquaintance in the armourer John Stevens, his chances of being able to arrange an informal session on the odd occasion were immensely improved.

However there was one other motive to his visits to the armoury. Deep in the bowels of the solid Victorian building that constituted Wellbury's police headquarters, the armoury was as good a place as any for keeping out of Frieda's way.

'I'm worried we might be being a little too harsh on Frank,' Susan said as they sat in the Hangman pub near Heading Square that evening. 'After all, it wasn't really his fault. We did tell him we were all unavailable on his birthday. All he wanted was some company. And he was injured after that motorbike crash.'

'We need to make sure he understands his place,' Frieda replied determinedly. 'Inviting my new secretary around to his place was breaking not only our rules, but also office rules. My office rules. I have to train young Tricia up to be what I want, and she has a great deal of potential. I don't want her wasting that because of that ... Because of some silly man.'

Gertie took a sip of gin and tonic and stayed silent. She had pretended to agree with Frank's isolation, knowing that she would be working with him and could ignore it. So long as Frieda and Susan froze Frank out, she had a free hand – apart from that little tart, Tricia Leigh. Tricia, she suspected, had even fewer morals than her where Frank was concerned.

One of the problems with Frank was that he had, at some stage, taken a solemn vow never to get emotionally involved with any woman he worked with. From one or two things he had said she had concluded that that was a result of some affair that had gone disastrously wrong sometime in his past.

The first stage of his recovery and her game plan was to convince him that he was mistaken. Or, to be more accurate, that she, Gertie, was the one true exception. Otherwise he might open his eyes and realise that Frieda was also in the race.

How he had managed not to realise so far that he was being pursued by all three of them was frustratingly incredible. It was almost as if, having decided that he would not go out with a colleague, he was able to follow some convoluted intellectual exercise whereby having amorous drinks with Gertie after work or going to a production by the National Orchestra with Frieda was not actually going out with them, since he did get involved with colleagues, and they were colleagues, therefore he wasn't going out with them. QED. It was the equivalent of a weather forecaster who had predicted sunshine refusing to believe it was raining and wondering where this wet stuff was coming from.

'Well, I vote we lighten up on him a little bit,' Susan said. 'Otherwise he might decide he fancies some little floozy, and there are plenty of those around. Look at Tricia. She slipped in under our noses.'

'Tricia is not a floozy,' Frieda protested, like a mother hen protecting a chick. 'She's a very competent girl who has yet to learn the ways of the world.'

'That makes it worse,' Susan pointed out. 'People who have yet to learn the ways of the world tend to play by their own rules, if they have any. And Tricia is an extremely attractive young woman. Especially for men who like their women to look like schoolgirls wearing lipstick.'

Frieda considered this important point. She didn't quite agree with the idea of Tricia looking like a schoolgirl who wore lipstick, but there was a certain vulnerability about her which could get to a man like Frank.

'True,' she said. 'I shall have a few words with young Tricia, make sure she understands what type of man she's dealing with. But I still think Frank deserves one last lesson before we bestow our forgiveness on him. Men have very short memories. If you don't keep them on a tight leash they forget and think they can get away with anything.'

'Phil Walthers of the Herald wants an interview and a photograph,' Gertie interjected. 'Frank hates having his photograph taken.'

'Good point, Gertie, I shall see that Frank co-operates with the local media,' Frieda said with a smile, not realising that she would be the one to give the order and receive Frank's displeasure while Gertie was left to comfort him, which was exactly what Gertie had intended. 'I think Frank deserves to have his lesson continued until Saturday. Saturday, if he's been a good boy, we continue the rota.'

Frieda had convinced the other two that going out with Frank on a rota basis would limit his range to the three of them, and remove their former antagonism amongst themselves. Fighting each other while trying to gain his affections gave Frank all the cards. The rota meant that he had none.

And it was fun.

Frank was totally oblivious to all this. He thought he was going out with Susan, and having occasional outings with Gertie or Frieda purely as work colleagues. The fact that these outings invariably ended with the sorts of kisses and clinches not usually exchanged between work colleagues he put down to the fact that women tended to go in for that sort of thing even on a purely platonic basis.

Despite the nicknames and the banter, he had at the station a reputation of being extremely intelligent and perceptive in his police duties. But all such positives are compensated for by negatives: in his personal relationships he was blinder than any bat known to modern science or ancient mythology.

For the three women it had turned out rather well. Frieda and Susan were both professional women with a great deal of work to do, and couldn't spare every night to be with Frank. Gertie was studying for a law degree with the Open University, and was in the same predicament. The rota meant that they didn't have to wonder what he was up to, anxiously worrying whether he wasn't out wining and dining some other woman while they were busy. They knew he was with another woman, but someone they could trust.

Or perhaps it could be said that the other two were known quantities, they could trust how far they could distrust them.

Just so long as one of the other cows didn't take things too far.

Which was precisely what each intended to do as soon as they got the chance.

'We've got a French Captain coming tomorrow,' Frieda continued. 'No doubt he'll turn out to be middle aged, overweight and smelling of garlic and Gaulloise, but I've got Frank to believe that I'm expecting the height of Gallic sexiness. Presuming this French police officer doesn't turn out to be absolutely dire beyond redemption, I think if we all pretend that he's the epitome of charm we can teach Frank his lesson. Agreed?'

'So long as this Frenchman isn't absolutely dire,' Susan agreed dubiously.

'Gertie?' asked Frieda.

'We can try it,' Gertie replied, as dubiously. 'But, knowing Frank, he'll end up going out for a pint with this Frenchman and chatting about rugby or something. Football, maybe, apparently the French aren't bad at that, despite what Eric Johns believes. You know what Frank's like – he'd get one of those silent monks gabbing away fifteen to the dozen within five minutes of meeting him.'

'Don't worry about that, Gertie,' said Frieda confidently. 'I've got that covered. I'll be looking after our suave Capitaine Tromperie myself. Frank won't get anywhere near him. Frank is going to be very busy running around doing useless things. Tomorrow he will be going to the house Matisse was renting to investigate the break-in.'

'But I thought that had already been done,' Susan noted. 'Tracey and I did the forensics on it today.'

'Precisely. It's a total waste of time. And he'll have to write up a report about it. Frank will find it tedious in the extreme. And after that bit of brain-numbing he will be off to the Blue Bliss to investigate these stories of illegal drug selling.'

'The Blue Bliss?' echoed Susan. 'Poor Frank.'

'Exactly,' smiled Frieda. 'Poor Frank. He isn't going to enjoy that at all. And if he does manage to find any spare time there are complaints about milk theft in Old Merrick.'

'Milk theft?' asked Susan incredulously.

'Just the sort of high-level crime Frank would enjoy. Every single bottle needs to be accounted for. And documented. I shall keep Phil Walthers and the Wellbury Herald's readers thoroughly briefed about Detective Sergeant Summers' hard work and earnest efforts in tracking down the milk thieves of Wellbury. It should make interesting reading.'

'Poor Frank,' Susan repeated. Gertie giggled.

'Fearless Frank versus the milk muggers of Wellbury,' she said.

They all had a good chuckle over their drinks. Each felt personally a little guilty. Though it was a good laugh, after all, wasn't it? And Frank had a good sense of humour, didn't he? And it would be over by Saturday.

'To Saturday,' toasted Frieda.

'To Saturday,' the others chorused, raising their glasses.

Interestingly, none of them looked any of the others in the eyes. The phrase "I can't wait until then" was going to prove literally true. It was just a case of making sure the others didn't find out.

Wednesday: Capt. Tromperie, a turn up for the books

'I don't believe it!' Frieda cried incredulously as she tried the ignition on her Range Rover for the fifth time. 'Come on, Abighail, come on, you can do it, just a little bit of power. Come on, my sweet.'

Abighail the Range Rover whimpered and refused to start. Frieda cursed herself. She knew she hadn't had too many gin and tonics the previous evening, but somehow she had forgotten to switch Abighail's lights off. The battery was completely flat. She had been too caught up in her own thoughts of Frank's punishment, that was what had happened. It was all Frank's fault. Everything was that expletive-deleted man's fault.

It was not so much a pleasing thought as a palliative one, but her conscience still pricked her. She wondered whether she was been just a tadge too silly about the whole business. After all, she was supposed to be a professional police, and senior, officer, not some love-lorn teenager taking revenge because of a minor slight. She was a grown woman.

Something that that idiot seemed to be obtusely unaware of, blast his cotton socks!

And his smart suits and loud ties and expletive-deleted twinkling eyes!

She had long accepted, however much she might dislike it, that to be a woman police officer was to be a woman police officer – the prefix would never disappear in people's minds, even though officially the designation was redundant. The world might be a different place many years hence, but in her life and career she would be judged as equally on appearance as performance, and not only by the men. She had never expected to meet anyone immune to this feeling. It was just a way of life. You had to accept it and move on.

And then along came Frank, a man who did not seem to think he should address his words to her chest, nor scan her legs as if rating them in a beauty contest. He had somehow trained his mind to regard other officers as colleagues, a gender-neuter noun which removed any potential romantic interest and, at the most, allowed them to be friends. And, as so often happens in these situations, having found a man who acted precisely the way Frieda would have preferred all officers to act, in his case she wanted exactly the opposite.

In her case, anyway.

Privately Frieda thought she had rather good-looking legs. Other men seemed to appreciate them. Frank could at least glance at them now and then.

She scrubbed these thoughts from her mind and tried the ignition one last time. The whimper had all but died. She gave up, took out her mobile phone and stabbed at the buttons impatiently.

'Sergeant Bute? Inspector Garold here.'

'Morning, ma'am,' replied a surprised Sergeant Keith Bute, manning the early-morning reception desk of Wellbury police station.

'Keith, my car won't start. I won't be able to get in for an hour or so. I'm expecting a Captain Tromperie from the French Sûreté any minute. I want you to make sure he gets looked after until I come in, okay? It's extremely important.'

'Yes, ma'am,' replied Keith Bute. 'I finish up in twenty minutes, but if this captain hasn't turned up then I'll pass the message on to Eric Johns.'

'Eric Johns, heaven help us,' said Frieda shaking her head slowly, her eyes closed as she contemplated this latest bad news. 'Just make sure he gets the message, very, very simply and very, very clearly. He has a bad habit of translating plain English into his own version of reality. The last thing I need is a diplomatic incident. I want the Captain treated with all due respect, make sure that Sergeant Johns understands that. If he messes this one up he will be walking the beat for the rest of his career. Got that?'

'Yes, ma'am,' replied an unhappy Keith Bute. He had never become accustomed to the reactions of senior officers to what he described as "visiting dignitaries", words he pronounced in such a way as to leave no doubt of his opinion of their dignity or the worth of their visit. Basic police work suddenly came a distant second to clear desks and clean, preferably empty, cells. One Chief Constable's visit could waste five days' work, even if that Chief Constable only popped in for five minutes and a cup of tea and had absolutely no urge to view the cells, which extremely few did. One of the reasons that Keith Bute had taken permanent early shift was to avoid this sort of nonsense. His ideas on the relative importance of police matters were often radically different to those of senior officers pursuing a political agenda, or, to be more accurate, practising the art of climbing the greasy pole of promotion.

You can run, he thought to himself, but you can't hide. Fate will find you. Or that karma thing. Never trust karma. It even sounded foreign.

Still, it would be Eric Johns' problem once his own shift ended. That thought cheered him up somewhat. Eric Johns was a good bloke, mostly, but when it came to a game of passing-the-pinless-grenade – well, it would be a far, far better thing that Eric Johns did in holding the baby.

The metaphor made him shake his head to clear it. Another reason he had taken permanent early shift was an attempt to reduce his wife's predilection for pregnancies. That hadn't worked either. So far she was up to number five. If anything could be said, it was that it was Keith Bute was left holding the baby, literally.

Still, it was better than being left holding a Frog. Especially one with the title of Captain. Typical foreigners. A Captain was something you found in the army, not in the police force. Foreigners always got these subtleties wrong. No wonder the Frogs were always going on strike and rioting and such. No subtlety, that was their problem.

'Morning, Eric,' Frank said, strolling into reception half an hour later. 'You don't have anything for me, by any chance? Something to avoid paper-work. A couple of bank robberies and an international crisis should do the trick.'

'Not quite an international crisis, Frank,' Eric Johns replied moodily. 'But we do have a Frog in interview room three. Keith put him in there just before I came on duty.'

'Captain Tromperie, by any chance? I thought Wonderwoman was going to look after him.'

'Apparently Fabulous's Range Rover won't start. She wants someone to look after the Frog until she gets in. I guess that means you.'

'Wonderwoman's Range Rover won't start?' asked Frank in simulated amazement, his mocking eyes wide open. 'I'm surprised it has the temerity. No doubt she'll send it straight to the knacker's yard. Get a new one which behaves itself. She'll probably get a kick from seeing the old one in the crusher.'

'Er, if you say so, Frank,' said Eric nervously. He was beginning to think that he preferred Wellbury in the pre-Summers and pre-Garold era. At least the explosions went off in a more controlled manner in those days. 'But you'll do it?' he asked, a certain amount of pleading in his voice. 'Look after the Frog?'

'Okay, Eric, no problem. After I've had a coffee. It gets me out of the paperwork for half an hour or so. Say, what does this Frog look like? Inspector Clouseau or Hercule Poirot?'

'God knows, Frank, I didn't ask. All I know is Keith put him in the interview room. I think he was trying to wind me up, so I didn't listen to his waffling. I need at least two cups of tea before I could face a Frog first thing in the morning, especially one with the rank of Captain. Arrogant and smarmy with it, I can do without that.'

'Known many Frogs, Eric?' Frank asked, amused.

'Everyone knows what the Frogs are like, Frank,' Eric replied, burying himself in the study of a tabloid newspaper.

Frank whistled as he strolled to interview room three after he had refreshed himself with a slow cup of coffee. He didn't share Eric's hang-ups about the French. But they did come in quite usefully at times. Times such as when he had had a French girlfriend and wished to wind her up.

He paused and blinked his eyes to clear the memory. It was one he spent most of his time avoiding. He had thought he had managed to suppress it entirely. Precisely because of that it took him by surprise when it invariably resurfaced.

Get on with life, he told himself. Leave the past behind. It's a beautiful summer's day, Wellbury is the closest thing to paradise you've lived in, what more could you ask for?

Not having a spat with Frieda, for a start. Frieda was using this Frenchman to wind him up, but that didn't faze him. Life was far too short to let such little things get one upset. And he never did. Not these days.

Okay, he admitted to himself, yesterday he had let Frieda get under his skin, just a little bit, but now, after a good night's sleep, he was back on form. If he found himself losing it he would just start singing "The sun will come out tomorrow". It didn't do anything for him, but boy did it get on other people's nerves.

"Tomorrow, tomorrow," he began humming as he approached the interview room.

He opened the door to the interview room and came to a sudden stop, his eyes almost popping out.

A young woman sat at the interview desk, tapping away at a laptop. She had short, black, bobbed hair with a fringe, and wore an unzipped black leather bunny jacket with a badge on the left side. Next to the laptop lay a navy-blue kepi with gold braid circling the bottom. Under the jacket she was wearing a light-blue shirt with breast pockets either side, and a neatly tied black tie. It was obviously a uniform of sorts. As with many men, Frank found the tie and male shirt disorienting, almost erotically so.

She finished what she had been typing into the computer and looked up at him slowly, with an expression which suggested she was not expecting to be impressed. Not by anything, and even less by him. It was the face of a very young Queen

Victoria not at all being amused at the sight of something a dog might have left as a keepsake, and not the best of breed either. Despite this Frank noticed that she had an extremely attractive face, or would have if she exchanged the sneer for a smile.

'I'm sorry,' he said, 'I was told Captain Tromperie was here.'

'I am Captain Tromperie,' the woman replied in a French accent, with heavy emphasis on the "I".

There was a pause as Frank took in this development, his mind already working on the amusement it could provide.

'That's unusual,' he noted.

'Unusual for a woman to be a captain? That is what I would expect from you English sexist men.'

Frank paused again, slightly bemused at this sudden and unexpected assault.

'I must confess I was expecting someone rather older and male, not a beautiful young woman,' he said, gathering his wits and charm about him. 'I thought Jean was a man's name in France. I'm Frank Summers, by the way, Detective Sergeant Frank Summers.'

'A sergeant?' asked the woman with an expression so full of utter disbelief a lesser man might have automatically promoted himself, however temporarily. She ignored his flattery and looked him up and down as if he were an interloper pretending to belong to the human race. 'I was expecting someone of rather higher rank. No doubt this is what is called a calculated insult. Purely because I am French.'

'Not at all, Captain, some of my best friends are French,' Frank said with a grin. 'It's just that Inspector Garold has been unavoidably detained – her car wouldn't start, I believe.

But she is looking forward to meeting you enormously. I just can't wait. I mean the Inspector can't wait to meet you.'

'Until then,' Captain Tromperie said, standing up and snapping her laptop closed, 'I wish to see the prisoner, Guillaume Matisse. Now.'

Frank smiled, folded his arms and leaned against the doorpost languidly.

'I'm afraid that won't be possible at the moment, Captain,' he said reasonably, his eyes not looking anywhere near the skin-tight grey uniform trousers with navy-blue stripe down the side that had been revealed when the woman stood up. She was also wearing highly polished, military-style black combat boots, but so small as to make them look like a child's. 'He'd have to have his lawyer present, for a start. That could take a little while to arrange. In the meantime, would you like a coffee or something? Perhaps some breakfast. Our canteen offers a very good breakfast. Egg and bacon on fried toast is a speciality.'

'Your canteen?' asked Captain Tromperie in more disbelief. 'Do I look like the sort of person who has breakfast in a canteen, Sergeant? Do I need to remind you that I am an officer – a Captain? A French Captain of the Sûreté?'

'We have this strange belief in égalité, Capitaine,' Frank replied, smiling easily, resisting the urge to point out that she'd hardly be likely to be a Bolivian captain of the Sûreté.

'Coffee, black, no sugar. I will have it here,' the woman snapped, sitting down and re-opening her laptop, effectively dismissing him, or trying to.

'How would you like that?' asked Frank.

'Pardon?'

'Your coffee. How would you like it? Large, small, medium, extra-strength, normal, organic, non-organic, filtered, non-filtered, Brazilian, Argentinean, Kenyan, roasted, de-caff or latte? Or does latte have milk in it? I can never remember. Anyway, normally it comes in plastic cups, but I'm sure we could rustle up a mug for you somewhere. We keep some for special guests.'

Just for a moment, a flicker of a nano-second, there was a look in her eyes. Then, just as suddenly it disappeared and she looked down her nose at him, appraisingly, like a long-dead and disgusting toad she needed to dissect but would prefer not to, an impressive trick for someone sitting down while he stood quite a few feet above her. He returned it with a look of dispassionate helpfulness. They were interrupted by the arrival of Frieda.

'Ah,' she said pleasurably, bursting into the room. 'Ah ...' she continued, looking from the other woman to Frank. 'I was told Captain Tromperie would be here.'

'Allow me to introduce you, Inspector,' Frank said, not managing to hide the deep pleasure in his voice. 'Captain Jean Tromperie of le Sûreté, Inspector Frieda Garold of Wellbury police force.'

'You're Captain Tromperie?' asked Frieda in incredulity. 'Ah, of course, you're Captain Tromperie,' she added quickly, as if the fact were obvious, recovering her poise with eminent speed.

'A pleasure to make your acquaintance, Inspector,' Captain Tromperie said, standing up again and shaking Frieda's hand. 'I do not wish to appear to be rude, but there is much work to be done and little time to do it in. Firstly I would like to see M Matisse, as he calls himself.'

'I've explained that M Matisse's lawyer needs to be present,' Frank interrupted evenly. 'Regulations.'

'Well, yes, of course, naturally,' Frieda said. 'You go organise that, Frank. I mean Sergeant Summers.'

'Yes, ma'am,' Frank said, leaving. He stopped in the corridor to eavesdrop. It wasn't something he would normally do, but this time he couldn't resist it.

'I apologise for being late,' he heard Frieda say. 'I hope my officers have looked after you?'

'Very well. Your Sergeant Frank Summers especially. He is obviously stupid, but, how would you say, sexy in a cute way? A bit of rough, I believe the expression is in English.'

There was a pause. Not so much pregnant as storm-laden and ominous. A silence which heralded the sharpening of swords and the bringing up of cannon. Or, in this case, the preparation of handbags, the sight of which would have many yearning for something less threatening, something quieter, like standing naked in the middle of the Charge of the Light Brigade.

Frank almost laughed out loud. He shoved his knuckles in his mouth to stop himself.

'Perhaps you'd like to come to my office, Captain?' suggested Frieda in what could have been mistaken for a level voice, but one which Frank recognised as containing half the arctic icebergs, unaffected by global warming.

Frank grinned and left before he could be discovered eavesdropping. He doubted whether Captain Jean Tromperie found him sexy in any way; that comment had been purely to wind Frieda up. Why, he didn't know. But he had had a lot of experience in such matters. Being able to recognise the sound of two women getting their talons ready was a survival technique. In such circumstances you didn't hang around to ask for whom the bell tolled, you just ran like the clappers.

And there was that very brief look in Capitaine Jean Tromperie's eyes. He was sure it had not been an illusion.

It had been a look of surprised amusement. For a moment she had let her guard down, like a boxer pleasantly surprised to find their opponent might not just be the pushover they had expected. Frank was not entirely sure of what it meant, but he rather suspected Jean Tromperie was going to be fun.

Oh, yes, Capitaine Tromperie was going to be fun. More fun than a bucketful of drunk ferrets dropped into the middle of a St Trinian's bunfight.

Whether she was going to share the sentiment was another question.

He decided it was his duty to remove that sneer from that pretty little face. Everyone should have a hobby.

'I was bo-orn under a wandering star,' he sang in a gravelly voice as he entered the office he shared with Gertie.

'Morning Sarge,' she said, a surprised look on her face. 'You're a bit cheerful, aren't you?'

'And why shouldn't I be, my dear Gertie?' he asked. 'It's a glorious day, the sun is shining, Wellbury is displaying its usual wealth of summer colour. The birds are singing in the trees, swans and geese and ducks swim serenely on the river, while lovers canoodle along the canal. Daisies blossom and roses bloom. Just breathing the fresh air gives you that tang of a wonderful, wonderful world. Makes one glad to be alive. Oh,' he added as an afterthought as he dropped happily into his chair, 'our French Captain Tromperie has turned up. He's a she.'

He smiled at Gertie.

'Isn't it just wonderful to be alive?' he asked. He sat looking at her, humming happily.

'A she?' asked Gertie suspiciously, after a short pause.

'Indeed, impossible to mistake, even if I weren't a trained detective. About twenty-six and what some might describe as drop-dead gorgeous. Wearing trousers so tight you can leave your imagination at home. And the cutest little booties you ever did see.' He gave Gertie another grin. 'You know, I don't think the Inspector likes her very much. Not so that you would notice.'

Gertie considered this news for a few moments. There was a certain malicious enjoyment in Frank's voice which would have made anyone wary.

'Fancy a coffee, Sarge?' she asked finally. 'I was just about to get one.'

'A coffee sounds like just the thing, dear Gertie. I'd love one.'

Frank smiled to himself as Gertie left. Frieda and the Captain would have been seen on the way to her office. Already the gossip would be flying about. "Have you seen that French bird? Talk about a stunner! Those legs on her go right up to her waist!"

Gertie was not only going for coffee. She was going to the gossip watering hole. The male and female rival views on the French were about to be reversed. Eric Johns would be "ooh-la-la-ing" again.

Along with that he was going to totally ignore the legal requirements and paperwork for handing M Matisse over to the French. Scotland Yard were interested. Because of the antagonism between himself and Frieda he had not realised the obvious immediately, as he would normally have done. There was no way Wellbury police force would hand over Matisse to the French while Scotland Yard were in the queue. Wellbury police would pass him to Scotland Yard and let them decide whether the French should have a look-in. It had been just another way for Frieda to wind him up, and damn close she had come too. He had only fallen for it because he had been so tired.

He stood up and looked out the window. There were two things trying to get into his mind. One was a thought niggling away in his brain. The other was a memory he had managed to suppress ever since arriving in Wellbury. But it was refusing to be suppressed any longer. He knew that Gertie thought that his refusal to become romantically entangled at work was the result of an earlier affair which had gone sour. She was wrong about that. That philosophy was based on seeing others making that mistake. But she was right about a previous relationship, and now the memory had come back with a vengeance.

Jean had been the name of his French girlfriend. French father, British mother, christened Jean after her mother's mother. Jeannie, he called her when he wanted to tease her, which was often. It had been his way of avoiding the fact that he was totally and utterly in love with her. Besotted. Being besotted was entirely against his philosophy of life. Languid walks in the autumn, hand in hand, confidential exchanges of quiet looks, small smiles, yes. Heart-breaking passion was just not his thing.

It could have been said to have been love at first sight. She had tried to belt him even before they had been introduced. It had been nothing personal. Although then a Detective Constable, he had been pressed back into uniform to help control a demonstration of people who insisted on Saving the Whales, or something similar and as such was guaranteed to be peaceful. The demonstration had got out of hand when the news spread that the police were bringing up the Riot Squad with teargas, water-cannon and dogs. The fact that this was totally untrue wasn't relevant. Frank and nine other officers found themselves confronted with about a hundred extremely unhappy protestors. The other nine officers backed off faster than Frank, who had always believed that his charm and the innate pacifism of the average British protestor could resolve any situation, without realising that some might not share this idealistic belief, in this case about a hundred of them.

Jean, at the forefront, had somehow misinterpreted his upheld hands and request for calm, and had swung her bag at him, completely missing and falling over.

He had stepped forward to help her, with the memorable phrase of the sort one comes out with when faced with a large mob determined on beating the merry hell out of you, "You okay, love? Bit of a tumble you took there. Not hurt, are you?".

Leaning over her probably saved him. Another demonstrator took the opportunity to thwack him over the head with a poster, the stave catching him on the back of the head and knocking him semi-unconscious. Jean, either because his considerate and rather old-fashioned charm in one so young had already caught her fancy, or because she regarded him as "her bobby to beat up", had sprung up and loudly berated Frank's assailant. Then she had helped Frank to wobble over to the pavement, where he sat, dazed, as she tended to his wound, mopping up the blood streaming down his neck. The sight collapsed the demonstration. Protestors milled around, uncertain of what to do, and wondering if attacking such a charming young policeman was really the right thing to have done. The issue had been resolved when a distinctly overweight and middle-aged sergeant had forced his way to the scene. He had reviewed the sight, turned to the protestors and issued the stern command:

"You daft pillocks! Look what you've done. And on his birthday, too. And him hoping for a quiet day and a couple of pints in the evening while opening his pressies. Now look at him. Go on, bugger off the lot of you!"

They duly buggered off, but Jean didn't. Not even the revelation that the Sergeant had lied about the birthday bit made any difference to her sudden, intense and passionate feelings for Frank Summers, a feeling that was reciprocated by a puzzled Frank. They were like chalk and cheese. It was a strange sort of heaven. A tempestuous heaven.

The break-up, when it came, and he knew, although he tried to deny it to himself, that it would inevitably come as winter follows a summer you never want to end, came in a totally unexpected way. She had accused him of having affairs behind her back. He had been gobsmacked. He had actually used the word "monstrous" to describe the accusation. The reason he had not seen her as often as he wanted was that work was hectic at the time, and police officers couldn't always work nine-to-five. Then she claimed that he did not love her, if he did he would not be teasing her all the time and treating her as a plaything.

How could he explain to her that his teasing was a front for his deep love, a way of dealing with emotions he found difficult to handle?

She had walked out of his life, slamming the door. And, as it turned out, she had walked out of life permanently. She had been driving too fast. It was the onset of winter, and the roads had not been gritted in time for an unexpected flurry of snow and sleet which had turned to black ice. Her car had skidded, hit the safety barriers, flipped over and burst into flame. She never stood a chance.

He never had the chance to tell her he really loved her.

Or, to be honest, he had had that chance, and squandered it.

It had been a stupid, silly accident, the sort that rarely makes the news, but leaves those behind shattered. Not even a ripple in the traffic accident statistics, but a wave of devastation for those affected.

It had taken him a long time to blot out the memories. It was a combination of Frieda's needling him and the sudden jolt of meeting this Jean Tromperie that had breached the defensive dyke of his memory, he decided.

He sat down again, trying to erase the memory. There was no comparison between his Jean and Jean Tromperie. His Jean was gone. Gone forever. It was in the past. He had loved and lost. So be it. The living had to continue living. Coming to Wellbury had been a chance to start anew, which he had done. The past was a foreign country. They did things differently there. He had no urge to learn the language, nor apply for a visa.

'Mr Summers?' asked a voice from the doorway. He looked up. A thin, smallish man of indeterminate age stood there, a clipboard in his hand, cap pushed to the back of his head, a pencil behind his ear.

'Vic Brown!' Frank exclaimed. 'What are you doing here? More to the point, how is that you're wandering around the nick without an escort?'

Victor Brown was an ex-petty criminal who had relocated to Wellbury after finding London too dangerous for his health as an "honest criminal". Frank had apprehended him in the course of what appeared to be a break in, but, since the door to the house in question was unlocked, Vic Brown had not actually taken anything and the owner had shown absolutely no interest in the affair – and because it was obvious that Vic Brown was probably the most incompetent criminal to hit the streets of Wellbury – Frank had let him off. Frieda and Gertie had been with Frank during the arrest, and had frightened the life out of Vic Brown, who had turned to Frank for protection. Ever since then he had treated Frank with a devotion that Frank sometimes found hard to deal with, though he could not help but like the cheerful man who had a bad habit of over-playing his Cockney street-urchin role.

'Well, looked like they was a bit busy in reception,' Vic Brown said, 'so I sed to meself, well, you know, let's not bother poor Sergeant Johns, let's just go see Mr Summers like.'

Why Eric Johns was "Sergeant Johns" and Frank, of the same rank, was "Mr Summers" was probably something only Vic Brown could explain.

'How did you get in though? Didn't anyone stop you and ask you where you were going?'

'Nah, they wouldn't do that,' Vic Brown replied confidently. He held up the clipboard. 'People don't see you when you've got a clipboard or a piece of paper and you look like you knows wot you're up to.'

And especially not, thought Frank, when there's a stocktake going on which everybody was doing their level best to avoid. The sight of a clipboard would have them hiding in cupboards rather than be accosted by the carrier. Vic Brown was well known to himself and Eric Johns, along with Frieda and Gertie, but for most of the others he was just some vague person who popped in to see Frank on the odd occasion. For all they knew he was official. For certain they could see he was carrying a dangerous and potentially damaging clipboard. And he had a pencil behind his ear. That was the clincher. You didn't walk around with a pencil behind your ear unless you were on official business.

Frank had to smile. Vic Brown's thought processes might seem strange to others, but they seemed to work in practice.

'Okay, Vic, come in,' he said. 'I'll give you two minutes, but that's it.'

'Cheers, guv,' Vic Brown said, humbly advancing into Frank's office, 'I've always said that you were a diamond geezer –'

Frank held up a warning hand.

'And what have I said about overdoing the Cockney blarney?' he asked.

'Er, you said you'd rip me into tiny little pieces and feed me to the moggies while I was still breathing.'

'Not quite an accurate rendition, but I like the thought. So, you now have one minute and thirty seconds left.'

'I've come to report a sort of burglary,' Vic Brown said quickly, recognising that arguing over the time elapsed would be counter-productive.

'A sort of burglary?' Frank asked. 'What sort?'

'Fags, guv, fags.'

'Fags? Cigarettes, you mean.'

'Yeah, that's right guv, fags.'

'I haven't heard of any major heists of cigarettes recently. This something you picked up on the criminal grapevine? Something that's going down soon?'

Frank tended to pick up some of the Londoner's slang when Vic Brown was around. Everybody did.

'No, Mr Summers, these have already bin stolen. And they was stolen from me.'

It took Frank a few seconds to take this in.

'Someone nicked a pack of fags from you, and you've come to the nick to report it?' he asked slowly.

'Not a pack, guv, I'd hardly waste your time on just a single pack. I'm talking big time. Thirty cartons.'

'Thirty cartons?' Frank asked in astonishment.

'Yes, guv, thirty bleeding cartons, right from under me nose. I still can't work out who done it or how they done it. Whoever it is, they're right crafty bleeders. Right from under me nose it was.' He shook his head sadly at the thought that someone more clever than him, obviously a master criminal, had outwitted him.

'Well, Vic, not quite the crime of the century,' Frank said, 'but thirty cartons does constitute a reasonable amount. What I don't understand is why you've come to me. You know the ropes, a theft like that goes to uniform first.'

'Well, guv, it's a little tricky, you see.'

Frank leaned back in his chair, nodding understanding, a wry smile on his face.

'I should have known it would be,' he said, 'since you're involved. Okay, I'm listening, much as I think I'm going to regret this. Come on, what's it all about?'

'Well, guv, see, it's like this,' Vic Brown said slowly, choosing his words carefully. 'Now I popped across the Channel, like, for some shopping like, you know, French stuff, cheese, wine, some perfume for the missus, that sort of thing.'

'And found out that you had accidentally bought thirty cartons of cigarettes which are dirt-cheap in France, and could be sold for a nice little profit over here? Which just so happens to be illegal?'

'It's legal if they're for your own personal use,' protested Vic Brown.

'Thirty cartons? And how many do you smoke a day, Vic?'

'Well, I don't really smoke, meself. Not as such, just the odd roll-up now and then. But I thought, what if one day I suddenly had this craving? So while I was there I might as well stock up, just in case.'

'As you do,' Frank replied sardonically. 'Come on, Vic, I hope you don't expect me to believe that. You illegally brought thirty cartons of fags back from France to flog over here and now they've been stolen. Sounds to me like you're in a no-win situation. You can't officially report the theft because you shouldn't have had them in the first place.'

'Aw, come on, Mr Summers, it's only a little financial transaction. Government wants everybody to be entry-reppy-neurs, I was only doing me little bit for the free market. These big companies get away with it all the time. Bleeding unfair, that's what it is, bleeding unfair.'

'Oh, I agree, Vic, totally unfair. What I don't understand is what you expect me to do about your missing cigarettes.'

'Well, all I need is a number, Mr Summers, you know, a case number for the insurance.'

'A case number? Let me get this right, Vic. You want me to open a file on your missing fags just so that you can claim on your insurance? You don't think certain questions might be asked? Such as why you had so many cartons in your possession, and where they came from?'

'They're legit, Mr Summers, even got that death warning on them, proper fags, not that Turkish rubbish other people try to flog.' He paused, noticing that Frank was not overly interested in the quality of the merchandise. 'Anyway, you know what it's like, something gets nicked, coppers come around, make a few notes and forget about it cause there ain't enough evidence and they're too busy with other things. Only reason they bother is so someone can claim the insurance.'

Frank shook his head in despair.

'Vic, apart from the fact that you'd end up getting a visit from Customs, if I tried to open a file on your fags and then bury it, do you know what would happen to me when they found out? Which they would. We have computers these days, Vic, they flag up things like that.'

Vic pondered this sadly.

'What would happen to you, Mr Summers? Just being curious?'

Frank looked at him.

'In normal times I'd probably be quietly fired. At the moment Inspector Garold wants to make a study of my internal system with a very blunt knife and while I'm still alive to feel the pain. I don't know what she'd do if she caught me fiddling things, but she has a very good imagination, and I'd rather not find out what she's capable of, if you don't mind.'

'I'm sorry about that, Mr Summers,' Vic said earnestly. 'I always thought you and the Missus Inspector got on like a house on fire.'

'We do, Vic, we do. But to understand that you have to think of what the phrase "a house on fire" means. It means a burning house. Flames crackling, walls falling down, gas pipes exploding, you know, death and destruction, to put it in a nutshell. I've never understood why people use it in the context they do.'

'Doesn't make sense, when you put it that way,' agreed Vic Brown. He sighed. 'Oh, well, I'll have to think of another plan. Sorry to have bothered you, Mr Summers. I hope you and the Missus Inspector sort your problems out, guv, honest I do. I'll see myself out, don't want to trouble you no further, guv.'

Frank watched the small shape leave as if he were a wraith disappearing into smoke. Vic Brown was the sort of person who could blend into the background when he wanted. All people would see would be the clipboard and pencil.

He smiled to himself. Missus Inspector? When had Vic thought that one up? Another bow to the image of a cheerful, yet respectful, Cockney sparrer, with just a soupçon of suggested mockery. Frieda would belt Vic one if she heard him using that expression.

He must remember to repeat it to her when next he saw her.

Vic Brown was like a tonic. He never failed to make Frank feel just that bit more cheerful. And now he had taken him out of his earlier dark thoughts.

And there was that little something else. Actually, a very big something else. Vic Brown put on the act of being the quintessential Cheeky Cockney Chappie. That reminder had crystallised a thought in his mind, that second thing that had been niggling at his brain. Someone else was also putting on an act, a bigger and more dangerous act.

If that woman with the tight trousers was Captain Jean Tromperie of the Sûreté, then Frank Summers was Napoleon Bonaparte of the Salvation Army.

He was convinced of it.

He looked at his telephone. Maybe he should warn Frieda.

No, sod it. Wonderwoman deserved to be taken down a peg or two.

But he could telephone the Sûreté to confirm his suspicions. And then stand back and watch Frieda making a total ballsup of things.

She deserved it.

The last of Frank Summers' mental defence voices packed its bags and left for a well-deserved and long-awaited holiday.

Frank wasn't smiling when Gertie returned with two coffees after half an hour, an inordinately long time to fetch just two cups of coffee.

'You okay, Sarge?' she asked as she put a mug in front of him. 'You don't look happy all of a sudden. Not having mood swings are you?'

'Oh, nothing serious, Gerts. Just hacked off with trying to make a simple phone call. You think it's going to take no more than a minute. Until you hear a voice asking you to press one if you want this, two if you want that, three if you're a Cornish trawlerman with a lisp, four if you had measles as a child, five if your big left toe has rheumatism, and so on and so on, and you don't want any of the options.'

What he didn't mention was that, while he could more or less read French, he hadn't understood most of the rapidly spoken options. He had spent half an hour pressing buttons and listening to machines giving him further choices, until he ended up speaking to a woman who apparently represented some sanitation department in the Loire Valley. Or maybe something else. He could have sworn she had suggested something which sounded a bit too much like colonic irrigation for his taste.

To be fair they did sound efficient. The person had promised that a drain-purging operative would be with him in less than a day. They had seemed rather perplexed by the address that Frank had given, but the tone of her voice suggested that they would give it a damn good go.

'Wellbury,' the woman had said thoughtfully. 'Perhaps maybe more than one day, but do not be constipated, relief will arrive.'

Or that was what Frank thought she had said.

Just to be on the safe side, in case it was something to do with enemas, he had given Inspector Percy Hanson's name and number instead of his own.

'Can't stand them myself, those talking machines,' Gertie sympathised, sitting down in front of his desk and taking a sip of coffee. 'Here, this Captain Trumpet sounds a bit toffee nosed.'

'Does she?' asked Frank, hiding a smile. 'She seemed rather attractive to me.'

'Looks like a little French tart, according to Allison Hardbury,' Gertie sniffed.

'What does Harry think?'

Constables Allison Hardbury and Harry Wheatley were going out together. It had all started after a passionate hatred during which Allison had belted Harry with her handbag and then fallen deeply and instantly in love with him as he lay on the ground with a nose-bleed. These days the two were almost inseparable, despite Harry's insistence that Allison at the time had checked her handbag for damage before deciding to fall in love.

'Harry's looking for trouble,' Gertie replied. 'He said he thinks that French tart looks pretty sexy. You don't say that sort of thing in front of your girlfriend, unless you're looking to be thumped.'

'I think he's wrong,' Frank noted easily, leaning back and looking at the ceiling. 'I think she looks very sexy. Those tight trousers she's wearing. I might have dreams about those.'

Frank Summers was obviously looking for more than trouble.

'That reminds me,' he said as Gertie sulked at him, 'I need to organise Matisse's lawyer. Foxy Fillette wants to speak to him rapidement. Matisse, that is, not his lawyer.'

'Foxy what?'

'The little French bint,' Frank translated, dialling a number.

'Ah, Mrs Smith, you sound as attractive as ever,' he said when his call was answered.

'Of course not, Mrs Smith, I would hardly try to chat up a

married woman, no matter how good-looking she was. I was just wondering when Mr Jadbhur could find a little time in his diary to pop down to the station. We need him to sit in on an interview with M Matisse.'

'Yes, yes, I know his diary's full, Mrs Smith. Mr Jadbhur really does work too hard, doesn't he? Perhaps tomorrow, or the day after? Possibly next week? How about a Sunday in August? I'm sure I know a song about that. Or was it a Tuesday in September?'

'This afternoon? Are you sure? We wouldn't like to trespass on Mr Jadbhur's busy schedule. Tomorrow would be just as good.'

'Tomorrow it is, then, Mrs Smith. Regards to Mr Smith. Tell him from me he's a very lucky man.'

He put the phone down and smiled at Gertie.

'Such a pity, M Matisse's lawyer can't make it until tomorrow. Do you suppose that will upset Wonderwoman? I'll ask Tricia to pass on the sad news.'

Gertie returned the look with one of mixed concern and pleasure. Pleasure that Frieda was firmly in Frank's bad books, concern that Frank might be pushing his well-known luck a little too far this time. He put her in mind of a cat testing its nine lives all at the same time. Only in this case he was gambling his career on it. It was only recently that she had realised that Frank's easy-going, boyish charm hid an obstinacy that had decided on all-or-nothing. There would be no quiet posting to a different police station to resolve a personal dispute. It was either win or leave the police force. The trouble was that Frieda herself would never accept losing.

'What say, Gertie,' Frank said, having spoken to Tricia,

checking his watch. 'There's that break-in at Lords Acres at the house Matisse was renting, that should take up the morning. Wonderwoman has so ordained that we should attend the scene of crime, total waste of time as far as I can see, but there you go. Then lunch, a visit to the Blue Bliss about the rumours of drug dealing, that'll take up the afternoon, and then time for a couple of drinks after work. Should keep us out of the station and out of trouble for the day, if we stretch things a bit. How does that sound to you?'

The Blue Bliss was a gambling-cum-strip-club on the outskirts of Wellbury. It had acquired a new owner after the last one had been murdered. It had also acquired a reputation for being a source of some of the more mentally stimulating drugs on the market, according to Frieda. And, also according to Frieda, the Chief Constable wanted it stamped on immediately. So did the good citizens of Wellbury. The Blue Bliss when it had originally opened had been an affront, accepted only because many Wellburians needed something they could be affronted by. Such a club was heaven-sent for the "I don't know what the world is coming to" brigade. But drugs? If you really did that sort of thing you did it privately or went and lived in a commune in Amsterdam. There was such a thing as propriety.

'Sounds good to me, Sarge,' Gertie said happily. Susan and Frieda would not look kindly on her for having drinks with Frank after work.

If they found out. And they weren't likely to. Frank wasn't about to mention it, now was he? He was hardly speaking to them. Or, to be more accurate, they were hardly speaking to him.

They were just about to leave when an irritated and harassed-looking Frieda appeared in the doorway with Captain Tromperie behind her.

'I understand Mr Jadbhur won't be able to get here until tomorrow,' Frieda said grimly. By the look on her face she was only just holding on in the face of the onslaught of the French woman, Frank thought. The briefest of small smiles, another nano-second, crossed Jean Tromperie's eyes as he looked at her. Again came that flicker in her eyes. An amused look, almost as if they were secret combatants in a duel, and whoever won, it would be theirs alone. And then the look was gone, replaced by the eternal sneer.

Frank had the urge to warn her that her face might need plastic surgery to remove the look if she weren't careful.

'A very busy man, our Mr Jadbhur,' he said, pushing the thought aside. 'I only managed to book him for tomorrow after quite a bit of charming his secretary,' he replied. 'It was hard work. She's not easy to flatter, our Mrs Smith.'

Frieda looked at him in a fury that showed she believed none of it. Frank returned the look complacently, challenging her to push the issue.

'In that case Captain Tromperie has some time on her hands,' Frieda said. 'I've offered her the chance to see Wellbury police in action. You will take her around with you this morning to M Matisse's house. You will return her for lunch in my office at twelve thirty precisely. At one-thirty you will take her with you to the Blue Bliss, returning at four on the dot. Understood, Sergeant?'

'What time did you say again?'

'Don't push it, Detective Sergeant.'

'If you so wish, Inspector.'

They indulged in a further bout of eyeballing before Frieda turned and swept away, back to her office. She walked up the stairs, passed Tricia without a word, slammed her door closed, and walked over to the window, standing back so that she could not be seen from outside. She watched Frank, Gertie and the other woman walk to Frank's car.

Damn you, Frank Summers! she thought, tears welling to her eyes. Damn you to hell!

Having rebuilt her life after a traumatic marriage to a wife-beating fellow police detective, having established herself as an extremely professional and efficient police officer, having achieved the rank of Inspector at a relatively young age, having learnt to handle men as arrogant but rather stupid creatures in need of firm control, she had come across Frank, a man who had little ambition but the enjoyment of life, a man whose self-deprecation and sense of humour had stolen her heart away.

She had once believed in love. She had married a man she was in love with. She really had loved him at one stage. The harsh realities of life had opened her eyes. After a long battle to recover her very self, she had decided that love was an illusion. And then along came Frank. It would be her last chance. She was reaching the age when life stood at a crossroads: a few years more without a man and she would be left childless, her only role as a woman to act as the mature woman seducing and inducting young men in the art of the bedroom, until left embittered and alone, a single woman with little but the political battles of the police bureaucracy to keep her interested, her only comfort being that she was a Mrs rather than a Miss, and what very little comfort there was in that.

She had not meant it to turn out this way. She had become used to controlling things. Too used to controlling things. Susan had been right, it had not been Frank's fault. Not entirely.

Now they were involved in a battle of wills, and Frank was showing the steel she had always known was there. He was easy-going up to a point. Now they stood at that point. Frank was inviting her to cross a line. She was doing the same to him.

And for what?

So that they could end up destroying each other? Facing one another with wounds, torn clothing, like two wild animals who cannot win but refuse to lose?

She shivered. The thought was a little too arousing.

She watched Frank and Gertie get into the front seats, Gertie in the driver's seat. That little French bitch with the tight trousers got into the back as if she was being chauffeured.

She went back to her desk. On it she had a swear box, one that received a fifty-pence piece any time anyone swore in her presence.

She put it away in a drawer. It would become too bloody expensive for her over the next few days if she left it out.

But she was not going to give in to Frank. Neither as his superior officer nor as a woman. Not even if Hell should freeze over, the Winter Olympics be held there and Frank be a part of the British bobsleigh team – as the bobsleigh.

Of course that did present her with a small problem. Given the circumstances, how was she going to arrange that she and Frank went out on Saturday? Which they were going to do, whatever low plans and cunning tricks Susan and Gertie might be thinking up. Better that she and Frank should go out and have an argument than that he should go out with one of the others and enjoy himself.

How to arrange it, that was the question. Still, she was an intelligent woman, no reason not to come up with and carry out some devious plan. The more devious the better. It would have to be.

Gertie was fuming as she drove. That little French tart with the stupid hat was treating them like minions. She could handle that, she was used to senior officers doing the same. But she wasn't going to allow some French bitch to humiliate Frank. Not her Frank.

Frank, as usual, seemed totally unperturbed and unaware. He idly wound his window down and played with the mirror on his side of the car.

'We're going to the scene of a burglary,' he said evenly. 'A suburb called Lords Acres. Very wealthy part of town. Not what you would call an ordinary *banlieue*.'

Captain Tromperie sat in the back, disapproving. Of everything. The smart and colourful summer streets and avenues of Wellbury no doubt compared not at all with her own native town, wherever that might be.

'You know some French, Sergeant Summers?' she asked haughtily.

'Used to be able to speak it fluently once upon a time,' he said, to Gertie's surprise. 'A bit rusty now, but now's c'est la chance, n'est ce pas, Capitaine? I'll parley le francais and you can correct me where I go wrong. Deal?'

'I prefer English,' the woman replied with her usual sneer. 'After all, if you English are to be dominated by the Americans we need to be able to speak in what the Americans think English should be. You English do not like us purely because we are not prepared to be treated by the Americans like a preferred prostitute. An occasional whore, to be given the scraps from the table of the beneficent master.'

'Your English is superb,' Frank noted as Gertie took a corner at a speed above that of the accepted guidelines and on fewer than the recommended number of wheels. 'Take it easy, Gertie my sweet, no rush,' he added. 'But the idea of us as French-hating is somewhat of a stereotype, I think. After all, look at the marvellous women in French history we admire so much. Joan of Arc, Madame Curie, Marianne – who is the present Marianne, by the way?'

'I do not trouble myself with such outdated sexual irrelevancies,' Captain Tromperie said, looking out of the window.

'It's a bit like the French Prime Minister,' Frank continued. 'They seem to change all the time, almost as bad as the Italians. President what's-his-face seems to sack one a week. Who is the current incumbent, Mary la Pen?'

Captain Tromperie turned and looked at the back of his head.

'I think, as your English saying goes, you try to take the Mickey, Sergeant?' she suggested. 'There is no way le Pen would ever become prime minister of la belle France.'

Well, thought Frank, one to the sneering captain. At least she knew who the right-wing politician le Pen was. Perhaps she was French after all.

'Not at all, Captain,' he replied smoothly. 'I'm just a poor police sergeant trying to improve myself. They don't tell me nothing. All I know is what I read in the newspapers.'

'The, what you call them?' scoffed the young woman in the back seat, 'the tabloids? They would not even be called newspapers in France. Big pictures and small words. Little paragraphs that do not tax the little brains of their little readers.'

'Great British newspapers,' Frank said. 'You can trust every word. Not a single lie.'

Alongside him Gertie's anger dissolved slightly. Frank wouldn't trust a tabloid to get the date right. In a halcyon period a few weeks before she had lived in his flat while hers was being renovated following a disastrous leak from the flat above. It hadn't gained her the pre-eminent position in his affections she had so desperately craved – and worked bloody hard at, mind you – but she did remember that he never so much as glanced at a tabloid newspaper. His preferred reading, apart from non-fiction books, were the Guardian and Independent, with an occasional Times or Telegraph to balance things out. She also remembered seeing him sitting with the French newspaper Liberation, the Friday edition of which he bought on a semi-regular basis, and a dictionary, tongue sticking out slightly like a schoolboy at study, earnestly trying to understand news from a different viewpoint and culture.

Frank knew exactly who the current French prime minister was. He probably even knew the name of the Italian under-secretary of garden gnomes, if there was such a thing. He was baiting this French bitch. Gertie didn't know why, but she realised that Frank had his own strange reasons. It wasn't that he was more intelligent than her, just that he had a lot more experience, something she intended to tap into.

And it wasn't only his experience she intended to tap into. Frieda was sidelined. She could deal with Tricia by pointing out to Frank how young the girl was, repeatedly if necessary. Susan had agreed to Frieda's suggestion of cold-shouldering Frank for a while, so she was out of the race. That left only one woman on Frank's active radar.

Herself.

Which is why she was extremely not happy to find Doctor bloody Susan Pleadle standing outside of the house in Lords Acres.

'I thought you'd finished up here,' Frank remarked mildly. Since Susan hadn't spoken to him for over a week he presumed he was still in her bad books. He had come to the decision that he would always be in her bad books, no matter what he did. He intended to shrug it off and maintain a purely professional relationship with her. She could have her little tantrums, he would politely ignore them and merely read her reports. If she wanted to act like a child he would treat her as a child. So there.

Nah boo sucks.

'I have a very professional approach to my work, as you know,' Susan replied, trying not too obviously to inspect the French woman. 'I like to make sure everything is completed properly. There are one or two loose ends to tie up.'

'Ah, this is Captain Tromperie of the Sûreté,' Frank introduced her, as if only just remembering her presence. 'Captain, Doctor Susan Pleadle, our forensic expert.'

After an initial look of surprise Susan nodded a less than warm welcome.

'The French police are of course world leaders in forensic matters,' Jean Tromperie said. 'I doubt if a little town like this has much awareness of the latest procedures. Perhaps I could arrange a short visit to Paree for you at some stage in the future, you would learn much.'

'I doubt if I'll find any spare time,' Susan replied through gritted teeth.

'Let's take a look inside,' Frank said, concealing a smile. Jean Tromperie was doing a class act as an arrogant French woman, the stereotype to beat all stereotypes. Susan, like the others, had immediately fallen for it. Had anyone stopped to think they might realise that not even the French would send someone like Tromperie over to antagonise a brother police force.

He was sure of it.

At least, he was pretty sure of it.

Unless, of course, they had done what he would have done: sent her over to get rid of her.

The problem was, if he had got it wrong, and he did something unwise, he would not come out smelling of roses, and Frieda had already prepared a noose for him, just waiting for him to stick his neck into it.

He would have to play this one pretty carefully.

He opened the door and they stepped inside. He whistled.

> 'They must have cost a few bob when they were in one piece,' he noted.

In the hallway in front on them lay the remains of what had once been two large, impressive, waist-high vases in the Chinese style. Now all they were was a debris of broken shards scattered across the floor.

'The whole place is like this,' Susan said. 'It looks as if a cyclone went from room to room. The sitting room, dining room, upstairs, all wrecked.'

They moved into the sitting room. The brown leather couch and armchairs looked as if they would have been both smart and comfortable at one time, not to say very expensive. Before someone had taken a knife to them and ripped out the stuffing.

'Made in Britain,' observed Jean Tromperie, reading a label. 'No great loss then.'

This was met with looks of fury from Susan and Gertie, both of which the erstwhile captain affected not to see. Frank wandered out into the passage and into the dining room. The others followed, the French woman at the back. A brief and enigmatic smile played across her lips.

'Our M Matisse certainly had expensive tastes,' noted Frank. 'This furniture looks like it's Regency, or something like that. Or was.'

The dining room chairs had once been padded with striped green and cream material. They had received the same treatment as the furniture in the lounge. Cabinets at the sides had been broken open and their contents ripped out and strewn across the floor.

'It isn't Matisse's furniture,' Susan said. 'Apparently this is how the place was rented out.'

'With broken furniture?' asked Jean Tromperie with a superior air. 'You English have strange preferences in your lifestyle.'

'I meant the furniture came with the house, obviously, before it was broken,' Susan said.

'Well, you should have said so,' noted Jean, not bothering to look at Susan, whose face was turning the colour of hot fury. 'Accuracy is all-important for a professional.'

'Let me guess,' said Frank, 'there's a library and they trashed that too.'

'I'm afraid so,' replied Susan, trying to control herself, addressing her words to Frank and ignoring the French woman. 'The whole house has been taken apart.'

'And you found nothing, no useful fingerprints, strands of hair, pieces of clothing caught on a handy nail, nothing of that ilk?'

'No,' replied Susan. 'We went through everything with a fine toothcomb. As far as we can see they probably wore gloves and just ripped everything apart.'

A "Hmmph" sound from Jean Tromperie indicated that she wasn't impressed with Susan's fine toothcomb.

'Well, let's get it over with,' said Frank. 'I don't think I can take much more of this mindless destruction.'

The large study-cum-library was especially heartbreaking. Books, hardbacked and looking as if they could well have been collectors' items before, had been dragged from bookcases, riffled through, and then thrown aside. The bookcases themselves had then been ripped from the walls and their back panels smashed. Paintings and etchings lay on the floor amidst the other debris, the remnants of their broken frames scattered around like pieces of a child's broken, unwanted toy. Busts of ancient philosophers had been carelessly tossed onto the marble tiles in front of the fireplace, to shatter into smithereens. There was an air of wilful damage beyond any other purpose.

The sight of the bedrooms upstairs was consequently a lesser shock. Although mattresses had been disembowelled and cupboards ripped apart, the furniture was more modern and thus more replaceable.

'Well, I suppose nobody ever buys an ancient mattress to sleep on,' said Frank thoughtfully, scratching his cheek. 'A carpenter might create something and dream of it being still in use a thousand years later, but I can't see a mattress maker having such illusions.'

All three women gave him strange looks.

'So, that's it?' he asked finally.

'Just the kitchen downstairs,' said Susan. 'It made me want to cry. Someone had really put a lot of hard work into making it a real kitchen, a place to cook and to relax, lovely and large with a real fireplace. The type of kitchen you'd love to come home to. It nearly broke my heart to see what they'd done to it. Come on.'

They followed her downstairs. Only Gertie amongst them knew what Susan had meant. The message had been aimed directly at Frank's subconscious. "I'm a good little woman who loves to cook for her man. Wouldn't I make a nice little wife?"

Knowing Susan, Gertie also knew it was complete rubbish. She was pretty sure that Susan wouldn't recognise an egg-timer if you hit her over the head with one. She probably thought vermicelli was some Italian composer.

But that was okay, two could play at that game.

The kitchen had indeed been taken apart like the rest of the large house. The floor was littered with pans, pots, broken crockery and glassware. Just as elsewhere, cupboards had been ransacked and brutalised. Had it been some ancient kitchen with smoke-glazed frying pans and wooden spoons deeply worn and imbued with the sauces of years, Gertie might well have agreed to a certain extent with Susan's alleged feelings, but this was a modern kitchen, the only reminder of earlier days the large fireplace which the owner had surprisingly not ripped out to make way for an Aga, possibly because there had been sufficient space for both the fireplace and an Aga. Expensively equipped, yes, but as it was it looked storm-wrecked but not destroyed totally beyond recovery.

'Not very efficient, were they?' mused Frank, idly pushing at a piece of a broken glass measuring-jug with the tip of his shoe.

'I think they were very efficient,' Jean Tromperie said. 'I cannot see anywhere they have missed. The entire house has been taken apart piece by piece. I have seen many such scenes, but never one as efficient as this.'

'Au contraire, ma Capitaine,' Frank said. 'They obviously missed whatever it was they were looking for. They were looking for something they believed was hidden. You don't go around slashing mattresses and breaking cupboards when something's been hidden. You use your brains. Subtlety, mon Capitaine, subtlety, toujours le subtlety.'

'Subtlety?' asked Jean Tromperie scornfully. 'You would not know subtlety if you were hit over the head with it, Sergeant.'

He nodded at the broken glass at his foot.

'You don't hide something in a glass,' he pointed out. 'So why break it? It just lies on the floor and gets in the way, apart from the danger of cutting yourself. No, my guess is that two things happened here. Firstly they tried to find what they were after by using brute force. Then, frustrated at being thwarted, they went the whole hog. They were sending a message to Matisse. Not a very polite or pleasant one.'

'Your guess?' enquired Jean Tromperie. 'I think you should stick with following orders. Your mind is too small for guessing. Let someone else do the thinking, Sergeant Summers.'

She turned to Susan.

'They were looking for a painting called The Blue Studio,' she said. 'Perhaps you stumbled across it while blundering around here?'

Susan's face turned red as her blood hit boiling point.

'As far as I'm aware you do not have any jurisdiction here, Corporal Strumpet,' she said in fury. 'I'd advise you to watch your step. In fact I'd suggest you get on the next flight back to your greasy little country. Go beat up a few Algerians, that's your national sport, isn't it?'

'You appear to have lost your self control, Doctor,' Tromperie noted with disdain. 'But then I was not expecting a professional approach in such a rural village. I think I will take another look around. No doubt you have missed much.'

Susan couldn't speak as they watched the pert backside and shiny boots leave the kitchen.

'The little bitch!' she exploded finally. 'She's looking for a good slap and she's going to get one. I'll kill her, so help me I'll kill her!'

'Now, now,' Frank said mildly and ironically, 'she's just being French. You don't expect anything better of them, do you?' He paused. 'Sexy little thing, though, isn't she?' he added. 'I quite like her, as it happens.'

Susan's fury turned towards him.

'Oh, you fancy her, do you? Well you can have her! I don't ever want to see you again, you bastard! You absolute shit, you! Chase after that little French tart if you want, Frank Summers! See if I bloody care!'

Frank and Gertie watched Susan stomp out of the kitchen, kicking pots and other cooking debris out of her way, not at all the image of a good little housewife.

'Her little tootsies are going to hurt like hell tomorrow,' noted Frank with a smile. 'I bet you she'll blame me for ruining those shoes, too.'

Gertie looked at him warily.

'You aren't mad at me as well, are you?' she asked in a small voice. 'Only if you are I'd like to go hide somewhere until you get over it, please? Pretty please?'

'Course I'm not, Gerts,' he said, squeezing her shoulder gently. 'I'm just teaching Wonderwoman and Doctor Death a little lesson.'

'You don't really think that French tart is sexy, do you?'

He considered this idea.

'Depends on your definition of the word, I suppose. What I do think is that's she's rather interesting. Do you think she knows what she's looking for, and where to find it?'

'You've lost me, Sarge.'

'Don't worry, Gertie. She can't hide it in those tight trousers she's wearing, there isn't any space. Just keep an ear open for the sound of canvas rustling coming from that jacket of hers.'

He looked around.

'However, if she hasn't found anything ... Yes, that will do nicely.' He picked up a box containing a roll of tin foil. 'I said they were inefficient. Didn't even bother to check something as obvious as this.'

He opened the box, took the roll of foil out and held it up to the light, looking through the cylinder as if it were the barrel of a rifle.

'Nope, didn't think so,' he said, returning the roll to its box. 'But that doesn't mean our Captain Comedy shouldn't think so. Come on, let's see how she's doing and whether she's ready for dejeuner with Wonderwoman.'

Gertie shook her head, wondering whether Frank had taken leave of his senses.

'Speaking of dinner,' she said as they left the kitchen, 'I've taken up a course in Spanish cooking. I wondered if I could experiment on you, say supper Saturday night?'

'A cookery course? Along with your law studies? Where do you find the time, Gerts?'

'It isn't easy,' admitted Gertie, hoping he wouldn't ask for any further details of the non-existent course, but knowing she had once picked up a book on Spanish cooking at a Oxfam shop a few years previously, and being sure that she'd be able to find it before Saturday. 'I suppose not having a boyfriend helps. Will you come?'

'Absolutely, Gertie. I look forward to it. I love Spanish food.'

He could at least have picked up a little on that "not having a boyfriend" bit. What did she have to do, dance naked in front of him while carrying a sign that said "Take me"?

'Only don't tell anyone else,' she said instead. 'Not until the course is over. I don't want to find that I'm useless at Spanish cooking and everyone knowing it.'

'Course not Gertie. I'm sure you'll be brilliant at it. You're always good at anything you decide to do.'

'Not quite everything,' Gertie said sadly as they entered the sitting room.

'Any luck, Captain?' asked Frank. The French woman was standing in the centre of the debris, rubbing her chin slowly, looking thoughtful.

'Mmm?' she asked absent-mindedly. Suddenly she started as if waking up. 'I was thinking. You have interrupted my thinking, Sergeant. Now it will not come. You should not interrupt your superior officer while she is thinking.'

'Ah, well, fortunately you're neither of those. Ready for a bang-up meal with the Inspector?'

'What do you mean, Sergeant? What is this "neither of those"?'

'I meant you're neither my superior nor my officer, mon petite Capitaine.'

She looked at him with contempt.

'I see you are very rude as well as very stupid, Sergeant. I shall speak to your Inspector about that.'

'You do that, Captain. You can do it over lunch. Sausage, mash and baked beans today, I think. I'm sure you'll love it. Sometimes they also throw in some overboiled cabbage as well. My favourite. Come on, Gertie, let's drive the nice little Capitaine back to the station. If we're lucky it might be roast beef instead of sausages. We British do love our roast beef.'

The Captain's attention was distracted by his slapping the foil box against his leg, as if in happy anticipation of lunch.

'You have found something, Sergeant?' she asked.

'This? Oh, I've run out at my flat. I thought I'd borrow some. I'll replace it with another box when I remember to buy some. Very handy for wrapping stuff in, this stuff.'

'That is removing evidence from the scene of the crime,' she said, her eyes locked on the box. 'I think you should give it to me. I will give it to your Inspector.'

'Nonsense, Capitaine Jeannie,' Frank replied, turning to go. 'We British coppers always borrow things here and there. Nobody misses them. Come on, I'm starving. Can't wait to get at that cabbage.'

Gertie smiled as she drove. Frank sat whistling nonchalantly, tapping the dashboard with the box in time to the tune. In the rear-view mirror she could see the French tart's eyes locked on the box. Gertie didn't know what Frank was up to, but he had obviously got the measure of the arrogant little bitch.

Which was something the others hadn't. And while Frieda and Susan had their eyes on the French slut, she, Gertie, would have Frank all to herself. It was just a question of not letting your attention get distracted from the important things.

After all, hadn't she just finessed Saturday right from under the other two's noses?

'Eric, I meant to ask you,' Frank said as they joined Eric Johns in the canteen, 'any idea who took over the Blue Bliss after Bagley copped it? We're supposed to be going to have a word with the new owner about the inadvisability of allowing drug selling on the premises. Just rumours at the moment, but it would be nice to stop it before it gets serious.'

'Haven't you heard?' asked Eric Johns in surprise. 'I thought everybody knew. Mrs Blower's running things now. She and Phil Walthers bought the place.'

'You're joking!' Frank exclaimed, his eyes opening wide in amazement.

Mrs Blower had been a suspect in his previous case, a woman who ran the local vicarage until Frank had revealed the vicar to be a psychopath on the run. Mrs Blower could have three conversations at the same time, and had a memory far worse than any sieve ever invented.

Phil Walthers was the editor, chief reporter, sub-editor and photographer of the Wellbury Herald. He was the Wellbury Herald. A chameleon type of man, at times effeminate, mincing, but highly intelligent. And a man who couldn't stand Mrs Blower.

'Not a word of a lie,' Eric replied. 'They seem to think it's some sort of artistic revue. We were taking bets on how long it would be before the place went bankrupt.' He paused. 'Strange thing is, what with everyone going there just to see how awful it is, they seem to be doing quite well.'

'Well, well,' said Frank thoughtfully. 'Today is becoming better and better.' He looked at Eric Johns. 'You haven't popped in there for a look, by any chance?'

Eric looked down guiltily.

'Keith and I were just passing the place last week and, well, we thought we'd have a quick pint and maybe see what the fuss was about, you know?'

'Without telling your wives, of course?'

'Course not, Frank, don't be daft. As it was, it was quite interesting. They were doing a re-enactment of some women's thing, votes or something. Women taking their clothes off and chaining themselves to rails.'

Frank whistled and shook his head in amazement.

'I'll bet Emmeline Pankhurst was turning in her grave,' said Gertie sourly.

'Emily who?' asked Eric.

'Oh, only one of the most important women in the history of women's liberation,' said Gertie, having managed to remain silent when Eric Johns had confessed to keeping the truth from his wife but finding the latest revelation of this misrepresentation of the Suffragettes too much to accept. 'That's probably why you haven't heard of her.'

'Women's lib?' commented Eric dismissively. 'That's ancient history, love. Been there, done that. Lost a helmet to one of them in the Seventies when they were demonstrating. I'll never forget that. I had to pay for that bloody helmet.'

He turned to Frank.

'Here, you didn't half miss a right to-do this morning.'

'Oh? Wonderwoman discover the ceilings hadn't been polished properly?'

'Nah, Frank, be serious. You know that bloke who's checking out the armoury downstairs?'

'John Stevens? Nice bloke. Knows his firearms.'

'He knows something more about something else now. Guess what he found.'

'From the sounds of things so far, a pike, a couple of swords and a musket, I would imagine.'

'Worse than that. A hand grenade.'

For the second time that lunchtime Eric Johns had managed to surprise Frank.

'You're joking. A real hand grenade? Not one of those tear-gas ones again?'

'A real hand grenade, Frank, no word of a lie. And you know what? The pin was out, lying next to it. I tell you, that poor bloke came flying up the stairs like a scalded cat, shouting for everyone to evacuate the building immediately. Almost put me off the cream bun I was eating.'

'So what happened?'

'Well, we just ignored him, you know, to save him from embarrassment. Poor bloke had lost it, probably being doing too much overtime or whatever. You know what these people from large towns are like, work too hard, get stressed out, then have a breakdown over some little thing. Then Fabulous comes down to find out what all the fuss was about, not looking too happy, you know? When our gun chum has managed to explain she orders us to evacuate the station, all calm but pissed-off like, as if that grenade was going to wish it had never been made when she gets her hands on it. Tells young Tricia to call the bomb squad. Trish calls up the army, not knowing better, and around they come, quick as you like, as if they were just waiting for the call. Lazy buggers sitting on their backsides with nowt to do, I reckon. The fortunate thing is, this army lot had an old sergeant in charge, the old type who doesn't let things like unexploded grenades put him off his tea. He goes down on his own, no blast jacket or anything, has a look, comes back up the stairs with the bleeding grenade in his hands. Only person who wasn't hiding where they could was Fabulous. He explains to her as how it's a dummy for throwing practice. There's some sort of coded colour on the top of the grenade which tells him that. It was probably left over from the war, along with those Lee Enfields.'

'And then?'

'Fabulous gets everyone back inside, lets this army Sergeant explain everything to our gun chum, and sends both of them back here to the canteen for a cup of tea and a chocolate éclair. I reckon our gun chum was about ready to leave and never come back, poor sod. But the whole time we're outside hiding, Fabulous is standing in reception as if daring that grenade to go off. So gun chum, well he's a bloke, he can't run away when a woman has stayed, can he? Even though he doesn't rightly know our Fabulous like we do.'

'Marvellous,' said Frank acerbically. 'I can imagine Wonderwoman in the role.'

'Oh, come on Frank,' Eric Johns protested. 'Be fair. I know you and her are having an argument, and I don't know what it's all about, and I do wish you'd stop it, but you have to admit she's got balls.'

'Biologically, Eric, I think I might just be able to refute that argument.'

Eric rolled his eyes in exasperation and decided that it would be best to change the subject. He paused in his consumption of lunch and noticed the box containing the roll of foil in front of Frank.

'Thinking of wrapping something up for later?' he asked. 'A snack to keep you going? Not a bad idea. Wish I'd thought of that one. One or two of Agnetha's drumsticks would do nicely at about mid-afternoon.'

'No, Eric, I just didn't want to leave it in the office where someone with itchy fingers could nick it.'

'Tin foil?' asked Eric in amazement. 'Who would want to nick a box of tin foil?'

'Me for a start, Eric. I nicked it from the place Matisse was renting.'

Eric Johns shook his head in despair. He looked at Gertie.

'You'd better keep an eye on Frank, love,' he said. 'I think he's really lost it this time.'

'Oh, you'd be surprised at the lengths some people will go to get their hands on this box,' Frank told him. 'I'm expecting someone to try all sorts of tricks just for that purpose. What is going to be truly fascinating is what those tricks will be. I'm looking forward to finding out.'

After lunch Frank went down to the basement armoury. John Stevens was sitting on a box eating a door-stopper of a sandwich.

'Hi, John,' Frank said. 'I hear you had a bit of fun this morning.'

John Stevens rolled his eyes and swallowed.

'Tell you what, Frank, I won't need a check-up for a few years. If my heart can take that it must be in good nick.'

Frank looked around the solid walls of the small armoury.

'Not much consolation I suppose,' he said, 'but I would imagine if it was real and did go off in here you wouldn't know anything about it. Here one minute, splattered across the walls the next.'

'Cheers for that, Frank. You don't know how much better that makes me feel. Here,' John Stevens added, putting his sandwich down, standing up and pulling a long, slim box from underneath the counter. 'I've found something else. Take a look at this.'

He undid two clips and opened the lid of the box. Inside a rifle lay awkwardly, the box originally designed for a different model.

'Bloody hell!' exclaimed Frank. 'That's an FN. How the hell did one of those turn up here?'

'Same way as the rest of the stuff here, no doubt. Ever used one?'

'Indeed I have. When I was doing one of the firearms courses the instructor – Jack Gilly, ever heard of him? Big chap, about six-four tall and four foot wide?'

'Of course. I trained under him myself. Still see him from time to time. One of the best.'

'He let me stay on in the evenings after the others had left. Let me try a number of different firearms. The FN was his favourite.'

John Stevens nodded.

'Funny bugger, Jack,' he said. 'The original gentle giant. He loved firearms, loved target shooting, but hated the idea that they could be used against anything living.'

Frank nodded agreement, holding the rifle up to the light, admiring its form.

'There was a story that that was because he had had to take out someone in a hostage situation once.'

'Nah, Frank, he never liked the idea before that. What happened is that afterwards he refused to ever go out on the streets again. Couldn't face it.'

'Can't say I blame him. I could never get used to the idea myself.'

'Pray God you never have to, Frank.'

Frank was tempted to ask John Stevens whether he had ever been in that position. Somehow he had a feeling that he knew what the answer would be, and that the other man would prefer not to discuss the matter.

He handed the rifle back and checked his watch.

'Lovely, isn't it?' he asked. 'I'm afraid I have to go, though, time for afternoon babysitting.'

'Rather you than me,' John Stevens said, picking up his sandwich. 'I prefer bolts and breeches to people. You know, I might take this beaut to the firing range this afternoon. Just to make sure it's in full working order.'

'You're just trying to make me jealous.'

'Jealous? What I heard is that you're babysitting a gorgeous French piece.'

'I wish I knew just what it was I'm babysitting, John. All I can say for sure is that I'm pretty sure it is a woman. Apart from that I wouldn't bet a penny on anything, not even with somebody else's money.'

'You'll be interested in this case, Captain,' Frank said as they drove to the Blue Bliss. 'It's a night-club we suspect is involved in dealing in drugs brought over from France. Inspector Garold tells me you're well known for your interview techniques. Perhaps you could give us the benefits of your greater experience by interviewing the owner, a Mrs Blower.'

Gertie's mouth twitched as she restrained a giggle. Frank hadn't spoken to Frieda since first thing that morning. For all he knew the only thing the French tart was known for was wiggling her tight little backside. But the French tart didn't know that. Nor did she know that the rumours of drug-selling were only that so far – just rumours – and there had been no suggestion that the drugs, if they existed, came from France or outer Rumania.

'This is not, as you have so strongly pointed out, Sergeant Summers, my jurisdiction,' the French woman in the back of the car pointed out with a sneer. It was a sneer that came with a little smile of triumph, as Frank noticed in the rear-view mirror. There were rumours that Frieda had not enjoyed entertaining the Captain to lunch in her office. It was more than just the food that had stuck in the craw. France two, Frieda zero, he thought. And Frieda hated losing.

Correction. Frieda never lost. Ever. It was something that sat at the back of his mind constantly, now that he and she were having their own private little war.

'You mean you're afraid of making a fool of yourself,' he replied to the French woman, deciding not to point out that it was Susan who had commented on the question of jurisdiction and not himself. 'Very quick to treat us like country bumpkins, but as soon as you're offered a chance to show how good you are you run away like a scaredy-cat. Scaredy-cat, scaredy-cat,' he repeated, a little like the boy Pike in Dad's Army.

There was a short silence. Frank noticed in the rear-view mirror that this approach had somewhat thrown Jean Tromperie.

'You think I am scared, Sergeant Summers?' she asked finally, in a voice containing just a slight tadge less than her normal arrogant confidence.

'Your choice, Captain,' Frank said easily. 'It's called put up or shut up.'

Gertie was amazed. Frank was the original diplomat. Normally he could tell people to go to hell in such a way they looked forward to the journey, as the saying had it. Now he was bluntly taking on Frieda, Susan and this stuck up little French bitch. And he was winning.

So far.

That's my Frank, she thought happily.

He would lose, of course, in the end, especially against Frieda. But it would be a fun ride. Afterward she, Gertie, and Frank could leave the police force and go live somewhere such as Cornwall, maybe growing daffodils on a farm. It was a half-dream she often had. While she loved her job as a police officer, and had always planned on achieving a top post some day, there was also part of her that yearned for a quiet life in the country somewhere not far from the sea. She could imagine herself, belly enlarged with their first child, looking out of the kitchen window at Frank contemplating rows of daffodils on a chilly spring morning, ready with a mug of warm, home-made soup for when he came indoors, her own loving husband.

It was a nice dream. She wished she could have both that dream and a highly successful career as a police officer, but not even an eternally optimistic Gertie could honestly see a way of reconciling the pragmatic necessities involved in the two options. But it was looking increasingly certain that Frank was determined on a course which would see the end of his police career.

Unless Frieda were to be posted away from Wellbury for

some reason ...

'Pah!' exclaimed the French bitch as if with regained confidence, interrupting Gertie's thoughts. 'If you cannot interview a drug dealer yourself I shall do it. We have many of these in Paree. We treat them like the scum they are.'

'Oh, good,' said Frank, smiling.

As they drove in silence Jean Tromperie appeared to be increasingly looking forward to the challenge. She began to quietly tap a tune on the armrest next to her.

'Lovely music, that,' Frank said. 'I've always thought the Mayonnaise was one of the better national anthems. Not as good as ours, but not bad.'

Jean Tromperie paused before continuing tapping.

'The Marsellaise,' she said, emphasising the word, 'is the only real national anthem, Sergeant. Unfortunately you British have never been musical. It comes of having a barbarian history – if it can be called history. You will never understand anything but beer and fish and chips. Culture is foreign to you.'

Not for the first time that day Gertie was puzzled. She didn't know what tune the French tart had been tapping to, but it certainly wasn't the Marsellaise. She knew that, and Frank would definitely have known that.

'Not true, Capitaine,' Frank said. 'For example, I had a glass of red plonk only a few weeks ago. Maybe a couple of months. Australian it was, lovely stuff. Two quid off in the local supermarket.'

Jean Tromperie was about to reply when she realised that Frank had begin softly singing the words to the same tune she had been tapping. It was a tune from a re-run of a film on television he had seen some years before, "A Funny Thing Happened On The Way To The Forum".

"Something appealing, something appalling, something for everyone: a comedy tonight."

Jean Tromperie stopped tapping. Instead she was studying the back of Detective Sergeant Frank Summers' head with a thoughtful look in her eyes. After a while she seemed to come to a decision. She nodded slightly and turned to look out of the window, a brief smile passing across her face.

Yes, thought Frank, watching her face in the rear-view mirror. If you haven't already realised it, now you know you aren't up against some dense country plod, don't you Capitaine Jean Tromperie, or whatever your real name is. You wanted a battle of wits, now you've found one. The only question is, how long will it take you to realise that you've already lost?

And of that he was quite sure.

Or pretty sure, anyway.

Catching a fish, Inspector Percy Hanson had once opined – several times, in fact, to anyone not fast enough to get away in time to avoid his obsession with angling – was the easy bit. Landing the bugger was another matter altogether.

Frank had a worrying suspicion that landing this particular fish wasn't going to be the easiest thing in the world. But he was going to have fun trying. If he thought about it, and was honest, a combination of events unlikely to happen in this case, he was becoming intrigued with Jean Tromperie.

If intrigued was the right word.

The first thing they encountered, once they had entered the

doors of the Blue Bliss and advanced to the main bar area, was a yawning young woman wearing a see-through nightdress, pair of panties and nothing else. She was sitting at a table with a cup of coffee and a newspaper as if enjoying breakfast some hours later than others might consider the normal hour.

'You're early,' she pointed out, 'we don't open until six.'

'Detective Sergeant Summers, Wellbury police,' Frank introduced himself. 'Frank Summers. We're here to see Mrs Blower. She knows us.'

'Does she, now?' the young woman asked, her sleep-laden eyes clearing as she looked Frank up and down, appearing quite pleased with what she saw. 'I'm Sonia, by the way. Maybe I can be of assistance.'

'No, thanks,' Frank replied, 'welcome as your assistance would be, I'm afraid it's Mrs Blower we need to talk to.'

'Oh, well, takes all sorts,' replied Sonia. 'She's probably in the kitchen. Just down that passage, two large doors with thin pipes the whole way up, they're the handles.' She giggled. 'And if you're ever here of an evening, tell the barman to let me know, I might let you check out my handles.'

'An offer no man could ever resist,' Frank replied, smiling. 'Thank you, Sonia, I might well do that.'

He noted something interesting as they left Sonia on their way to the kitchen. Gertie was pouting, as she always did when he was polite to attractive looking women, as if, he thought, she were his younger sister disapproving of his fraternising with someone who was no better than she should be. He was used to that. It was Jean Tromperie's look that intrigued him.

She was doing a good job of almost hiding it, but for a few

seconds she was pouting just as much as Gertie was. By the time they reached the doors described she seemed to have recovered her normal ebullient, sneering self.

Oh, boy, are you in for a surprise, thought Frank as he pushed open the swing doors to the kitchen. He noted that it was large and modern, a kitchen that any restaurant would have been proud of, brightly lit with powerful neon lights, gleaming steel tables and an almost hospital-like cleanliness. Mrs Blower stood in the centre, glasses hanging down from a chain around her neck, wearing a tweed skirt and jacket outfit, a strange garb to be wearing in such a kitchen, and in complete contrast to Sonia's more minimalist approach to attire, but then Mrs Blower was an unpredictable woman.

'Sergeant Summers! Gertie!' she exclaimed in delight as they walked up to the table she was working on. She immediately proved her unpredictability by grabbing Frank and gave him an ecstatic kiss on each cheek.

'Careful, now, Mrs B,' Frank said, disengaging himself and holding her wrist gently, the one connected to the hand holding a sharp butcher's knife. 'That thing could cause a nasty accident.'

'Oh, I am sorry, I forgot I was holding that,' Mrs Blower said, looking at the knife as if wondering where it came from. 'But I'm so glad to see you, I was hoping you'd pop in sometime. It's the first time I've ever had anything to do with the Arts, you know, not on this scale. I've been thinking of having windows put in. Now what was I saying?'

'May I introduce Captain Jean Tromperie of the Sûreté,' Frank said. Mrs Blower looked at the French woman.

'Well, that is interesting,' Mrs Blower said, scratching her head thoughtfully and lopping off a few stray curls with the knife. 'She certainly has the figure. I don't know about the funny hat, though. Are you sure you have it on the right way? You have been looking after our Frank, haven't you, Gertie my sweet? Take your jacket off, young lady, I can't take you on if you don't have decent nipples. My customers like good nipples for some reason. He needs feeding, you know. It's the natural light, you see.'

'Captain Tromperie is a French police officer, Mrs B,' Frank said. 'She's not here to audition.'

'Isn't she? Pity, she has a lovely derriere. You have lost weight, haven't you Frank? Bit flat chested, mind. Still, there are ways of hiding that, as I'm learning. What on earth are you feeding him on, Gertie, the poor dear. French, eh? Are you sure? What you see isn't always what you get, is it? He's almost a skeleton. Oh, dear, I wonder what's happened to the roast. I had it only a few minutes ago. Mr Walthers thinks it will be too expensive, though.'

'Captain Tromperie wishes to ask you a few questions, Mrs B.'

'Captain who?' Mrs Blower asked, looking around her. 'Oh dear, I haven't lost another one, have I?'

'All yours, ma Capitaine,' Frank said to the French woman looking in stunned silence at Mrs Blower scratching her head with a butcher's knife.

Frank and Gertie stepped back, leaned against a steel table and folded their arms as if waiting for a show to start. They knew Mrs Blower and her parallel conversations. The French woman didn't.

Captain Tromperie seemed to come to a decision and squared

her small shoulders.

'Madame Blower, we have had reports of drugs being sold here, drugs brought in from France. There is a heavy penalty for such actions. You would not like a French jail. They are not pleasant places.'

'I dare say I wouldn't like any jail, young lady,' Mrs Blower replied, squinting at the young woman's chest. 'You know you really should wear a proper brassiere. It's amazing how they can pad them these days. Have you seen my glasses anywhere? Good food and good exercise, Gertie, that's what a man needs, just like a dog. Are you sure you're a French police officer? You'd look good in lace, if you have the nipples for it. I got myself one, a dog, you know. Now, where did I leave it?' she asked, peering around the kitchen, underneath the shining steel tables. 'Falsies, that's what they're called, I think. I'm sure it's time for walkies again. There's some Neurofen in the cupboard if you need drugs. Or is it his dinnertime? So hard to remember these things, isn't it?'

'I am not here to discuss dogs, Madame Blower,' Jean persisted against the deluge. 'This is a most serious crime, drug smuggling. There are heavy penalties. Very heavy penalties!'

'Heavy? Not at all, he's hardly more than a puppy. Though I do think you should keep away from drugs, you know, especially at your age. At least one good meal a day, Gertie. You know, that's a thought! Discounted membership for special groups. Police officers, yes, that would be one. I'm not sure about the boots, though, a little too avant garde for my taste. Femininity, that's the theme. Old age pensioners, yes, we could have day outings, something like that. I shall have to take it up with Mr Walthers. Now, where did I leave that knife? I must write it down before I forget. He's very forgetful, you know. Did I mention the windows? No, I'm pretty sure he's just had dinner. It must be walkies then.'

'You are obstructing the law!' Jean Tromperie exclaimed in a high-pitched voice full of desperation, a last-ditch attempt at trying to get the older woman to make any sense.

'Obstructing the law?' Mrs Blower asked in amazement. 'Are you trying to suggest I'm fat? Really, Frank, bringing around this disreputable young thing. It's all your fault, Gertie, you're not feeding him properly. I was going to call him Fido, but that sounded too ridiculous. Instead I decided on Nelson. I've hired one of the best chefs in Europe, you know. A Frenchman. Though he's very lazy, just like the rest of them. Enrique!' she called out in an ear-splitting shout. 'Enrique! I need to speak to you about this fillet steak. Croutons.' She paused, a puzzled look on her face. 'Or is he Italian? So difficult to tell with these foreigners, you know.'

Enrique, Frank guessed, was lying down somewhere with a splitting headache, sucking Neurofens.

'You're changing the club's ambience?' he suggested, leaning back and palming something off a plate.

'Oh, yes, Frank, I knew you'd understand. He's very clever, isn't he, Gertie? Though where Nelson has got to I don't know. Clever isn't the right word, is it my dear?' she asked of a wide-eyed Captain Tromperie. 'Understanding, that's the word. Do you have that word in French? Not so much ambience, really. Just giving them a good meal. Men come to look at my young girls pole-vaulting, or whatever it's called, very artistic, very modern, but what they really want is a good meal. Gertie, Gertie, what have you done to my dear, poor

Frank? He looks half-starved, the poor thing. Of course Bumbles was another option, but do you really want a dog called Bumbles? Don't you think this kitchen could really do with some natural light?'

'I'm fine, Mrs B,' Frank replied, 'Gertie's a real martinet about food, won't leave me alone unless she thinks I'm eating properly. I'm afraid we must go now. Just popped in to make sure everything's okay and let the Captain here see some of the sights of Wellbury.'

'I could ask a couple of the girls to do a strip for you, on the house, as they say. They'd like that, some of them need the practice. I wonder if Bumbles wasn't such a bad idea. There's an art to taking your clothes off, as I've been discovering. Oh, where has Nelson got to? Enrique? Enrique, I need you!'

'Possibly the most frightening words a man has ever heard,' Frank murmured as the three of them slowly backed out of the kitchen, leaving Mrs Blower checking underneath the steel tables for Nelson, or possibly a missing French, or Italian, chef. 'I don't think we need worry about the Blue Bliss being involved in drug dealing. One chat with Mrs B and they'd think they'd been on the worst trip of their lives. What say, Captain T?'

Captain Tromperie did not reply. She looked too shell-shocked to say anything.

'There's just one thing I need to do before we leave,' Frank said as they exited the Blue Bliss's front doors.

He wandered around the side of the building. The Blue Bliss was set in a large acreage of rambling trees and bushes, a pleasant setting that served to enhance the nightclub's allure. It also provided a number of hiding places for possible trysts, which was what Frank was looking for. It took him a while, but he finally found it, a hiding place toward the front with a good view of the entrance.

'Thought so,' he said as he came across a particularly dense and low-hanging bush. 'Come here, Nelson, I have a treat for you.'

A young greyhound with frightened eyes lay on the ground underneath the bush, trying to hide, head down, eyes looking up at him in fear. It growled in a hopeless attempt to appear threatening.

'Here you go, son,' Frank said, tossing the dog the large piece of fillet steak he had appropriated from the kitchen while Mrs Blower's concentration was elsewhere. 'Mrs B won't miss that.'

Nelson looked at the steak with starving eyes. He looked at Frank as if wondering whether this was another trick life was playing upon him.

'Don't worry, son, I'll pop back every so often to make sure you're being looked after,' Frank assured the frightened pup. He walked away and Nelson took his chance to lunge forward and grab the steak before backing underneath the bush once more.

'Don't wolf it down, Nelson,' Frank warned as he walked away. 'You'll give yourself indigestion.'

Nelson wolfed the meat down, looking after Frank's disappearing back. As soon as he had made sure this meal was really his he was going to follow the human who had saved him from that mad woman, the one who didn't seem to remember whether it was time for walkies or din-dins.

But by then Frank had left.

Nelson burped and began howling.

'She is insane, that woman!' declared Captain Tromperie as they drove off.

'Not insane, Captain T, just British,' Frank replied easily. 'Eccentricity is what makes us different. Individuality. You might want to try it sometime.'

If you haven't already, he thought.

They drove in silence for a few seconds.

'And I do not need to wear a padded bra,' Captain Tromperie said indignantly. Frank smiled. He agreed with her on that one. Mrs Blower should wear her glasses more often. However it did tell him where one of the French woman's weak points were.

'Don't worry, Captain T,' he said, 'we just have to accept what nature's given us. It isn't your fault.'

Behind him Jean Tromperie glared at the back of his head venomously. She said nothing. But the phrase "you will pay for that" was written across her furious face.

Gertie could not help but smile, a smile of triumph. Her problem, in the breast department, was of excess rather than lack. It had often been a drawback. She would meet some young man, ready for a meeting of minds and a little romance, only to find that said young man's attention was somewhat below where her brain resided. Now, for once, she decided that emphasising her attributes was a positive thing. She could use them to put the little French bitch's nose out of joint. Figuratively, much as she would have liked to do it literally, with her fists.

Beside her Frank was not so self-assured. Internally he had to admit to himself that his jibe was, as one could put it, a bit below the belt, so long as the phrase wasn't examined too closely. But that was the name of the game. Whoever lost it first lost it all.

Not that it made him feel any better about what he had said.

'Frigid wants to see you,' Eric Johns said as they walked into reception. 'She's not in a good mood.'

'So, nothing new, then,' Frank remarked.

'I wish you two would sort your problems out, Frank,' Eric said. 'You're making the rest of us very nervous.'

'Nothing to do with me, Eric. You know me, anything for the quiet life.'

'Yeah, sure,' Eric said, disbelievingly. 'Oh, and there's been a couple of London boys wandering around this afternoon. I don't think that's made Frigid any happier.'

'London boys?' asked Captain Tromperie, showing an unexpected interest. 'What is this "London boys"?'

'Scotland Yard, Captain.' Frank said. 'They also have an interest. Look, I'm just going to see what Wonderwoman wants and then knock off for the day. Why don't you two girls finish up and go out for drinkies or something?'

'I have too much work to do,' the Captain said. 'I will be at my hotel if anything happens. And I am not a girl. I am a Captain of the Sûreté. You will do well to remember that, Sergeant.'

She nodded curtly and walked out. Frank smiled. Gertie's face showed a mixture of appalment at the idea of having "drinkies" with Jean Tromperie, and relief that it was not to be. Sisterhood, she had long decided, for at least twelve hours anyway, did not cross national borders. And, besides that, she was supposed to be having drinks with Frank that evening. Alone. He had promised. She would never forgive him if he broke that promise.

'Be back in five minutes, Gertie,' Frank said, giving her a wink.

Gertie smiled back in relief. Of course! Frank knew that the French tart would never agree. He was just winding her up again. She made her way back to their office, scolding herself for ever doubting Frank. A woman must have explicit and undoubting trust for her man, she told herself, otherwise how could love survive?

Well, most of the time, anyway.

Frank walked up the stairs to Frieda's office slowly, tapping the banister thoughtfully as he went.

'Is the wicked witch of Wellbury in?' he asked Tricia as he entered the ante-room to Frieda's lair, putting on a cheerful face.

'The Inspector is waiting for you, Sergeant,' Tricia said disapprovingly, emphasising the word "Inspector". Frank smiled again. Frieda had obviously been working on Tricia. From an affectionate kiss to disapproval in twenty four hours. Not his record by any means, but not bad going all the same.

'You shouldn't scowl so, Trish, love,' he told her. 'Attractive women like yourself should never scowl. There should be a law against it.'

She pouted instead, and concentrated on the computer screen in front of her, hitting the keys on the keyboard with an aggressive energy they did not deserve.

'Frieda is right,' she said, 'you are a complete bastard, Frank Summers. I don't know what she sees in you.'

'At the moment I rather think what she sees in me could be described in medical terms. Or perhaps those of an abattoir. And her intentions can be compressed into one word,' he said, leaning over and gently putting into place a lock of her golden hair that had slipped astray.

'And what would that word be?' Tricia asked, typing furiously and erratically.

'Evisceration,' he whispered as he opened the door to Frieda's office.

'I don't blame her. The thought had crossed my mind too.'

'Oh, and you've got a spelling mistake there,' he said, pointing at the screen before hurriedly entering Frieda's office.

'You wanted to see me, Inspector?' he asked as he closed the door behind him. He could have sworn he heard something hit the door behind him. One of Tricia's fluffy toys. No doubt she would blame him for that too. If it had been Danny the Dinosaur he could retrieve the situation. If it was Pooky the Bear he was dead meat. Making her throw Pooky the Bear at him would be unforgivable.

Frieda looked up from some paperwork she was doing, her face set.

'Sit down,' she said. He obeyed. He noted that he was neither "Sergeant" nor "Frank". That suggested to him that her guns were temporarily trained on someone else.

Temporarily.

'I presume you have heard that two officers have arrived from Scotland Yard?' she asked.

He nodded.

'A superintendent and a detective sergeant,' she continued. 'I was busy, you weren't here, so Inspector Hanson took it upon himself to look after them.'

Frank struggled to keep a straight face.

Percy Hanson and Frieda were in a race to become Chief Inspector. They had co-operated on the last high-profile case to hit Wellbury – or, to be more accurate, Frieda had talked Percy into acting as second fiddle to her commanding-officer role. Now it sounded as if Percy was trying to muscle in on the Matisse case. Or, more likely, was hoping to portray himself to the visiting Superintendent as a model of a professional police inspector, while Frieda was running around in circles trying to cope with a police station which appeared to be suffering more than its fair share of important visitors, right in the middle of stocktaking chaos.

'He said he was trying to lighten the workload on my shoulders,' Frieda continued. She looked at Frank as if hoping that he would share her outrage at this blatant lie.

Frank merely looked back neutrally. He normally tried to avoid getting caught up in what he saw as political manoeuvring amongst senior officers. Despite this he had found himself supporting Frieda's cause on the odd occasion, but this time she was on her own. If she wanted to treat him like an errant schoolboy, so be it, she would get no support from him outside of his own duties. He was a copper, she could play politics on her own.

'Which means that you are going to have to look after that French Captain again tomorrow,' Frieda said, realising that Frank was not going to say anything. 'I will see that the Superintendent receives all the co-operation he requires from Wellbury Police force.'

Frank nodded acquiescence, as if he looked forward to it.

'She's quite cute, in a way, Jean,' he commented. 'Presumably the Jean is the English version. I wonder where it came from.'

'Cute? That thing?' demanded Frieda in what was close to a roar of disbelief, a sound like a bear would make which had come home to find its porridge taken.

'Sexy, almost,' Frank continued as if unaware of the cranking sound of cannon traversing rapidly in his direction. 'Makes me wonder if I shouldn't sign up with the Sûreté. There aren't any exchange programmes available, are there?'

Frieda glowered at him.

'That is not a professional approach, Sergeant Summers,' she growled. 'Captain Tromperie is a police officer from another country, not some little piece of fluff for you to admire. Under the circumstances I think I will look after the Captain and you can see that the Superintendent is looked after. Just don't do anything to upset him, understand? He is a Superintendent, after all.'

Frank shrugged his shoulders.

'Okay,' he said mildly. 'I'll take him around the watering holes. Show him Wellbury's finest ales. I'll bet he's never had a pint of Old Stoat before.'

Frieda almost shuddered at the idea. Old Stoat was a locally manufactured brew made from apples. It had a very pleasant oak-smoked taste which belied its potency. Tourists had been known to finish just a single pint, smack their lips and say "I think I'll have another one of those" before standing up and keeling over, wondering why their legs were no longer working while their brain still was. Or appeared to be.

The last thing she needed was Frank and the two London officers reeling drunkenly around the Old Town singing dirty rugby songs, which, in her experience, was what men tended to do once merrily drunk, even if they had never laid hands on a rugby ball in their lives. There was the often retold story of a bus of elderly American tourists who had made the mistake of treating a few pints of Old Stoat as a benevolent beverage. They were singing dirty rugby songs when taken off to the cells to recover, and they had never heard of rugby before.

'Jeannie wasn't too keen on the idea,' Frank continued happily, almost making Frieda gasp at the idea of offering to take a French police captain on a pub crawl, never mind his rather over-familiar use of "Jeannie", something she found repugnant at the professional level and seriously worrying at the personal level. 'Actually she was quite rude about English pubs. About anything English, really. English women, especially. She doesn't seem to think highly of the way they dress. Or much else. What were the words she used? "Cold, emotionally and physically dead", I seem to recall. Strange comment to make.'

No doubt Jean Tromperie would have found it strange as she had not made it. But, Frank justified, she would have if she had thought of it.

Frieda was silent. Frank could almost hear the cogs in her brain working, her thinking about having to put up with the French woman for an entire day. While Frank gaily destroyed any notion that the Superintendent might have of Wellbury's – read Frieda's – professionalism.

'Thinking about it,' Frieda said through clenched teeth, her feelings divided between her career and Frank's apparent enthusiasm for that French thing, and concluding that the latter was unimaginable whatever Frank said, 'I think my original decision was the correct one. You will look after that Captain and I will look after the Superintendent.'

'Okay,' said Frank easily. 'Suits me. Oh, by the way, she refuses to eat in the canteen. If I have to take her to lunch at a restaurant, I presume I can claim it back on expenses? It will have to be one of the more expensive, mind. Somewhere that has a good wine list. You know the French attitude towards wine. Nothing but the best. You should have heard her when I suggested the Australians made the best wine in the world. Worse than a football supporter defending his team after losing a home match.'

The idea of Frank taking the French tart out for lunch did not sit easily with Frieda. The two of them sitting cosily while deciding which wine to have with an expensive meal? Out of her budget? How Frank could put up with the little French cow's rudeness she didn't know, but she was damned if he was going to spend her budget wining and dining Miss Little Pert Bottom.

'I will arrange for the Captain and the London officers to have lunch with me here in my office,' she said. 'It will be a chance for the Superintendent and the Captain to exchange views on modern policing methods.'

'Good thinking. I doubt she'd be rude to a Superintendent. Not from Scotland Yard, anyway.'

Yet again Frieda was stumped. She had no doubt that Jean Tromperie would be extremely rude to the Superintendent. The French woman seemed to be ruder the higher the rank. Frank was the only one who hadn't threatened to thump the little cow. In fact things appeared to be going in entirely the other direction, and that, she decided finally, was definitely not going to happen. But she couldn't see a way out. She would have to have the French woman and the Superintendent to lunch to avoid Frank either enjoying himself or jeopardising her career.

She really, really did not need this now, she thought to herself. She didn't have time to look after the stocktake, unexploded dummy grenades, visiting Superintendents and foreign Captains as it was. The Chief Constable was, as usual, dumping all sorts of extra work on them, expecting them to cope without any added resources. Whitehall seemed to come up with a new requirement in reporting crime figures every week. Instead of concentrating on basic police work they were being snowed under by bureaucracy. And they could expect more foreigners to float in within the next few days – the Spanish, Italians and god knew who else. She had to admit that things were beginning to slip out of her control.

With the Chief Inspector off fishing somewhere Frieda had thought she had the opportunity to take control and demonstrate her efficiency. She had jumped at the opportunity. And now, when she needed Frank on her side most, he was giving her absolutely no support whatsoever.

Well, he was going to pay for that.

'I have the perfect solution,' she said, smiling evilly as an idea came to her. 'I shall ask Percy to handle Captain Tromperie. You can deal with the Superintendent and the Sergeant. But no excursions to pubs or any other drinking establishments. You will keep them occupied until Matisse's lawyer turns up, they will have their interview and then return to Scotland Yard. Understood?'

'Okay,' Frank said as if he was quite happy with the idea, thoroughly irritating Frieda with his easy-going attitude. 'What are their names?'

'Detective Superintendent Campbell and Detective Sergeant Hovis.'

Frank paused before chuckling.

'Did they say what flavour?' he asked.

Frieda looked at him in astonishment.

'What on earth are you on about?'

'Oh, nothing,' he said, standing up. 'Anything else, or am I dismissed?'

Frieda scowled at him.

'Dismissed,' she said curtly.

To his relief Tricia appeared to have left when he exited. Though he had put on a good performance in Frieda's office, it had been quite draining, especially after a long day playing mind games with Jean Tromperie, and he was quite pleased not to have to battle through another round with Tricia.

Frieda, Tricia, Susan and Jean Tromperie, he thought as he walked down the stairs. A sane man up against any one of those would have legged it long ago, never mind all four.

Still, at least Gertie was still loyal. And it was time to knock off for the day. Now he could relax and take it easy for at least twelve hours. He perked up.

Gertie looked up in surprise as Frank walked into their office whistling the theme tune from The Sting.

'Come on, Gerts, grab your coat, drinkies time,' he said.

'You're in a good mood again, Sarge,' she said, hurriedly picking up her coat and handbag and following him out.

'I'll tell you about it once I have a pint in front of me,' he replied. 'It might be a cliché to say I need it, but need it I do. Toute suite, ma cherie!'

'Ah, that's better,' Frank said, having taken a long and grateful pull at his pint of ale in the Sergeants Arms. Gertie sat next to him and sipped her gin and tonic, a concerned look on her face.

'You haven't been having a go at Frieda, have you Frank?' she asked in a tone of concern.

She was allowed to call Frank by his first name when off duty. She thought of it as her "Frank" time. A question that occupied her mind from time to time was what she would call him when he opened his eyes and they finally became official partners, in more than the work sense. And then what when they were married? It would be a bit difficult calling your husband "Sarge" at work, wouldn't it?

'I know you're angry with her,' she continued quickly, blotting out that wonderful thought, because she wasn't quite there yet, 'but she could make our lives pretty miserable if she wanted to. I think you should just ignore her. Just do the job and keep out of her way.'

'Excellent advice, my dear Gertie, and advice I am already following. We were supposed to be babysitting Capitaine Jean tomorrow, but Frigid changed her mind. About three times, in fact.'

'You were baiting her, weren't you?' Gertie accused. Frank smiled.

'Only a little,' he said. 'But, instead of the French Captain with the pert little bottom, we're going to be babysitting the Superintendent and the Sergeant from London. One Superintendent Campbell and one Sergeant Hovis.'

'Sounds a bit like a light lunch,' Gertie observed. 'Hovis bread and Campbell soup.'

'Precisely, Gerts. I asked Frieda what flavour, but she didn't get the joke. Unusual that, her mind must have been on something else.'

'So who's looking after Miss Bottom?' asked Gertie, fully aware of what matters Frieda's mind would have been on.

'That's the best bit. Percy was looking after the London boys today, as a favour to Frieda, only without actually telling her. She wasn't impressed when she found out, as you could imagine. She's decided to reward him by giving him Miss Bottom tomorrow. Boy, I'd love to be a fly on the wall listening to those two, Percy the bloodhound and Trumpet the strumpet.'

Gertie gasped.

'She'll never get him to agree to that, he's not that stupid,' she said. 'He must know what a little cow that French tart is, surely. Everyone in the station does by now, they must do.'

'Oh, I think she will, knowing our Frieda. She'll thank him for being so kind as to help out and would he have a little spare time tomorrow to do the same? He'll agree, thinking she means the Superintendent. Before he knows it he'll be suffering the slings and arrows of an outrageous French woman. Soi-disant.'

'Swa what?' asked Gertie, not overly happy at Frank's admiration and his use of the phrase "our Frieda", and beginning to wonder whether Frank's amused descriptions of Miss Pert Bottom didn't have the echoes of someone a little too involved with the French piece of fluff. She was becoming increasingly aware that the only weapon Captain Strumpet had, that of her rudeness, was not affecting Frank at all, in fact he appeared to find it amusing. Take away the rudeness and you were left with a woman many men would find attractive. Too attractive.

'Soi-disant, Gerts. It's French. It means "so called". As in the sense of something not being what it pretends to be.'

'You mean you don't think she's French?' Gertie asked, hoping he would say something to alleviate her worries about his feelings for the French tart.

'Appearances, my dear Gerts, appearances. Appearances are not always what they seem.'

'You can say that again,' she said, nestling close to him, trying to turn his words into some form of comfort, and not quite succeeding.

Frank smiled and put his arm around her. He could always rely on Gertie. She was like a younger sister. They made a good team. So long as Gertie was with him – a mate, had she been a bloke – he had nothing to worry about. It was knowing that his back was covered by the totally reliable and utterly loyal Gertie that he could face Frieda, Susan and Jean Tromperie with confidence, whatever came his way.

He had a feeling that he would need Gertie supporting him in the next few days. At that moment his life was not as simple and easy-going as he would have liked, and he had a hunch that things were quite likely to get much, much worse.

Even so, just as anyone who knows that things are likely to get much, much worse, he didn't realise just how much, much worse they were going to get.

Thursday: Special Welsh blueberry muffins

Frank sat at his desk, feet on the windowsill, the window open, to an observer a man lost deep in thought, so obviously so that he hardly noticed the sweet smell of an early summer's morning wafting in.

In fact he was trying to get a tune out of his head. The Battle Hymn of the Republic had been plaguing him since the moment he had woken up. It wasn't unusual for a tune to take up residence in his mind, but the Battle Hymn of the Republic? The Americans had a lot to answer for.

He dropped his feet from the windowsill, stood up suddenly and looked out of the window. There was only one way to handle this. Sing it out of your system. That way it wandered off and found someone else to irritate.

'We'll meet again in the spring, sometime,' he sang softly in a deep baritone.

Frank Summers and music were perfectly compatible if he had the lyrics or the score in front of him, preferably both. Without either he was the musical equivalent of Mrs Blower.

'So, you are a fan of Chubby Checker, Sergeant Frank Summers?' asked a voice behind him.

He spun around to find Jean Tromperie.

'Chubby Checker?' he asked in surprise. 'As it happens, I do like Chubby Checker's songs, why do you ask?'

'I do not recognise the words, but I do recognise the tune,' she said. 'Though the title, I think, is "There will be a time and place for us". Not so?'

It took a few moments for the penny to drop.

'That wasn't Chubby Checker, that was the Battle Hymn of

115

the Republic,' he protested.

'Battle Hymn of the Republic?' she queried in amazement. 'I would not like to know which republic. One which only exists in that tiny little brain of yours. I know the hymn well.'

She began singing.

'Mine eyes have seen the glory of the coming of the Lord

He is trampling out the vintage where the grapes of wrath are stored,

He has loosed the fateful lightening of His terrible swift sword

His truth is marching on.'

Frank grinned.

'Ah, but you don't know the chorus.'

He took a breath.

'The sergeant major jumped from forty thousand feet

The sergeant major jumped from forty thousand feet

The sergeant major jumped without a parachute

And he ain't gonna jump no mo-or-ore!'

'Tchah!' she exclaimed. 'Typical! Boys will always be boys.'

But the words belied her emotions. For a moment there was a pleasant smile on her face as they faced each other, but in a blink of an eyelid it was gone.

'Your baritone is not as bad as it might be,' she continued, advancing towards his desk, dropping her handbag on it and sitting down, crossing her legs. 'But you lack training.'

'And you know all about such things, naturally,' Frank said, taking his own seat opposite her.

She looked at him for a moment, as if considering whether to reply.

'As it happens I do,' she said. 'You English have no concept. You lack the culture. To appreciate music you must be born into it, you must – what is the word? – imbibe it, from your mother's breast.'

'And what would your favourite piece of music be?'

She considered this for a moment.

'Naturally there is only one singer who can be called the greatest – Edith Piaf.'

'Je ne regrette rien?'

'Precisement. She is incomparable, both as a singer and in her philosophy. She may have been small physically, but she walked through life as if she were a giant.' She paused. 'However, if we are talking about musicals, English musicals, as that seems to be about your level, as pale and insipid as they appear against Edith Piaf, then I would choose the song from Cabaret.'

'Life is a cabaret?'

'Non. The one that goes, "I used to have this girlfriend known as Elsie".'

'She died of drugs in Chelsea.'

'Life, Sergeant Frank Summers, is both comedy and tragedy. In comedy there is tragedy. In tragedy there is comedy. One must enjoy life to the full, or one has not lived it.'

'And you, Captain Jean Tromperie, are living life to the full?'

A smile twitched across her lips.

'More than you are, little Englishman.'

Frank did not reply. He merely looked into her eyes. She returned the gaze evenly.

'So, to where do you take me today, Sergeant Frank Summers? Yesterday it was a nightclub. Today it is perhaps your red light district, another, how you call it, slight? Insult? Does the little town of Wellbury have a red light district, or are all the women as frigid as the ones I have met so far? Tchah! They are like ice, these English maidens. How a man like you can stand them I do not know. You should come to Paree with me. You will meet real women, women burning with passion.'

Frank paused before replying. Wellbury did indeed have its own small areas known for what could be politely defined as commercial trade in intimacy. The idea of taking the French woman for a tour of these appealed. He was sure he could think up some way of making her life more interesting in the process. Such a pity he wasn't taking care of her today.

'I'm afraid I won't be escorting you today, ma petite Capitaine,' he said instead. 'That task has been handed to someone more suitable.'

'More suitable? You mean more dull. Your Inspector Frigid is afraid, I think.'

Frank did not answer the accusation. Jean Tromperie stood up and picked up her handbag.

'Tell, me, Sergeant Frank Summers, what is your favourite music above all?'

Another pause.

'Albinoni's Adagio.'

She nodded.

'Just as I thought. You smile much, but in your heart is tragedy. You must learn how to enjoy life, Frank Summers, it is short but beautiful if lived to the full.'

'I will live my life the way I see fit, mademoiselle. However, I will give you some advice. Get out of Wellbury. This is no place for a French police officer, not a French police officer such as you. Not now.'

She gave him a last, sneering smile.

'The race goes to the swift, n'est ce pas, cherie? I wonder which of us shall triumph? I think it might be me.'

Frank made no reply.

'Yesterday,' Jean Tromperie continued, 'you spoke of subtlety – subtlety, subtlety, toujours le subtlety, you said. It shows your lack of understanding. The correct quotation is, l'audace, l'audace, toujours l'audace. Frederick the Great said that. With your so-called subtlety you will never be great. Audacity is what you lack, Sergeant Frank Summers.'

She made a show of consulting her watch.

'Sacré bleu!' she said mockingly. 'Nom de dieu. I am late. I must present myself to your Inspector. Do you think she is ready for the race? Perhaps she hopes that I have had the maladie during the night. I think she does not like me too much, your Inspector, non?'

Once again Frank made no response. Jean Tromperie shook her head sadly.

'That one is too old for you, Detective Sergeant Frank Summers. Perhaps not in the body, but in the head. And that Susan, she too has not the fire, she is too selfish. Your Gertie, she has the sense of humour, but not the understanding. You should find yourself a real woman. A woman who understands passion.'

Frank merely looked at her as if he were a teacher humouring an outspoken child.

'Pah!' she said finally. 'Perhaps I throw myself at this other man who escorts me today! You are a monk, Detective Sergeant Frank Summers! No, you are a eunuch! I waste my time with you. You do not need a woman, you need a mother!'

With that she swept out of his office.

Frank was mildly amused. For most historians there was a simple test to see which side had won a battle. The side that left the field first had lost. And Jean Tromperie had left first. Admittedly, as he was in his own office, he had nowhere to retreat to, but he still felt as if he had won.

On the other hand, those stinging barbs she had launched without feeling for their target had hurt. A eunuch? He would show her.

How? Strap her to a bed and ravish her? Don't be stupid, man, she was having her revenge for your comments on her attributes yesterday.

Forget it, he told himself. You're letting her and Frieda get to you. If they achieve that, they've won.

He pulled his computer keyboard towards him irritably, and punched in his username and password. The visits to the house in Glenbourne Avenue and the Blue Bliss would have to be documented, no matter how useless they were. He would have to give the dry facts, no more. Suspicions of the supposed French Captain would appear nowhere.

Suddenly a thought struck him and he smiled. While he could not give his suspicions, he could relate Mrs Blower's conversation, word by word. Anyone reading it – perhaps in fifty years' time – would need their own headache tablets, whatever those might be called in the future.

And there was another reason to smile. The idea of the Miss Pert Bottom throwing herself at Inspector Percy Hanson. She would have to dress up as a fish first, and even then he would be confused.

The thought comforted him. He was well into his description of Mrs Blower's one-sided multiple conversation when he was interrupted by a voice at the doorway.

'Slacking as usual I see, you useless excuse for a copper!'

Frank looked up from his computer. Pete Phillips stood in the doorway, a broad smile on his tanned face. Frank was amazed. Pete was Percy's Detective Sergeant. Normally the two of them sloped around the station like two hungover bloodhounds who hadn't slept for three weeks. The Pete Phillips standing in the doorway looked as if he hadn't a care in the world, and was thoroughly enjoying life.

'Pete! You're looking well. How was the holiday?'

'Bloody marvellous, mate, bloody marvellous,' Pete Philips said, slinging himself down in the chair in front of Frank's desk and putting a box on the desk.

'And the missus?'

Frank had advised Pete Phillips to take his wife on a second honeymoon in order to save his failing marriage. Pete was an ambitious man who hadn't had a real holiday in five years. He had let himself fall into a habit of working all hours, letting the job take over his life. He had been drinking too much, and was well on his way to losing both job and marriage.

'Bloody marvellous,' Pete repeated. 'She's half Welsh, you know, the missus. So we spent two weeks at Aberystwyth, lovely place. She got to see her family. I even made up with her dad, you know?'

'Oh? What happened?'

'Oh, usual silly thing, I belted him one at our wedding. Hadn't seen him since. But we made up. Now we're greatest of friends, and he's even forgiven me for being English. Oh, by the way, these are Welsh blueberry muffins for you. The missus said I had to get something to thank you. The story is that, if you share one with someone, that's the one you're going to marry, so you should only share one with you dearest sweetheart. Which rules me out,' he laughed.

'I'm amazed,' said Frank. 'I've never seen you look so cheerful.' He also wondered how belting your father-in-law at your wedding could be construed as the "usual silly thing". It begged the question of what constituted an unusual silly thing.

'Never realised what a miserable bastard I'd turned into,' admitted Pete. He leaned forward conspiratorially. 'Listen, Frank, just between you and me?'

He looked around in case someone was listening.

'The missus reckons she's pregnant,' he whispered. 'How's that, now? Married five years and nowt. Two week's holiday and she reckons she's bearing. Don't tell anyone, mind. How she knows, I can't tell. She could be totally wrong about it, I reckon.'

'Women seem to know that sort of thing,' agreed Frank, leaning forward, also whispering. 'God knows how.'

'You two fallen in love?' asked Gertie, sweeping in with two cups of coffee, one of which she placed in front of Frank, eyeing Pete Phillips suspiciously. The two men drew apart quickly.

'Aye, no, love,' Pete said expansively, 'I was just telling young Frank here about my little holiday.'

'Good, was it?' asked Gertie, looking at him over her cup of coffee. She had had run-ins with Pete Phillips before, and had never really liked him.

'Bloody marvellous, Gertie, my love, bloody marvellous. Thanks to Frank my marriage is again heaven, and I intend to take a holiday every year from now on. Sod promotion. Percy can stick it. Some things are more important in life.'

'Just a pity Frank is better at recognising other people's problems rather than his own,' Gertie said caustically, going to her desk.

The two men looked at her back in puzzlement. Pete scratched his head and turned back to Frank.

'Here, Frank, I hear I have to take on something you couldn't handle. Some French bird? Sex on legs, they say. I'm supposed to keep her occupied until that bloke's lawyer turns up, Matisse, or whatever he's called. Percy reckons she was too much for you.'

Frank laughed.

'That's how Percy sold it to you, is it?' he asked.

Pete Phillips smiled back as a man who knows how to treat women, or at least as a man who thinks he knows how to treat women, however contrary the evidence might be. Then his eyes narrowed as a man who suddenly suspects that someone has led him a long way up the garden path, away from the pretty plants and into the stinging nettles and poison ivy.

'What do you mean, "sold it to me"? What's wrong with this French bird? Everyone says she's a right looker.'

'Oh, she's a looker, alright,' Frank agreed. 'But put it this way, Pete, if she was worth the effort wouldn't Percy have kept her to himself? Take my advice, act the dumb plod, say as little as possible, and check the time left to going home to the missus.'

Pete stood up angrily.

'That's all you think I am, isn't it?' he asked. 'Just a dumb plod. You've got your university degree, you think we're just – dumb plods. Thick. Well –'

Frank held up a hand to stop him.

'Ask anyone you like, Pete. We had to put up with her yesterday. She likes winding people up. Ask Gertie if you don't believe me.'

Pete turned to Gertie. She nodded.

'She's a right little bitch, if you don't mind me saying,' she said. 'You won't find anyone on the station who has a good word to say about her. And she does it deliberately. Thinks she's superior to the rest of the world.'

'Fancy a bet, Pete?' asked Frank, leaning back in his chair and putting his hands behind his head.

'A bet?'

'Yup, a bet. Ten quid says that, as soon as she learns you're a sergeant she'll look you up and down and say "sergeant" as if she were thinking of maggots. Not very nice maggots, either.'

Pete Phillips paused, thinking about it. Finally he nodded.

'Okay, Frank, I'll take your advice. I must say, though, if what you're saying is true, it's a pretty low thing to do to a man who's just got back from two weeks' holiday.'

'Oh, I agree, Pete,' Frank said, smiling, 'a very low thing. All in all it's a good time to keep your head down. There are certain things going on which everybody thinks they understand, but nobody does. If that makes sense.'

Pete nodded again, and a rueful smile lit his face.

'No sense whatsoever, but I'll take your advice,' he said. 'Hope you enjoy the muffins. Remember, you must only share one with the one you're going to marry.'

'What's this about muffins?' asked Gertie after Pete had left.

'Oh, Pete brought some blueberry muffins back from holiday,' Frank said, tossing the box into his out tray. 'They've invented some ancient Welsh legend that, as far as I understand, if you share one with someone else, you end up falling in love with them, marrying and living happily ever after. Fifteen kids and a little country cottage made out of gingerbread, no doubt. I wouldn't be surprised if the Welsh hadn't started cooking blueberry muffins until someone came up with that story. You can try one if you want.'

'Aren't you going to try one?'

'Bit early in the morning for me. Maybe later.'

'What about half a one, Sarge?' Gertie asked hopefully.

'Later, Gertie, later. I've been doing some research on our friend in the cells, Guillaume Matisse.'

'Just a little one, Sarge? You need to keep your strength up, you know.'

'Gertie! Later.'

'But they're special Welsh blueberry muffins, Sarge,' Gertie protested. 'You can't let them go stale.'

Frank was about to bang his head against his desk in frustration when the telephone rang.

'Hello, Sergeant Summers here,' he said grimly. As he listened a smile lit his face.

'That's terrible, Mrs Smith. I quite understand, Mr Jadbhur really must stay in bed, summer colds and flu are the worst.'

He listened again.

'Yes, I quite understand, Mrs Smith, tomorrow then.'

He put the telephone down and smiled at Gertie.

'Sad news, Gertie, M Matisse's lawyer has gone down with a bad cold or flu or something. His partner's going to stand in for him, but he's already drowning in work, so he won't be able to turn up until tomorrow. M Matisse will just have to enjoy our hospitality a little longer.'

'We'll have to ask for an extension soon,' Gertie pointed out.

'I don't think we'll have any bother getting an extension, Gertie. Somehow I don't think M Matisse will object either. Not too much.'

'What's this about needing an extension?' asked Frieda, walking into the office with a frown on her face. Frank explained briefly.

'By the time we get a lawyer in we should have the Spanish and the Italians here,' he said happily. 'Get it all done in one go. If the Norwegians and the rest turn up we might have to hire the town hall to fit them all in.'

Frieda looked at him thoughtfully.

'I'm surprised they haven't been in contact already,' she said. 'From the Interpol poster they seemed very eager to get their hands on him. Still, it is the Italians and Spanish we're talking about. They're probably still having a siesta. God knows what's wrong with the Norwegians.'

Frank paused and rubbed his jaw thoughtfully.

'Well, now there's a thought,' he said softly.

'A siesta? You are not going to have one, Sergeant. Superintendent Campbell and Sergeant Hovis are waiting for you in the canteen.' She paused, noticing the box of muffins. 'And I don't want to see your breakfast lying in your out-tray, Sergeant, it gives a very bad impression.'

'That isn't my breakfast, Inspector,' he said, standing up and putting his jacket on. 'They're some muffins Pete Phillips brought back from Wales.'

'Special blueberry muffins,' Gertie said. 'There's an old Welsh legend that says you get to marry the first person you share one with.'

'Which just goes to show the Welsh must have caught up with the Irish in inventing blarney to sell to gullible tourists,' Frank said, walking towards the door. 'Come on, Gertie, babysitting time. Our London friends await.'

Gertie paused as she followed him out. She looked at Frieda looking speculatively at the muffins. Frieda noticed the look.

'Amazing what silly things people will fall for,' Frieda said in a bluff voice. 'Like believing in horoscopes.'

'Load of nonsense,' Gertie agreed, unconvincingly, having, as usual, consulted her own horoscope first thing that morning.

'Anyway, who ever heard of sharing a muffin with someone when you have a box of them?' continued Frieda. 'Unless they were cut in halves to start off with.'

'Gertie, have you got lost?' came Frank's voice from down the corridor. Gertie hurried out with one last suspicious look at Frieda.

'Not until Saturday,' she reminded Frieda as she left.

'Of course not,' Frieda agreed.

She looked at the box. It was obviously unopened. Frank had presumably tossed it into his out-tray without a thought. It was one of the things they shared, the ability not to fall for such hocus-pocus.

She quickly checked Frank's desk drawers, finding a clean knife belonging to the canteen. She slipped open the box lid. She wasn't too sure what she had expected, but these looked unlike any muffins she had ever seen. Smaller than she had expected, and flattish, almost like four-leaf clovers. The thought crossed her mind that they had been given the title muffins rather arbitrarily.

Still, there wasn't time to ponder on that. She carefully cut a dozen muffins into halves in such a way that might suggest that that was how they had been made – if you didn't look closely, and weren't of a suspicious mind. She closed the box, wiped the knife on a handkerchief and replaced it.

Of course she didn't believe that twaddle about sharing a muffin leading to love. Absolute nonsense. Like crossing your fingers for luck.

She crossed her fingers and left Frank's office wondering how she was going to arrange to be there when Frank opened the box to try out a Welsh blueberry muffin. A special Welsh blueberry muffin.

After all, it couldn't do any harm, and a girl couldn't afford to waste chances, however silly they might seem.

'The house has basically been trashed,' Frank said as Gertie drove them back to the house in Lords Acres which Matisse had been renting. Superintendent Campbell had voiced a wish, since they could not yet interview Matisse, to visit the scene.

He and Sergeant Hovis had turned out to be two tallish, stocky men, wearing suits and ties. They looked what one might imagine two London coppers to be, close-cut haircuts and serious faces, two bruisers with a hint of menace in their eyes and the suggestion that they did not always play by the rulebook.

Campbell looked the shrewder of the two, well dressed, urbane and intelligent. Hovis looked like a plod, somewhat stupid and coarse, wearing an ill-fitting suit, his face bearing the imprints of a number of fists, his nose broken in at least two places. When Frank and Gertie had walked into the canteen he had looked Gertie up and down with a leer. Both Frank and Gertie had had to individually restrain an initial urge to give his nose another kink.

'Local criminals?' asked Campbell, in the back of the car.

'Probably,' said Frank. 'Mindless junkies desperately searching for something to flog to pay for their habit.'

'You have a drugs problem here?' asked Campbell.

'It's very recent, but growing very quickly,' Frank said, somewhat to the surprise of Gertie to whom this was news. 'We can take you to a place called the Blue Bliss after lunch. That's where we think the drugs are coming from. But we have to take a very softly-softly approach. The owners could be part of a larger organisation. Dangerous people. Your London experience could come in quite handy.'

Gertie just managed to restrain a giggle at the thought of Mrs Blower and Phil Walthers being described as dangerous. Mrs Blower might deserve the appellation, but not for the reasons Frank was suggesting. Privately Gertie wondered what Frank was on about this time.

'I heard about this Blue Bliss place,' said Sergeant Hovis with barely disguised interest. 'Strip club, innit?'

'Arts,' replied Frank.

'Arse?' asked Hovis 'You prefer arses?'

'No, Arts. It's apparently being re-invented as a modern performing arts establishment.'

'Sort of Frenchified, you mean?' asked Hovis. 'They still get their tits out, only it's all artistic like and you get to pay more for it?'

'Something like that,' said Frank. 'We're still trying to get used to the idea. Not the sort of thing we in Wellbury find easy to understand.'

'Quiet sort of a place, Wellbury,' Campbell noted.

'Very,' agreed Frank. 'Unusual place to find an international criminal hiding away. But not surprising if you think about it, you could probably hide out in a house in Lords Acres for years without your neighbours showing too much of an interest. M Matisse was just unlucky.'

'I understand you were the one who made the arrest,' Campbell said. 'On your own, off duty, unarmed. I think we could organise a medal for that.'

'I've always fancied the George Cross,' Frank said. He could hear Frieda behind Campbell's words. She would be very happy to portray him to the Superintendent as a brave, efficient and single-minded officer of hers, no matter what she might think privately. Brave, efficient and single-minded officers were very good for the career prospects of their superior officers.

'George Cross it will be,' said Campbell. Frank smiled and wondered whether he should have gone for the Victoria Cross. He had a suspicion that that would be pushing things a little far.

There was a puzzled look in Gertie's eyes. Why would a superintendent from London offer to confer a medal for just an arrest, and not a particularly dangerous one? And what was Frank up to? Normally he would have brushed the offer aside, he wasn't the type to go after medals. Or was there something in his character which she had missed?

She shrugged mentally. There was something going on that she didn't understand, and the best thing to do, until she worked out what it was, was to keep quiet and out of view as far as possible.

The large house remained unchanged when they entered, its interior lined with wreckage. To Frank's surprise and Gertie's displeasure Susan was there again.

'Not finished yet?' Frank asked.

'Er, no, just one or two things I needed to finish off. Could I have a word with you?'

'This is Superintendent Campbell and Sergeant Hovis from Scotland Yard,' Frank introduced the other men. 'Doctor Pleadle, our forensic expert.'

They exchanged greetings, Susan taking little heed of the London men.

'Just a quick word, Frank,' Susan repeated. 'I just want your advice on something. In private. Rather than making a fool of myself.'

'Okay,' Frank said, his eyebrows raised. 'Gertie, could you take our London cousins around? They'll probably be bored by seeing another wrecked house, probably see one a week in London, I would imagine.'

'Oh, we get our fair share,' Campbell said as he and Hovis wandered away. Gertie flashed Susan a warning look before following them, a look Frank totally missed as was his wont.

'Come into the kitchen,' Susan said. Frank followed her obediently.

'New evidence?' he asked.

'Pretend it's Saturday,' she said, turning to face him.

'Saturday?' he asked, puzzled. 'I often wish it was Saturday, especially on a Monday.'

'Good,' she said, stepping up to him, putting a hand behind his neck and pulling his face down. A pot went rolling loudly as she gave him a deep and lengthy kiss.

She stood back from him, breathing deeply, holding on to his arms.

'I didn't know how to say it,' she said. 'I thought that would say it better than any words.'

'Well, I'm not sure of the translation,' he replied, trying to get his breath and mind back. 'Could you repeat that?'

She smiled and gave him a peck on the cheek.

'Better not,' she said, 'Gertie might be here any moment. Saturday, Frank, Saturday, just wait until Saturday. I didn't want you to think I was ignoring you.'

'Well, you've certainly blown any such illusions away,' he admitted. 'I have to confess that I'm finding things somewhat confusing. I thought you were still angry with me.'

She smiled a half-grimace and looked at him contritely.

'I know, I'm sorry,' she said. 'We haven't really had much luck, have we? And I admit a lot of it was my fault. I think it was because I hated you for making me fall in love with you.'

Frank's mind made a "Yerl Glew?" noise.

'I did? I what? I when?' his mouth asked, having decided that his brain wasn't up to it.

'When I first met you, silly. Didn't you notice?'

No, his mind replied honestly, the first thing I remember was you threatening to take a scalpel to parts of my anatomy.

'Was that before or after you offered to dissect me?' he asked. She laughed and gave him another kiss on the cheek.

'You'll never change, will you, Frank?' she asked. 'Give me a hug to last me until Saturday.'

He put his arms around her and hugged her, wondering what Saturday had to do with it. Presumably she was too busy at the moment.

'I must fly, Frank,' she said, giving him a final kiss. 'Love you.'

'Love you too,' he murmured. She stopped at the door to blow a final kiss to him.

Frank scratched his head. Then he put a hand through his hair. Then he scratched his head again.

He was in love. She was in love.

But every time they got together he was on the receiving end of slammed telephones and slammed doors. And yesterday kicked pots and pans.

He had meant to ask her how her toes felt.

He would give her one last chance, he decided. One last

chance.

No, he wouldn't. It would end up just the same as all the other times. She would leave in a huff and he would be back in the dog box.

But, what the hell, third time lucky. Or in her case, fifty-millionth and first time lucky.

No, only a fool would go out with her again. And he was no fool. No, he would telephone her and tell her that it was off. Much as he liked her, possibly more than that, it was obvious that they could never be happy together.

Oh, what the hell! One more date wouldn't matter. It couldn't be that bad, could it?

Maybe he should ask Gertie. Gertie would be able to give him good advice.

Gertie!

She was upstairs wandering around with those two London bruisers. He shouldn't have left her alone with them. The man called Hovis was a particularly unpleasant specimen of the species.

He jogged quickly up the stairs. There was no sign of them. He ran back downstairs and found them in the ruined library. Gertie was keeping her distance while Campbell and Hovis looked around moodily. The two London men seemed little interested in investigating the damage.

'Have you found out what was stolen?' asked Campbell, hands in pockets, nudging at a broken bookcase with the point of his shoe.

'No,' replied Frank, slightly out of breath. 'We'll have to bring M Matisse here to draw up a list. At the moment I imagine he's got other things on his mind.' He paused. 'I hear he's flogged quite a few fakes in his time. Goya's Nude Mistress In Her Bath, Cezanne's Naked Lady In The Shower, to mention only two.'

'Sounds like you know a little about art, Sergeant,' Campbell said.

'Not really, no. Just bits and bobs you read in the newspaper, that sort of thing.'

'Any pictures stolen from here?' asked Campbell.

'We don't know. All the ones here had their frames broken, but the pictures seem to be still here, strewn around the place. They look like they'd be worth a few bob, but I don't suppose drug addicts could tell the difference.'

'Unless it was a professional job,' Campbell said. 'Matisse has flogged some fakes in his time, but he's also dealt with some of the real stuff. Ever heard of a painting called The Blue Studio?'

'The Blue Studio? Strange title for a painting.'

Gertie glanced at Frank's face. It was totally innocent of any notion that Jean Tromperie might have mentioned The Blue Studio the previous day, or Matisse the day before that.

'That's artists for you, I'm afraid. Anyway, it was painted by Matisse's great uncle, the original Matisse – you have heard of Matisse, no doubt?'

'Yes, one of the major Romantic painters, if I recall correctly.'

'Precisely, the, er, Romantic period. He painted a work which he called The Blue Studio. It disappeared for a long time, until just after the Second World War. The Nazis had looted it from somewhere. Then it disappeared again for a long time.

But Matisse – the one you arrested – got hold of it somehow, recently. Stole it, probably.'

'And you think that's what the thieves might have been after?' asked Frank dubiously. 'I can't see it, to be honest. Professionals going after something like a painting wouldn't tear the place apart like this. It's too messy. If the painting had been here they could have damaged it along with everything else.'

'Well, there is that, I suppose,' Campbell said. He paused for a few moments. 'But you definitely didn't find anything that might be The Blue Studio?'

'No, sorry. We haven't removed anything, so if you didn't notice it I doubt that it's here.'

Campbell nodded slowly.

'Oh, well, he must have hidden it somewhere else I suppose,' he sighed. 'So what did your forensic expert – Doctor Pleadle, was it? – want to speak to you about? Did she find anything new?'

'Er, no, um, fingerprints.'

'Fingerprints?'

'Yes, a bit of a cock-up, really. Turns out they were mine. She just wanted to double check.'

'These things happen,' Campbell said. He checked his watch.

'Better get back, I suppose,' he said. 'Your Inspector Garold is expecting us for lunch.' He looked at Frank. 'Any chance we could have a quiet word with Matisse without his lawyer present? We need to move on this one. We don't have a lot of time.'

'Sorry, sir. Strict instructions from the Chief Constable. We have to play this one by the book. We can't give Matisse the slightest chance of claiming any irregularities. You know what lawyers are like, and Matisse's Mr Jadbhur is one of the worst. Once he gets his teeth into something he's like a bulldog. We're rather lucky that his partner's going to be standing in for him.'

Campbell grunted.

'What's his partner's name?'

'Heathwaite, Samuel Heathwaite. He normally does divorces and such. He shouldn't give us many problems.'

A mild-mannered and inoffensive Mr Jadbhur would have been shocked to find himself described as a bulldog. His secretary Mrs Smith would have been most indignant at such a suggestion. Her high estimate of the young Sergeant Summers would have plummeted.

After Frank and Gertie had left the two London men with an increasingly irritated-looking Frieda, Frank sent Gertie on to the canteen while he went down to the cells to have a word with Matisse. He knew he shouldn't do it, not only because he was getting involved in something his instinct warned him to keep clear of, but also because he shouldn't be speaking to Matisse without his lawyer present, or, at the very least, another officer who could provide witness that no foul play or abuse had occurred. He wouldn't be the first police officer to be accused of such, even if nothing had happened. He was giving Matisse a chance he shouldn't, and if Frieda got to hear of it Frank might end up swinging on the end of her carefully prepared rope, attached noose, Detective Sergeant Summers' neck for the purpose of.

'So, M Matisse, what's this all about, then?' he asked. Matisse looked at him in innocent confusion.

'I have told you, Sergeant, my political enemies wish revenge for something which is not of my making. I am sure that once you have spoken to London you will realise that this is an unfortunate mistake. I do not understand why I have been kept here for so long.'

'Ever hear about a French police officer called Captain Tromperie? She's popped over from Paris just to have a chat with you. She's from the Sûreté.'

Matisse shrugged his shoulders, a surprised look on his face.

'I can think of no reason why a French policeman would be interested in me. No doubt this is another mistake.'

'Oh, it isn't a French policeman, M Matisse. She's a French policewoman. About twenty-six, bobbed black hair, pert little nose, lovely figure, likes wearing very tight trousers. Ring a bell with you?'

For a second the surprise was replaced by a look of shock in Matisse's eyes. A large and very loud bell had obviously rung in his head.

'I think you should speak to London,' he repeated, a definite hint of nervousness in his voice.

'We don't need to. London have come to us. A Superintendent Campbell and a Sergeant Hovis. Big lads, crew-cut hair. Ever been interviewed by them before?'

By now there was no doubt about it. Matisse was worried, if not fearful.

'Please, Sergeant, I beg of you. Speak to someone in Scotland Yard. They will tell you that there has been a terrible mistake.

I am not a wanted man.'

'Yes, I know, I know, you're innocent as a new-born babe, it's just that your political enemies have it in for you. So you say. For your information Campbell and Hovis are from Scotland Yard.'

'You are sure these men are from Scotland Yard?' asked Matisse anxiously.

'Oh, definitely.'

The news seemed to relax Matisse. There had been hardly a hint of doubt in Frank's voice, nothing of the heavy doubt which was growing in his mind.

'Ah, in that case I am grateful,' Matisse said. 'This matter will be cleared up very quickly. I presume they wish to speak to me?'

'In due course, M Matisse,' Frank said. 'But I think it would be a much better idea if you told me what this is all about. Now would be a good time.'

Again Matisse shrugged his shoulders and smiled, all nervousness having left him.

'A pure misunderstanding, Sergeant, I can assure you. Your colleagues from Scotland Yard will confirm this. No doubt they are as confused as I am.'

Gertie slipped back to their office before going to the canteen. Of course she didn't believe that story about sharing a muffin making two people fall in love. But you could believe in fairy tales even if you knew they weren't true. And when she handed Frank his half of a muffin he wouldn't know it was only a half. She would only mention it afterwards, as if surprised.

'Hey, Sarge, looks like we've just shared a muffin,' she would say offhandedly. 'Doesn't that mean we're going to fall in love and get married?'

He would scoff at the idea, but it would sit in his mind and niggle away, especially as she would remind him as often and subtly as possible. She would talk him into believing it, even if only subconsciously.

She hunted through his desk drawers for the knife she knew was there, the one he kept asking her to remind him to take back to the canteen. She opened the box of muffins carefully, trying not to make any creases, making sure no-one would suspect it had been opened.

She looked at the contents in surprise. She had never seen a Welsh blueberry muffin before. She had presumed they would be in some form of round shape. These were almost like two-leaf clovers, if such a thing existed. Maybe it was symbolic.

She shrugged her shoulders and hurriedly cut each two-leaf muffin into single leaves, arranging them afterwards carefully so that she would know which belonged to the other. Then she closed the box carefully, cleaned the knife and replaced it. She hurried off to the canteen, a smile on her face. Frank's fate was sealed. Or it would be shortly.

Half an hour later another figure walked into Frank's office. Captain Tromperie seemed mildly disconcerted not to find Frank at his desk. Then she looked out into the corridor, found it empty, closed the door and began quickly to search Frank's desk. She found nothing of interest, and commenced the same operation on Gertie's desk. The only thing that attracted her attention there was a spare lipstick of Gertie's.

'Cherry red,' Jean Tromperie noted with a smile. 'I'll bet you wear that especially for your Sergeant when you're off duty, you little tart.'

The search ending otherwise unfruitfully, she stood and looked around the office for a few seconds. She noticed the box in Frank's out-tray, and opened it purely out of curiosity. The contents surprised her.

'And I'll bet you made these yourself, little Sergeant Frank Summers,' she said softly. 'That's the sort of man you are, you have to be different. And they'll taste gorgeous, no doubt.'

To test the theory she popped one of the quarter sections into her mouth.

'Not bad,' she said, swallowing and replacing the box. 'Just a pity I'm on a diet, or I'd have a few more.'

She moved back to the door, listened for a few seconds, and then slipped out into the corridor. She held herself up straight and began marching back to Frieda's office, ready to complain, should anyone have the temerity to ask her why she was wandering around and where she was going, that this silly little English police station had too many corridors, and that Frieda had deliberately misguided her as to where the Ladies' was. Another calculated insult to the honest citizens of France.

Pete Phillips joined Frank and Gertie at their table in the canteen. In a few hours he had lost the breezy enthusiasm that two weeks' holiday had brought him. He looked as if he hadn't slept for days.

'Thanks for that warning, you two,' he said tiredly. 'If I hadn't known I would have thumped that little French bitch before an hour was out.'

'Little Miss Muck still giving it her all?' asked Gertie.

'And then some. Apart from general rudeness, she told me I was too fat to be a proper copper. Hell, I've lost ten pounds over the last two weeks, what with hill walking and all. And she tells me I'm fat! Just like that! Bloody French. It's the first time I've met a woman with a bum like that and my only wish is to give it a good kick.'

Frank smiled.

'Anything about her strike you as odd?' he asked.

'She's French, isn't she?' replied Pete Phillips rhetorically. 'Probably thinks it's normal to be rude.' A thought crossed his mind. 'She keeps humming a tune to herself, when she isn't having a go. That American national anthem, or whatever it is. The Civil War thing. Now I can't get it out of my mind. Bloody irritating, it is. Driving me round the bend.'

This time Frank kept his smile to himself.

'Where is she now?' he asked.

'Up in Fabulous's office, having lunch. Thank god. Fabulous doesn't look too happy.'

'Along with our friends from London,' Frank noted. 'I wish I could be a fly on the wall at that meeting.'

'Percy reckons the London boys are right decent blokes. Don't throw their weight around, if you know what I mean. Not like that French tart.'

'Strange, that,' remarked Frank. 'You'd think they'd look down on us small-town plods.'

'Nah, a good copper's a good copper wherever he is,' Pete Phillips said. 'So long as he isn't French.' He smiled suddenly as another thought hit him. 'That French tart keeps trying to get me to let her speak to Matisse. Says it's important she speaks to him as soon as possible. I just shrug and say orders is orders. About the only time I feel I'm enjoying myself.'

'Old Matisse certainly seems to be popular at the moment, doesn't he? Everyone's straining at the leash to have a quiet word with him, preferably without his lawyer present.'

'Well, I can tell you one thing. That French tart isn't going to get anywhere near him if I can help it. With or without his lawyer. In fact, if she asked me the time of the day I wouldn't give it to her. I've been thinking of accidentally locking her up in one of the cells, if only I could work out a way to do it which wouldn't look too obvious.'

'Where are you taking her this afternoon?' asked Frank. Pete's shoulders slumped.

'I was trying not to think about this afternoon,' he moaned. 'I was hoping she'd choke on something during lunch. I don't think I could face a whole afternoon of her.'

'Why don't you take her to where that bloke disappeared, Cranley, wasn't it? Herbert Cranley? I seem to recall you mentioning him once. Went fishing at the river and never came back. An unsolved mystery.'

'Yeah, that was his name, but it wasn't much of a case. He probably ran off with his girlfriend, if what his neighbours said was true.'

'But from what I remember you searched the area. Very muddy, you said. Came up to your ankles, didn't it?'

'Yeah, that's right. Wet and muddy and a waste of time. Right pain in the proverbial, it was. I wouldn't like to have to do that again.' He paused at the look on Frank's face. He smiled.

'Wet and muddy,' he repeated.

'Be an awful shame if she should slip and land up on that pretty backside in the mud, wouldn't it?' suggested Frank.

'Terrible,' agreed Pete, smiling hugely. 'Course, me being such a clumsy plod, well, mistakes happen. Us fat blokes are always accidentally bumping into things.'

The three of them smiled.

'Can I come along?' asked Gertie. 'I could help push.'

'Fucking French bitch,' Hovis fumed, sitting in the back of the car as they drove to the Blue Bliss. 'Next time let's just get ourselves a MacDonald's, boss. If I'm ever in the same room as that bitch I swear I'll punch her lights out.'

'Now, now, Sergeant,' Campbell replied with a controlled smile, as if he had toothache and was trying not to show it. 'Patience. The French have a different approach to ours. And I don't think we'll be seeing the Captain again. I shall go out of my way to see that that does not happen.'

'Thank fuck our coppers are decent,' Hovis said. 'Say what you like about English coppers, they don't come across like that Frog bitch. Jesus!'

'Yes, Sergeant, we in the British police believe in manners. Such as not swearing too much.'

'Fucking right, too,' replied Hovis.

'Captain Tromperie's not that bad when you get to know her,' Frank said, sitting in the front seat, a smile playing on his lips. 'The French have their own ways of approaching things. She's an ambitious police officer. She wants to take Matisse back to Paris. It would be an extremely large feather in her cap.'

'Which won't happen, of course,' Campbell suggested smoothly. 'I presume we from Scotland Yard will have priority.'

'I don't know, sir,' Frank replied uncertainly. 'Normally, yes, but I hear from the grapevine that the Home Office are sending some civil servant along. He might decide that it's time to be friendly to the French. You know what these politicians are like. Especially with the European Union. They might want some favour or other in return, a bit of back scratching, that sort of thing. When politics comes into it right and wrong go straight out the window.'

Home Office? thought Gertie to herself. When had they entered the picture? And why not the Foreign Office, or whatever it was they called themselves?

'Bloody politicians,' Hovis grumbled, as if finally realising the need to moderate his language. 'They give everything to the bloody Frogs and Krauts. And the Eyeties.'

'Quite so, Sergeant,' Campbell interjected quickly. 'I'm surprised Inspector Garold didn't mention that, Sergeant Summers.'

He wasn't the only surprised one. Gertie was somewhat baffled as well. Frieda would have been speechless. And the Home Office would probably also have been somewhat perplexed had they known.

'Oh, she probably hasn't heard yet,' Frank said blithely. 'You know how it is, quite often we at the bottom hear things before senior officers.'

That was also news to Gertie. "We at the bottom" were invariably the last to know anything apart from football scores and even then only if they were lucky.

'Of course, Sergeant, of course,' said Campbell. 'Always the way, isn't it? Er, any idea when this person from the Home Office will turn up?'

'Oh, not before Monday I would imagine, sir,' Frank replied. 'Civil servants don't tend to act very quickly in my experience. They probably won't finish the paperwork before they go home on Friday, if then, and then there's the weekend. And, thinking about it, Mondays are normally a bad day for them, takes them a while to get up to speed. All in all I doubt whether we'll see them before teatime on Wednesday.'

It was fortunate that no civil servants were around to hear this calumny. But then they would have had to queue up behind the others Frank had so far blithely maligned.

'Typical civil servants, eh?' Campbell agreed. 'However, I'm sure we can sew this one up before then, with your assistance, Sergeant.'

'Oh, I'm sure we can work faster than the Home Office.'

There was a pause as Campbell thought about this.

'This place we're going to now, the Blue Bliss – it's a strip club, I understand,' he said, changing the subject.

'I could do with a nice bit of totty,' remarked Hovis.

'That's their cover,' Frank replied. 'We suspect that's it's a front for gun-running.'

'Gun-running? I thought Inspector Garold mentioned drugs.'

'That too, sir. A little of everything, really, guns, drugs, diamond smuggling. All on a very small scale, mind. At the moment, anyhow. We think they're testing their plans before they go in for something big. But the owners don't know we're on to them, so if you could just play along? We'll pretend it's just a routine check, security or something. We need to play it carefully, they're a shrewd bunch.'

'Of course, Sergeant,' replied Campbell, not noticing the shaking of Gertie's shoulders.

They found Mrs Blower and Phil Walthers in a room which had been converted into a studio of sorts. Phil Walthers was looking harassed as he fiddled with a camera on a tripod pointing at a young woman wearing the skimpiest of togas, draped over what appeared to be a marble bench in what might be considered to be the Roman style. Despite the minimally increased clothing Frank recognised her as Sonia, the girl they had met the previous day.

'Frank!' exclaimed Mrs Blower in delight, coming towards them, unknowingly dragging an electrical cable wrapped around her ankle. 'Twice in two days! How marvellous! We're doing a photo-shoot to advertise the changes we've made. Have you seen Nelson? Who are these? Not more French, I hope. Mr Walthers, I don't think she needs to show too much, there won't be anything left to show on the night. Gertie, he's growing thinner day by day, my dear.'

'Hello, Mrs B,' Frank said. 'Allow me to introduce Detective Superintendent Campbell and Detective Sergeant Hovis from Scotland Yard. They're here to give a training course on modern security. We're just showing them around, thought they might be able to give you a few hints.'

'Delighted,' Mrs Blower said doubtfully, peering short-sightedly at the two men. 'You haven't seen Nelson, have you, Inspector?' she asked a confused Hovis. 'Are you also French? Frank really does get involved with the most awful women, you know. Not you, Gertie, of course not, but you should look after him more. Would you like to start with the wiring cupboard?'

'Wiring cupboard?' asked Hovis, eyes wide open in confusion.

'Where the wires are,' Mrs Blower explained, noticing the cable around her ankle with some surprise and untangling it, almost pulling Phil Walthers' tripod over. 'You know, the ones for the cameras. Mr Walthers! Your tripod thingy! The TTCV cameras, not the other ones. Mr Walthers, where did we leave the wiring cupboard last? It's so easy to get lost around here, you know. No, don't worry, Mr Walthers, I think I can find it. Nelson might be there. Come along then, which one of you is the soup?'

'Soup?' asked Campbell weakly as they obediently followed the figure of Mrs Blower. Frank smiled as they left, and wandered over to Phil Walthers.

'A partnership made in heaven,' he commented. 'You and Mrs Blower running the Blue Bliss. If there was an award for incongruity you would get first prize.'

Phil Walthers shook his head sadly and rolled his eyes. He turned to the young woman on the marble bench.

'Take a break, Sonia. Be back in fifteen minutes.'

'Thanks, Mr Walthers, me bum was going to sleep there,' the woman said, walking passed them, giving Frank a come-thither smile. 'You want to wake it up?' she asked him playfully.

'Get along, Sonia, get along,' Phil Walthers said sternly. 'Honestly,' he continued, turning to Frank and Gertie when the girl had left, 'no respect, some of these girls, no respect whatsoever. You won't believe some of the offers I've had.'

Frank couldn't help but smile.

'So what inspired you to go into business with Mrs Blower?' he asked. 'I'm surprised you have the time.'

Phil Walthers looked at him mournfully.

'I was dragooned into it,' he said. 'Keelhauled before I knew it.'

'Don't you mean press-ganged?'

'Press-ganging would have been mild by comparison. No, Sergeant Summers, having to suffer Mrs Blower's conversation is like being keelhauled, mentally dragged through a swamp of misunderstanding.'

He sighed.

'I don't really have the time for it, as you say. The idea was that I would co-finance the operation and Mrs Blower would run the organisational side. I saw it as somewhat of an investment for my retirement fund. But you can't get partially involved where Mrs Blower is concerned. She drags you into everything.'

He gave another sigh.

'Don't get me wrong, she's a fine woman. A little too enthusiastic, perhaps, somewhat not entirely reliable as far as her memory goes, that is true, and her thought processes resemble a sackful of ferrets on speed, that cannot be denied, but a fine woman.' He paused. 'A misplaced sense of sympathy, perhaps. I felt sorry for her after that business with Sykes – when he tried to kill her. At the time I did not realise that sympathy for Mrs Blower is about as useful as offering a loan to Croesus. By then it was too late. Once wrapped in her coils it is impossible to escape.'

Both Frank and Gertie had the impression that, much as he bemoaned his fate, Phil Walthers was secretly enjoying being wrapped in Mrs Blower's coils.

'Of course the one I really feel sorry for is Nelson, poor thing,' Phil Walthers noted.

'How is Nelson?' Frank asked.

'I've taken him under my care. Mrs Blower does mean well, but I'm afraid it will take poor Nelson time to understand her. She takes him for a walk ten minutes after the last one, or not at all for days. She forgets to feed him and then suddenly he has three meals thrust on him in the space of a few hours. It must be quite confusing for the poor animal. But, as I say, I've taken on some of the responsibility. It will take time, of course, but I'm sure he will settle down. It is a little irritating, as I'm hardly an animal lover, but he seems quite affectionate when he isn't terrified.'

'I have to admit there's another reason I was surprised to hear that you and Mrs Blower had gone into partnership. I'm not sure how to put this diplomatically, but – to be blunt, I thought you couldn't stand her.'

'Oh, dear me, no, Sergeant Summers. That was during her religious period. Now she's decided she prefers the arts I find her a most attractive, if somewhat demanding, lady. However I do wish she would leave me to get on with my job. She's afraid the girls will appear like some page three tarts. As if I would allow anything like that in the Herald. Really!' A thought struck him. 'But while we're on the subject of photographs, I could do yours now. It would save time. And I need it for the next edition.'

'Photograph? You are not taking a photograph of me, Mr

Walthers. I thought I had made that quite clear.'

'But Inspector Garold, fine woman ...' His voice tailed off.

'Inspector Garold?' prompted Frank, almost growling. 'Inspector Garold what?'

'She told me ... um, how can I put this ... I understood she had ordered you to, um, co-operate with the local media.'

'Did she, by god,' muttered Frank. 'She'll have another thought coming. She knows how much I hate having my photograph taken. This time she's gone too far.'

'Please, Sergeant Summers, I have no wish to be the cause of a spat between the two of you. I will forego the photograph.'

'Police officers do not have spats, Mr Walthers.'

'If you say so, Sergeant.'

'I'll bloody well kill her for this, though,' Frank said grimly.

His mood lightened slightly when the two London men re-appeared, being almost dragged along behind Mrs Blower by an invisible rope. They looked desperate to be somewhere else. Anywhere else.

They never did find the wiring cupboard. According to Mrs Blower someone must have moved it again.

Back at the station, having left Campbell and Hovis in the canteen, they were in their office in the late afternoon when Eric Johns popped in to tell Frank that Frieda had ordered him to report to her forthwith.

'She's not in a good mood, Frank,' Eric said. 'If I were you I'd go in there, say yes ma'am, no ma'am, absolutely ma'am, and get out as soon as I could.'

'Well, fortunately I'm not you, Eric. I'm not afraid of Wonderwoman. She wants a fight, she's got one.'

He tripped up the stairs, whistling to himself. Frieda wasn't going to give, he wasn't going to give. The business about the photograph was the last straw. She knew how he hated having his photograph taken, and the idea of it appearing in the local newspaper was something he was not going to allow. They were going to have it out right now, and he was going to tell her exactly what he thought. He had had enough of her nonsense.

It would be the end of his career in the police force. The end of his life in Wellbury. He loved Wellbury. But, there you go. Life is transient. Maybe he'd move to somewhere like Cornwall. Start a daffodil farm. Settle down with some local girl. Or perhaps Susan would like the idea. He could imagine the scene: she bulging with their first child, watching him as he tended to the daffodils on an early spring morning, ready with a mug of soup as he came in from the cold. He'd always had a yen for somewhere far from the madding crowd.

But with a small village of the madding crowd nearby with a nice little pub of course, somewhere to go in the evenings after a hard day's work watching daffodils grow.

Tricia had packed up for the day, he presumed as he passed her empty desk and walked into Frieda's office without bothering to knock. She sat at her desk as if expecting him to enter in such a cavalier fashion.

'You wanted to see me, Inspector?' he asked.

'Close the door, Frank,' she said, standing up.

He did as bid and turned to find her looking out of the window.

'We have a problem, Frank,' she said.

'Oh? And what's that?'

'You know damn well what it is, Frank.' She turned to face him. 'You're angry with me, and I'm angry with you. It can't go on like this. We have to work together, if nothing else. I intend to put a stop to this nonsense. It's just plain childishness.'

'Oh? And how do you intend to do that?' he asked as she stepped up to him.

'Pretend it's Saturday, Frank.'

'Sorry?'

'Pretend it's Saturday. Go on, your mind is easily capable of that. What day is it?'

'Er, Saturday?' he asked, baffled. What was all this business with Saturday all of a sudden? First Susan now Frieda.

'Good,' she said. 'It's Saturday.'

She put a hand behind his head and drew his face down on hers. He found himself involved in a kiss of heroic portions, the sort never shown until after the nine o'clock watershed. After about a minute they had to come up for air.

'Phew!' he said weakly. 'Suddenly I wish every day was Saturday.'

'Maybe we could arrange that,' she said coyly, 'if you played your cards right. Not angry with me anymore?'

'I've quite forgotten what I was mad about. Er, do they teach you that sort of thing in Inspectors' school? I don't remember that from when I did the course.'

'Not even a little angry, still?' she asked, a coquettish look in her eyes.

'Well, now you come to mention it ...'

Before they could resume their clinch there was a knock at the door. Frieda stepped away, smoothing down her blouse. Frank quickly took an interest in a file he picked up from Frieda's desk.

'Come in,' Frieda ordered, sitting at her desk.

The door opened and Gertie stepped warily inside.

'Er, Superintendent Campbell asked me to pass a message on,' she said, looking from Frieda to Frank, a suspicious look in her eyes. 'He and the Sergeant have left for the day. They'll be at their hotel if they're needed.'

'Ah, yes, Superintendent Campbell, I'd quite forgotten about him. Thank you, Gertie.'

Gertie nodded, gave them a last suspicious frown and left. Frank realised the file he was pretending to read was upside down.

'Now, where were we, Frank?' asked Frieda.

Frank looked at her. He dropped the file he had not been reading onto her desk, put his hands in his pockets and wandered over to the window, looking at the setting sun.

'Campbell and Hovis,' he said. 'Have you checked up on them?'

'How do you mean, checked up on them? They're from Scotland Yard.'

'Who says so?'

'Their warrant cards say so. What are you talking about, Frank?'

'You can buy a machine for twenty quid on the Internet to print a plastic card saying you're a copper,' he pointed out.

'Or the Mayor of London, or whatever. I once went to a party with an ID card saying I was the Mayor of Casterbridge. You'd be surprised how many people fell for it, even when I introduced myself as Tom Hardy.'

He turned around.

'I think I first became suspicious when I heard their names. Yes, it's entirely possible that there were a duo called Campbell and Hovis, but it sounded too much like two people having a lunch and trying to come up with false names – Campbell after the soup, Hovis after the bread. And then Campbell offered to arrange a medal for my arresting Matisse. I said I wouldn't mind the George Cross, and he said, effectively, "no problem". I wasn't sure whether he was taking the Mickey or was just making it up to make me feel good – patronising the local plods, as it were. Either way, why come up with such nonsense? You don't get given the George Cross just for nicking an old man in a supermarket. So later I said to them that Matisse had faked Goya's Nude Mistress In Her Bath and Cezanne's Naked Lady In The Shower, came up with some rubbish about the Romantic period. There are no such paintings, but the only reaction from Campbell, as he calls himself, was that I obviously knew something about art. What's more obvious is that they haven't a clue about fine art. He changed the subject very quickly to disguise the fact. I'm sure Scotland Yard would have a Fine Arts unit, they wouldn't send down two coppers to interview an international con artist if they didn't know their subject.'

Frieda went to her desk and sat down, a grim look on her face.

'Why didn't you tell me of your suspicions before?' she asked.

He didn't reply. They both knew the reason. They hadn't

been on speaking terms. And neither was prepared to admit to such childish behaviour. So they didn't.

'I'll call Scotland Yard,' Frieda said, reaching for her telephone. 'If you're right you get a sweetie. If you're wrong ...'

'I'll be having a coffee in my office,' Frank said, opening the door. 'I don't have a sweet tooth, but if there's a bottle of ale on offer ...'

'Okay, Frank, if you're right I'll take you out and you can have as many ales as you want. How about Saturday night?'

'Saturday night sounds just fine.'

He tripped down the stairs, humming to himself. Life was back on course. He was back in Frieda's good books.

He paused. That kiss ... well, it had been a little passionate, almost as if ... No, you're being silly, he told himself. Frieda was a woman, women did things like that, they were forever kissing. Not normally on the mouth, and probably the tongue was a little unusual, but ...

Saturday night, he thought.

Oh, bollocks. He was supposed to be having a Spanish dinner with Gertie. Bollocks, bollocks and double bollocks!

And Susan had talked about Saturday as if they had a date.

He walked into his office, frowning. His only comfort was that he had only officially agreed to a date with two of them. Normally he would have managed to include Susan, but in her case there was nothing explicit. She had mentioned Saturday, but they hadn't actually agreed anything, had they? Not as such. And Saturday had been mentioned as a possibility, there had been nothing about Saturday night.

Of course the distinction between explicit and implicit with women was a very fine one. About the width of an extremely sharp razor blade that didn't actually exist. But was bloody sharp all the same.

Even that little comfort left him as he walked into his office and realised that Susan and Gertie were sitting next to each other, looking at him.

'You okay, Sarge?' Gertie asked in concern at his abrupt stop and the way his face suddenly went pale in the realisation that just one of them had to say anything about Saturday night and he would have a lot of explaining to do, and since he didn't understand what had happened and how it had happened he didn't have a clue of how he would start.

But he could take a pretty good guess at how it would end.

'Mmm? Yes, fine, fine. I'm surprised to see you here,' he said to Susan.

'I was passing and popped in to have a chat with Gertie,' she said defensively. 'You don't mind, do you?'

'Of course not,' Frank said, shaking his head resignedly and sat down behind his desk. A few hours previously Susan had been all passion and hugs, now she was being defensive. What was wrong with her?

To Frank's relief Frieda came into the office, beaming.

The relief suddenly plummeted into near panic. Now he was facing all three of them. The chances of Saturday night being mentioned had increased exponentially. That might not make mathematical sense, but then a group of women had their own, higher, form of mathematics. Fermat's Last Theorem probably had something to do with women, which is why it had been his last. Perhaps not the last theorem he had, but the one that got him in the end.

And what was the first thing a woman did when she had what could be construed as a date? Announced it to the whole world, including her enemies. Especially her enemies.

'Frank gets a sweetie,' Frieda announced happily as Frank measured the distance to the door. 'Or, in his case, an ale. A crate, in fact.'

Gertie and Susan looked at her in bewilderment. She turned to them.

'Wonderboy here,' she explained, 'was the only one of us not taken in by our visitors from London. I've just been on the phone to Scotland Yard. They don't have a Superintendent Campbell, nor a Sergeant Hovis. They probably are from London, but police officers they are not.'

'And we've got a team on the way to request their company and offer an explanation or two about why they're posing as good honest coppers?' asked Frank, cautiously beginning to hope that he might escape the Inquisition if he kept the discussion restricted to office business.

Frieda grimaced.

'Well, yes. I know I should have given it to you, but I asked Percy instead. He was the one who first met them and got taken in by them, so he's entitled to a little revenge.'

'Ah, well, every dog gets their day,' said Frank. He noticed the box of Welsh blueberry muffins. Another diversion. Keep their minds occupied with anything but the weekend, especially Saturday. 'Might as well open these as a celebration of sorts,' he said, picking up the box and shaking it gently, putting it to his ear. 'Just in case it's a bomb rather than muffins,' he joked, not noticing the aghast looks on Frieda and Gertie's faces as they tried to work out which halves might have fallen where in the shaking.

'What is it?' asked Susan.

'Welsh blueberry muffins,' said Frank. 'Pete Phillips brought them back from his holiday.'

'You wouldn't like them,' Gertie assured Susan quickly.

'Too fattening,' agreed Frieda.

'According to Pete they flog them with some story about an ancient Welsh legend that you fall in love with anyone you share one with,' Frank continued gaily. 'No doubt get married, have fifteen children and live happily ever after, or some such rubbish. Amazing what nonsense you can sell to people. I bet there are American tourists who honestly believe in a legend invented about three weeks ago. Still, the Eiffel Tower has been sold to dupes quite a few times, hasn't it?'

'Yes, amazing,' agreed Susan after a pause. 'But I do like Welsh blueberry muffins. Though they are a bit fattening, aren't they? I'll just have half of one.'

Frank paused, a look of surprise on his face as he looked into the box he had just opened.

'Be difficult to cut one of these in half,' he remarked. 'They seem to make them bite size. Oh, well, help yourselves.'

He passed the box to Frieda. She looked at the contents in more surprise than Frank had. She took a piece of muffin and passed the box to Susan.

'You could just about share one,' Susan said without much conviction, taking an unusually sized and shaped muffin and passing the box on to a wide-eyed Gertie.

'Come on, Gertie, hurry up,' said Frank. Gertie chose a piece and passed the box to Frank carefully. Frank took a piece and dropped it into his mouth.

'Tasty,' he said, swallowing, 'but the word morsel does come to mind. Fancy a Welsh blueberry muffin, Eric?' he asked as Eric Johns' portly frame appeared in the doorway.

'Don't mind if I do,' Eric said, taking a piece as the women watched aghast. 'Small, aren't they? Typical bloody Welsh, mean little b – er, anyway, I was just about to go off duty when your London friend turned up.'

'You're joking!' Frank exclaimed. 'Which one, Campbell or Hovis?'

'Oh, not those two. Vic Brown, Cockney tea-leaf.'

'That's all I need,' said Frank, spotting an escape route and jumping to his feet. 'Okay, I'll have a quick word with him and kick him out. Probably just wants a bit of company. Pining for the cells or something. Where is he? Not wandering around unescorted again?'

'I've put him in interview room two,' Eric Johns replied. 'I made sure the door was locked when I left. He won't wander far.'

'With our Vic Brown you can never be too sure,' Frank noted.

The three women watched Frank and Eric walk out. Then they turned to each other.

There was more than a hint of suspicion in the air.

'Vic Brown, am I glad to see you,' Frank said, entering the interview room after unlocking the door. Vic Brown looked at him warily.

'Are you, guv?'

'Not especially, Vic, no. I just needed an excuse to get out of rather tricky situation. I'd have been just as happy to see the tooth fairy. So, what's up? Not those cigarettes again, is it?'

'Well, sort of, guv, in a manner of speaking.'

'I told you, Vic, no way. I am not going to open a case file just so that you can claim on your insurance.'

'Oh, no, Mr Summers, honest, that's all sorted. That's what I came to see you about, to put your mind at rest as it were.'

'Vic, I can assure you that your stolen cigarettes were not giving me sleepless nights. But, since it may give me a few moments longer to live, go on, satisfy my non-existent curiosity as to the missing fags.'

'Well, you see, Mr Summers, it turns out it was the missus.'

Frank considered this statement.

'Your missus smoked thirty cartons of cigarettes without you noticing?' he asked.

'Oh, no, guv, she don't smoke. No,' Vic Brown continued sadly, 'she found them in the garden shed where I had hidden them. She thought I'd nicked em, and threw them away before they got me into trouble.'

'Your wife threw them away?'

'Yes, guv. You'd think she'd 'ave trusted me after all the years we'd bin together like. Years I've devoted meself to that woman, bleeding years, and still she don't trust me. You'd think she'd know me by now. Wot's a bloke to do, eh?'

Frank resisted the urge to point out that it was precisely because Mrs Brown knew her Victor that she didn't trust him.

'Years of devotion,' he said instead, 'apart from the periods when you were separated, with her at home and you residing in one of Her Majesty's clinks?'

'Well, I suppose, if you put it like that, Mr Summers. But I'm straight now, I promised her I'd go straight, that's why we moved to Wellbury, to get away from all that temptation in London. Everything I do these days is legit, honest, no word of a lie.'

'I thought you left London because it was becoming too dangerous even for honest criminals,' Frank said, refraining from mentioning that Vic Brown's notion of legitimacy was not necessarily shared by most of mankind.

'Well, there was that, too,' the small man admitted. He perked up. 'Still, it means I can claim on the insurance after all. Accidentally lost, that's wot I'll tell em. Me missus threw them out by mistake.'

Frank sighed.

'Vic, apart from what might technically be described as a fraudulent claim, you don't seriously believe the insurance company is going to quietly pay you for your missing cigarettes without enquiring as to why you had thirty cartons of – again, technically – illicit cigarettes in your possession?'

'Ah, well, Mr Summers, I'm ahead of you on that one. I'll tell em they were for me daughter's wedding. It's Cockney tradition, you see, making sure everyone has fags if they want.'

'I see. Tell me, Vic, how long has this, er, tradition, being going on?'

'Oh, only since I thought of it last night, Mr Summers, but they won't know that.'

'And you do have a daughter about to get married?'

'Sort of, guv. Close enough. She's been living wif her bloke for ten years, so I reckon it would make sense if they thought of getting hitched. At least they will when I tell them. Even if they don't actually do it, if you see what I mean.'

He stood up.

'I owe you another favour for that, Mr Summers, you kept me on the straight and level there, you know, I could have got into real trouble otherwise. But I'll give you some good advice from one wot knows, Mr Summers. Never get married. You'd think a missus would trust her old man, wouldn'tcha? Oh, no, not mine, no, she goes poking her nose into my shed, throws away me fags because she don't trust me. No, never get married, Mr Summers, women have suspicious minds, it's part of their nature. I'll leave you now, Mr Summers, I knows how busy you are. And again, I owe you one, Mr Summers, you just say the word. Anything you want.'

Frank watched the wraith disappear out into the corridor.

I'd like you to make me invisible, he thought. I might need to be, very shortly.

Inside Frank's office three women were living up to Vic Brown's prediction of female distrust.

'I don't understand,' said Frieda. 'Someone must have cut those muffins up after I'd ...'

'After you'd what?' asked Susan suspiciously.

'After I'd cut them up myself,' Frieda admitted. 'It was just a joke. Well, you don't really believe that story, do you?'

Susan's face suggested that, whether or not she was a doctor, she was prepared to give it the balance of doubt. A very large balance. She noticed Gertie's guilty look.

'Gertie?' she asked. 'Something you'd like to share with us?'

Gertie shrugged, shamefacedly.

'I didn't know they'd already been cut up once,' she said. 'I just thought ...'

'That if you cut them into two you and Frank would share one without his realising it?' asked Susan angrily. 'The same as you did, didn't you Frieda?'

'Nobody really believes the story,' Frieda repeated, 'it was just a bit of a joke.'

'Of course not. Except, you realise what's happened, don't you?'

The other two didn't appear to want to answer, so Susan continued.

'We've probably just shared a love muffin, the four of us. Us and Frank. At least I hope and pray it was us and Frank. It could as easily have been us and Eric Johns. Or even Frank and Eric Johns.'

The others shuddered at both thoughts. Susan stood up.

'I can't say I'm impressed by your behaviour, going behind my back like that. I think it's disgraceful. We were supposed to be giving him a hard time until Saturday. I kept my part of the bargain, you haven't.'

Frieda raised her hand in surrender.

'Okay, Susan, you're right. It's just that Frank did expose those two con men from London. He was owed a lot of thanks for that. On a professional basis.'

'Very well. Just no more until Saturday, okay?'

Frieda and Gertie nodded silently.

'Good. Tomorrow we can draw cards on who gets Frank on Saturday,' Susan said and stalked out of the office.

Once out she hurried along the corridor until she reached the end and waited. In a short while Frank appeared. She pulled him into a doorway.

'Eh?' he asked in surprise. 'What's wrong?'

'Shush, Frank, it's Saturday again,' she whispered.

'I'm beginning to like Saturday,' he said.

'Good boy,' she said and dragged his face down to hers.

It was a sense of deja vu with a different woman a second time. Or a third. He was losing count.

'Now,' she said after oxygen starvation forced them to part, 'I am going to take you out for dinner on Saturday to make up for acting like a right little cow these past couple of weeks.' She gave him a brief kiss on the cheek. 'Saturday night, Frank, you get to choose where. Love you.'

Then she was walking away, leaving a stunned Frank Summers thinking what nice legs she had and what the hell had happened? And what the hell was he going to do about Saturday? And why did they all insist on Saturday? And when was the next flight to Rio? Or Timbuktu. Or anywhere.

He made a mental prayer asking that Saturday night would never come. It was made in an offhand way, never believing that he really wanted it nor that it should come true. With his knowledge of the Classics he should have known that you do not ask the fates for such things. More often than not you got what you had asked for, without getting what you wanted.

He mentally limped back to his office. Frieda had gone, leaving a sorrowful looking Gertie staring at the floor.

'You okay, Gerts?' he asked. 'You don't look like the happiest bunny in the world.'

'Sorry, Sarge, just got a few things on my mind.'

'I know the feeling, Gertie my sweet. I was just thinking that the one woman around this place – apart from you, of course – that I could rely on was our Captain Buttocks. She is consistent. At least she's consistently rude.'

'The Strumpet? You've been thinking about her?'

'I've been thinking about her ever since she turned up, Gerts. Right now I could do with a drink. Fancy one, Sergeants Arms?'

'I could murder a gin and tonic. Though that's not all I could murder.'

'Come on, then, I don't think Frieda needs us. She's probably making sure Percy collars her man. Or men. Best we get out before she finds some work for us.'

Or someone mentions Saturday, he thought.

Frieda walked in to Frank's office ten minutes after they had left. She frowned. He should have told her he was going off duty.

She had intended to ask him if he fancied a drink. As long as Gertie wasn't around.

Gertie!

The little cow. She wasn't supposed to do anything until Saturday. If she had grabbed Frank for drinks she wouldn't hear the last of it. The cheating little ....

'So, what's this business with the French tart?' asked Gertie as she nestled next to Frank in the Sergeants Arms.

He smiled, took a sip of his pint, and felt relaxation set in. Unconsciously he put an arm around her shoulders.

'Same as Hovis and Clovis, or whatever they called themselves. Think about it, Gerts. She's tried to put everyone's backs up, and managed it pretty well. Would you send an arrogant little thing like that to liaise with a foreign police force?'

'The French would,' Gertie insisted. 'They still haven't forgiven us for not losing World War Two like they did.'

'Beware of stereotypes, Gertie, beware of stereotypes.'

'You mean she's not French?'

'I don't know. She might be. On the other hand she may not be. If only I spoke fluent French I could probably trip her up if she isn't. But what I'm certain of is that she's not a French police officer. That kepi? And those trousers? She probably has to oil herself to get into them. It's as if she walked straight out of a bad comedy on the telly. And she's all of about twenty-six. A captain at that age? If they even have the rank of captain in the French police, something I must try to find out as soon as I get a chance.'

He took another pull of ale.

'Tell me, Gertie, if you were going across to France as a representative of Wellbury police force – or, say, Scotland Yard – would you wear the tightest trousers in your collection, or would you wear something that looked smart, felt comfortable and travelled well?'

'She's French,' Gertie insisted dogmatically, not overly happy with the interest Frank was showing the in French tart's bum.

'Five quid says she's not a French police officer,' Frank said, abandoning logic for the less subtle, but more powerful, financial threat.

'If she's not, what is she? Why is she pretending to be a police officer?'

'Ah, now that's the question, isn't it? Notice how interested she was in that tin foil box I picked up?'

'She did seem a little fascinated with it.'

'The Blue Studio, Gerts, remember? It's a painting that doesn't exist, at least not as a real painting, just something Matisse claims was probably a student prank. I doubt that rolling canvas up does it any favours, but it's quite possible it could fit inside a roll of tin foil quite comfortably. Especially since, as it doesn't exist, or rather that it's never been seen before, no-one knows what size it's supposed to be.'

'That's what the burglars were after?'

'Precisely, Gertie my sweet. And it's what our soi disant Capitaine Tromperie is looking for. And Hovis and Clovis or Campbell or whatever they want to call themselves, who, I rather suspect, were the ones who did over Matisse's place in the first place – they showed far too little interest in the damage, probably because they had seen it before. The question is, is our Jean Tromperie in with the burglars, or running a solo operation? Hovis's reaction after they had lunch together suggests that they had never met her before, so it's unlikely she's in with them. Or perhaps, considering her insistence on speaking to Matisse at the earliest opportunity, could she be his partner?'

'But why would they take such risks for a fake?'

'Campbell and Hovis think it's real, I can only presume. I'm not sure what our supposed French friend's interest is. Jean Tromperie, that is.'

'Have you told Frieda this?'

A look of irritation passed across his face.

'Damn. I meant to mention it to Frieda when I told her about Campbell and Hovis. I forgot about our little Miss Buttocks. Remind me first thing tomorrow. I don't think she's about to run away overnight. Not while she thinks she still has Frieda conned.'

He decided it politic not to mention to Gertie why he had decided to reveal his suspicions of the London pair to Frieda. "She gave me a snog so I decided to forgive her" was hardly standard police procedure.

'Thanks for finally letting me in on the secret,' Gertie said with a certain amount of bitterness which Frank missed, his mind occupied with thoughts of that kiss from Frieda, then the one from Susan.

'Is there anything special about Saturday?' he asked, pulling at his earlobe, frowning. 'This Saturday, that is.'

Gertie stared at him.

'The cow!' she whispered. 'She told you to pretend it was Saturday, didn't she?'

Frank looked at her, an appalled understanding beginning to appear in his eyes. He still wasn't sure what was going on, but something was, and Gertie knew about it and hadn't told him.

'What is going on, Gertie?' he asked quietly.

'Nothing,' she said, turning to concentrate on her gin and tonic.

He squeezed her shoulder, not very gently.

'Cough up, Gertie. What's going on?'

'You're hurting me, Frank.'

'What's going on, Gertie? You and Frieda are cooking up something behind my back, aren't you? And I ... Oh, my god. Susan's involved as well, isn't she?' he asked, releasing his grip.

'Frieda wanted us to keep you in the doghouse until Saturday,' said Gertie tearfully. 'Then the rota could begin again.'

'Rota? What rota?'

'We were sharing you on a rota basis. That way we knew one of us would get you, it meant we could keep any competition out. I'm sorry, Frank, it seemed to make sense at the time.'

Frank took an absent-minded pull at his ale, an automatic reaction to buy time while his brain spun around as if there was a personal cyclone taking place in his head.

A rota! Frieda, Gertie and Susan valued him so much they were sharing him? He'd never imagined such a thing! Men would give an arm and a leg for less!

Though, on second thoughts, he rather thought he might give an arm and a leg to be out of it. Whichever way he turned he would be faced by one of them. It was a lose-lose-lose situation. He might well end up missing more than an arm and a leg.

'Forgive me?' pleaded Gertie tearfully. 'We did mean it for the best, Frank. Please?'

'I shall have to think about it,' Frank said, finishing off his pint. 'One more, and then it's home time.'

Frank went to the bar to get their glasses refreshed. His mind was in the kind of turmoil you only normally achieve by playing pinball with live grenades while smoking some of the less legal and salubrious tobacco purchased from a Rastafarian with a Cockney accent.

With a tube of glue stuck up each nostril.

His thought processes, always his strongest point, raced from divergent points straight towards the one and only obvious conclusion.

'Ghlow?' asked his brain.

'Gloop?' it answered.

If what he had understood was correct he had his choice of three gorgeous women. Susan, whose eternal suspicion of his motives he would have to take in check. Frieda, whose bossiness he would have to deal with. Or Gertie, who alternated between sex-siren, feminist, ambitious police officer and baby-girl modes.

And they were playing for keeps. This was your basic choose one of us and the others will hate you until your dying day and by the way we're talking marriage here scenario.

Oh, shit!

How would Epicurus have handled it?

Probably by emigrating.

How would Saint Augustine have handled it?

Probably by updating his social calendar and looking forward to adding a few more. At least before he became a saint, anyway.

Double shit! Triple!

In business seminars they stressed that a challenge was also an opportunity. Well, now he had three opportunities. Like having to choose between three doors, marked "Trouble",

"Abandon all hope" and a not very nice "Whoops!".

He sat down next to Gertie who looked not at all like a happy bunny.

'I'm sorry, Frank,' she said tearfully.

'Shush, Gertie, I need time to think.'

'About what?' she demanded.

The obvious expected answer was "How to explain to the other two that I've always loved you from the bottom of my very heart and the other two mean absolutely nothing to me when I think of you which I do constantly all the time in fact".

'Well, this has all come as a rather large shock to me, Gertie. I've always thought of you as a younger sister, someone I'm responsible for. I'm just a little devastated to find out what has been going on behind my back. I need time to consider things. It isn't easy, you know.'

'I'm sorry, Frank, really I am,' Gertie repeated, pressing her face into his chest.

'There, there, Gerts, have a sip of your gin and tonic, it's getting warm. It will all turn out for the best.'

Gertie sniffled and sipped at her drink.

'You won't forget I told you first?' she asked.

'Of course not, pet. Only I don't think we should let the others know that I know, not just yet, do you?'

'Course not,' said Gertie, making sure Frank couldn't see the smile on her face. The other two would never forgive her, but even Frank would have worked it out sooner or later, and she had got in first. Now that it was all out in the open it was just a case of reeling him in.

Thursday Evening

Frank took the stairs up to his flat slowly, feeling more tired and mentally bewildered than he had ever been in his life. He had dropped Gertie off outside her flat. She had said "Pretend it's Saturday, Frank", and given him a goodnight kiss which no younger sister would have given. Tonsil time for the fourth time in one day.

Or was it the fifth?

He was under no illusions. The other blokes at the station, had they known, would have called him a lucky bugger. Until he explained that any man with three women after him had zero choice and zero freedom. Every second of every minute of every hour of every day of every week of every month of every year at least one of them would be watching his every move. And sooner or later he would have to make a decision that would seriously displease at least two of them. There was every possibility he might end up displeasing all three. And it wasn't something that was likely to go away. You couldn't leave it in your in-tray and pretend it didn't exist. You couldn't file it away and close the drawer. It would come out to get you.

Still, he didn't have to do anything now. Not for twelve hours, at least. Not now, as he made his way to the sanctuary of his own flat. Now he was alone, his own man. Now he could relax and not worry that that French bint was sitting at the top of the stairs in front of the door to his flat gently swinging a full bottle of booze in front of her, holding it by its top as if tempting him.

He blinked and shook his head as if to clear an illusion.

'Tullamore Dew, Sergeant,' the illusion said, standing up.

173

'Good Irish whiskey. I was bored in my hotel room. I thought I would see how tough you English are. You seem proud to be able to drink eight pints of warm beer. Do you think you could manage a single glass of whiskey? I doubt it.'

'You're quite right, Jeannie, I'm teetotal myself,' Frank said, walking past her and opening the door to his flat. She followed him in, closing the door behind her.

'Of course,' she said, 'that is my imagination then, the smell of beer on your breath. Lager, no doubt.'

'Good old British ale, Jeannie ma petite.'

'A connoisseur then,' she said, holding up the whiskey and swinging it again, teasingly. 'You will appreciate good Irish whiskey, no doubt.' She held up a plastic bag. 'And I have some cream here, just the thing for Irish coffees. We can drink out of mugs, I would not like whatever cheap glasses you have to break.'

He turned, looked at her and smiled. He had three women on his case he could do nothing about. This little fraud was another matter. He had met women who could drink him under the table. Jean Tromperie wasn't one of them. He knew what her plan was, and if she thought she was going to get him blind drunk so that she could search his flat for The Blue Studio she had a surprise coming. Instead he was the one who was going to get her thoroughly sozzled and then start asking some penetrating questions, such as who exactly she was and what she was trying to achieve. It might not be considered standard police procedure, but the hell with it. He wanted to do it. He had had enough of being chased. Now he was going on to the attack.

'I have Irish Coffee glasses,' he said, taking the whiskey.

'Come in to the kitchen. There aren't any pot-plants there that you can throw your drink in while pretending you've downed it.'

'And why should I pretend, Sergeant?' she asked, taking her jacket off as she followed him.

'Oh, I can think of a good reason. Such as you're afraid I might out-drink you.'

'Pah! You? A little Englishman such as you? Quelle idée!'

In the kitchen he switched on the kettle and watched as she carefully arranged her leather jacket on the back of a chair before sitting down, crossing her legs.

'Expensive, was it, the jacket?' he asked as he poured the cream into a bowl and took out a whisk.

'Standard issue,' she replied after a pause, watching him beat the cream.

'Had a shower recently?' he asked, turning to make the coffees after the kettle boiled, making sure she couldn't see him pour in an extra-generous serving of whiskey into her glass.

'I do not understand.'

'Oh, very muddy in places, Wellbury River.' He put her drink in front of her and raised his. 'Slainte.'

'Salut,' she replied, taking a sip, her eyes locked on his, a slight wince as she realised how strong the bitter-sweet drink was. 'I had to go back to my hotel and change my clothes.'

'Very unfortunate,' Frank said, sitting down in the chair next to her. 'Pete's a bit clumsy.'

'Very clumsy. It took me a good deal of time to clean my boots.'

She lifted a leg to show a shining boot.

'Perhaps you could unlace it for me?' she suggested. 'These boots become very heavy.'

'Your wish, mademoiselle,' he said, bending over the boot and lifting it into his lap, apparently not spotting her inching her glass towards his.

'A toast,' she said, picking up his glass as he dropped the boot onto the floor, keeping her foot in his lap. 'To Sergeant Frank Summers of Wellbury police, breaker of a thousand hearts.'

They drank, eyeing each other. Frank put his glass down and suddenly massaged her foot roughly with one hand.

'A little massage. To warm your tootsies up,' he explained as she bent back in pain, putting her glass down. He took the opportunity to switch their drinks back.

'Very nice,' she gasped, 'but perhaps now the boot on the other foot.'

As she took her stockinged foot off his lap he had to bend down to pick up her other leg. She quickly moved her glass next to his.

She watched as he unlaced the second boot. When he had finished and dropped it ungraciously alongside its partner she raised his glass.

'Only a little sip left, Sergeant. Shall we finish off? I will make the next drinks. I am as good in the kitchen as I am in the office.'

They finished off the alcohol-fuelled coffees, eyes locked together over the rims of the glasses.

'It's my kitchen,' Frank said, standing up. 'I make the coffees.'

'I will give you a hand,' she said, standing up alongside him. 'I am, how you say, the good little woman?'

'I don't need a good little woman,' he replied, switching the kettle on again. 'I have too many of those already.'

'Ah, but of course,' she said, slipping her arm around his waist and keeping a careful eye on the portions he was serving. 'Gertie, Frieda and Susan. You are a lucky man to have such attractive women in love with you.'

He didn't reply. He had the urge to ask her why she hadn't warned him if she had known about it before. And why they had somehow suddenly become "such attractive women" instead of the emotionally and physically repressed harridans they had been earlier.

'Your drink,' he said, handing her the glass. She took a sip and looked up at him from underneath her fringe.

'I am sorry, Frank,' she said. 'I did not wish to be rude to you. It is not easy being a woman in a man's world. You are different. You are different from the French men I have to work with. Arrogant men, it is awful.'

'Really?' Frank asked disbelievingly, taking a sip of Irish Coffee, his mind in a new civil war of its own, one half reminding him that she was a complete fake, the other half pointing out that she might not have overly large breasts, but they were pert, and her nipples were straining against her shirt in a way that Mrs Blower might have approved of.

'I would not have minded so much if it had been you who pushed me in to the mud,' she said, looking down demurely.

Frank's mouth twitched. Great performance, he thought. He was tempted to suggest that they go back to the river where he could shove her into the mud if she so wished, as many times as she wanted.

'It looked a good river for fishing,' she said, looking up at him. 'Do you fish?'

Only when I'm facing a fake French policewoman, he thought to himself, one who isn't doing such a bad job of angling at the moment.

'No, but the Chief Inspector does,' he said, taking a sip of his drink. 'We hardly ever see him these days.'

Now why had he said that, he wondered. It was the sort of thing you might mention on a first date to keep the conversation going.

Good god man, get a grip! he told himself.

'You should try it. It is very peaceful. I go fishing whenever I get the chance. My father taught me when I was a little girl.'

'I might try it sometime. But tell me, how much do you know about Guillaume Matisse?'

'Oh! Forget Matisse! Forget everyone! It is just you and me together now. Forget the rest of the world.'

I'd love to, he thought.

No you wouldn't, one of his voices corrected.

'I saw a piano in your lounge as we passed,' she said, stroking his chest gently with a finger. 'Do you play?'

'It's only an electronic thing,' he said. 'And I've only had it a couple of weeks. I'm very out of practice. Have you met Matisse before?'

'Ah, mais non, mon cherie, no more Matisse. Come, you will play the electronic piano to me,' she exclaimed, dragging him by his shirt buttons.

'As you wish.'

There are some really low-down tricks men and women play on each other in this world. Using a person's love of music for an ulterior purpose has to be one of the lowest. Both of them privately felt terrible about it.

Frank sat down on the piano stool and began playing, his hands moving confidently and professionally across the keyboard.

'Beethoven!' exclaimed Jean Tromperie. 'I love Beethoven!'

'Piano Concerto Number 5 in E flat major,' Frank said. 'Otherwise known as "l'Emperor".'

'Ah, but you do not give it the, how you say, the oomph? You must be more firm. Come, like this.' She put her drink to one side, put one hand on his shoulder, leaned over his back, took his finger gently with her other hand and pushed it down forcefully. 'See, like that. That is how ...'

She paused as she realised that Beethoven was continuing on his merry way and that the key that she had pressed Frank's finger down on wasn't making any sound. She lifted both his hands from the keyboard. It didn't stop Beethoven. The keys depressed themselves as if a ghost was playing them.

'Frank Summers!' she exclaimed, putting a hand to his chin and turning his face towards her. 'You are a fraud! That music is recorded!'

He grinned at her.

'Okay, I admit it. This thing can play the music while allowing you to learn the keystrokes. I'll switch that off and play for real. Not as well as the machine, but I'm learning.'

'Hah! You fraud, Frank Summers, you absolute fraud! I would never have expected that of you. I am devastated.'

'You'd be amazed at what I'm capable of, cherie,' he replied with a happy grin.

He turned a switch on the electronic keyboard and started to play the piece. Badly. Soi-disant Capitaine Jean Tromperie stayed leaning against his back, correcting his playing a number of times with her free hand, chiding him as his fingers reached for the wrong keys, or failed to use the right pressure.

'I'll get there in the end,' he said as he finished the mangled music.

'I am sure you will, ma petite. But come, it is time for another coffee. Finish your drink and I will make another.'

'I'm better with Concerto Number 4,' he said enthusiastically, downing the remainder of his drink and handing the glass to her. 'Let me show you.'

As she went into the kitchen he launched into a spirited – in more than one sense – performance. Inside the kitchen she was making sure that his glass received at least a treble whiskey and her own just a smidgeon. She had to concentrate. Things were becoming a little fuzzy. But she wasn't drunk. Nefinitely not drunk. Definitely. Something like that.

'Ah, mais non, mais non,' she said excitably, returning to the lounge. 'You put the Oomph where the Pah is supposed to be. Come, move over, I will show you.'

He made space for her, and they sat on the small seat, pressed against each other, happily arguing over the keys, she smacking his wrist lightly on occasion.

Jean Tromperie did not realise that she was drinking the glass intended for Frank.

Frank managed to make it to the kitchen for the next round.

To his surprise there wasn't much left in the whiskey bottle. He supplemented what there was of it with some Glenlivet he had in a cupboard. He made sure Jean's glass received a convincing majority and his only a touch.

'The Entente Cordiale!' he declared as he was entering the lounge. He leaned against the doorpost, and raised his glass.

'Any cordial you care to mention,' she replied, taking her glass and a deep sip. Something in her brain alerted her to the fact that there wasn't much whiskey in it. It was somewhat of a waste of an alert. Her brain was no longer listening.

He sat down next to her. She put an arm around his waist. Automatically he put an arm around her shoulders. She giggled.

'You take the right hand and I will do the left,' she said. 'Come it will be fun!'

Obligingly Frank began to play with his right hand while Jean took the notes for the left. After a short while they were both laughing at the impossibility of producing any recognisable music. Eventually Jean gave up and leaned her head against his shoulder, giggling breathlessly. The movement caused his hand to slip slightly, until it was on her breast. Quickly he pulled it away.

'No, I like it there, put it back,' she said petulantly. He did so. And, seeing as it were there, he might as well give a gentle squeeze, which he did.

'Cheeky,' she said softly, but not in such a way that might suggest she had taken any great offence, especially since she had squeezed him in return.

'What say to another one of these and then a pizza, ma cher capitaine?' asked Frank, wondering why his drink seemed more potent than it should be, and whether he had said "What say" or "Waht shay".

'I could murder a pizza, Frank,' Capitaine Tromperie replied in a husky voice, raising her head and grinning lopsidedly up at him.

It seemed the most reasonable thing to do. He held her chin gently and kissed her.

Friday: The sirens of silence

Frank woke up at around three o'clock in the morning, eased Jean's arm off his waist, climbed out of bed and went to the bathroom. On his way back he paused in the kitchen to sip at a glass of water and look at the remains of two pizzas.

It was going to be very, very difficult to explain this one.

If it came to that.

Which it would undoubtedly do.

This was the sort of thing that had got him into hot water at his previous posting. Even without the added complication of Susan, Gertie and Frieda, explaining how he had ended up in bed with someone he knew to be impersonating a police officer would be a difficult task. If he could remember how it had happened in the first place.

"Well, we had a snog while waiting for the pizzas to arrive, you see, and then another while I was paying for them, and another before we tucked in, and then Jean fed me a slice with pepperoni on it, and I fed her a slice with anchovies, and an anchovy dropped down inside her shirt, and I helped get it out and then ... are you sure you want to hear any more of this?"

Oh, yes, they would want to hear it all, all of them. Every single little morsel and titbit.

In normal circumstances he would get a severe bollocking before being fired. Under the current circumstances ...

He finished the glass of water, went back to his bedroom, climbed into bed and wrapped his arms around Jean. She sighed happily and turned into him. Tomorrow was another day, thought Frank. Actually, tomorrow was already today.

But what the hell, there were still a few hours before he had to face the world. He fell asleep peacefully. He might as well. Carpe Diem. Seize the day. He wasn't likely to have another one. He was going to be the one seized, by his throat.

He woke up later with a start, sun streaming through the window. He turned to where Jean should have been, but the place in the bed next to him empty.

Damn! he thought. Damn! Damn and double damn! He scrambled out of bed and hurriedly put a dressing gown on. A thought struck him, and he slipped a pair of handcuffs into the gown pocket before hurrying into the kitchen.

Jean Tromperie sat at the kitchen table, her uniform not quite as uncreased as it had been the evening before, sipping a cup of black coffee. He noticed that she had cleaned up the mess from the night before, including washing the glasses.

She looked at him sourly.

'I think the less said about last night the better, Sergeant Summers,' she said in her French accent.

'Oh, I don't know,' Frank replied, smiling, as he took a mug from the cupboard and began making a coffee. 'Anyone ever tell you that you talk in your sleep?'

There was a pause.

'I do not talk in my sleep,' she said in a less than convincing tone.

'Rodean, I believe the accent is called,' he said cheerfully, sitting down opposite her. 'That's the problem, you can't keep up the French accent in your sleep.'

She looked at him bitterly and said nothing.

'So, are you going to tell me here, or do I need to take you down the station? Impersonating a police officer is a serious offence, you know,' he said.

She put her mug down slowly, her hand trembling slightly.

'It was just a joke,' she replied, all trace of French accent gone. 'I'm an actor. I wanted to see if I could get away with it. Anyway, I wasn't impersonating a British police officer, just a French one. Hardly that serious.'

'Maybe we'll send you over to France to be tried, then. And I don't buy this just a joke business. You were after The Blue Studio, weren't you?'

She looked at her fingernails and stayed silent. Frank gave a dramatic sigh.

'Oh dear. If you won't talk here it will have to be down the station.'

'You wouldn't dare! Not after last night. Frieda would kill you. So would Gertie.'

And Susan, he thought, don't forget Susan.

'Oh, I might not be flavour of the month for a while,' he said easily, deciding to bluff it out. 'It won't be the first time, and I dare say it won't be the last.'

What he had meant was that it wouldn't be the last time he would be in hot water. There was a perfectly valid way of misunderstanding the statement.

'You bastard!' she said, immediately misunderstanding. 'So that's how you treat women. Use them and lose them. Wait until I tell Gertie and Frieda. And I am going to. It's only fair they should know what a total son of a bitch you are. I can't believe I fell for you last night.'

He stood up and pushed his chair against the radiator.

'Yes, well, there is that too,' he said. He beckoned with a finger. 'I need to have a shower. While I'm doing that you're going to sit here nice and quietly.' He took the handcuffs from his pocket and swung them gently in front of her. She stood up, backing away, her eyes open wide.

'What are you going to do to me?' she asked.

'Nothing to get worried about. I just want to make sure you don't decide you've had enough of my hospitality while I'm in the shower. Sit down here like a good girl, next to the radiator.'

'Oh, come on, Frank.'

She looked down and then back up at him, her eyes peeking cheekily out from underneath her fringe.

'I enjoyed last night, you know,' she said. 'I was hoping something more long-term would come of it.'

He laughed.

'I think the less said about last night the better, Sergeant Summers,' he said in an atrocious French accent. 'Not to mention the bit about being a total son of a bitch. You seem to change your mind quite quickly.'

She made a moue and then laughed with him.

'Yes, well, I had to try to keep the pretence up, didn't I?' She sighed. 'I knew you were going to be trouble. You were the only one who didn't seem put out by my rudeness.' She looked at him. 'I suppose you put Pete Phillips up to pushing me into the river. He wouldn't have had the nous to think of something like that himself.'

Frank's smile answered the question.

'But you aren't going to take me in really, are you?' she

pleaded as if a child. 'After all, I haven't done anything seriously wrong. It was just a bit of fun.'

'You have a choice. Either you tell me what's going on and I might – might – let you off, or I take you down the station.'

'I told you. It was just a bit of fun. I saw the picture of you arresting Matisse and thought, well, I wonder if I could get away with being a French police woman for a few days. I'm resting, as the saying goes, and I was bored. My father was also an actor. He once told me you could get people to believe that you could dance on water if you tried hard enough. Passing myself off as a French police woman should have been easy, compared to that. And it would have worked if it hadn't been for you.'

'Yes, and the bacon currently landing on runway three is prime Danish lean.'

'Bacon?'

'Pigs might fly,' he translated. 'Now, make a choice. The truth or a cell.'

She folded her arms and remained silent.

'Sit,' he said, pointing at the chair next to the radiator. An arch look came into her eyes.

'If you are going to handcuff me, why don't you handcuff me to your bed?' she suggested. 'I won't be able to do anything. I promise I'll never complain if you take advantage of me while I'm helpless.'

As she spoke she was suggestively undoing a button on her shirt.

'Sit!' he commanded again. To his mind it was a desperate command trying to blot out her suggestions which his nonrational side was beginning to think might not be a bad idea. In fact, a very good idea.

'Speaking to me as if I was a dog!' she said, tears welling up in her eyes. 'I don't know what those others see in you. I'm glad you're taking me in. Lock me up for ever if you want! I don't want to ever see you again! You're insufferable! Arrogant! Overbearing! Pompous! They should invent a new word just for you!'

'You forgot "bastard",' he said as she sat down. She pouted at him and then looked away tearfully. He took her left arm and gently clipped the first cuff on, feeding the chain around the radiator pipe and clipped the second cuff on the same wrist just above the first.

'Ow! You're hurting me!' she exclaimed. 'That's sore, Frank! It hurts! Please! Please don't hurt me.'

'Sorry, love, I'll loosen it a bit. There we go.'

She looked up at him with tearful, pleading eyes. He patted her head gently and stroked her hair. For a few moments they looked into each others' eyes. Frank could feel his heart trying to overpower his head.

No, Jean had played and lost. It was his duty to take her in, no matter what had happened between them.

'I'll only be ten minutes, love, promise,' he said quickly, and headed for the bathroom before he could change his mind.

'Bastard,' she called after him. 'I hate you, Frank Summers. I hope you drown in your bath.'

'It's okay,' he called back, 'I'm having a shower. No need to worry.'

He stepped into the shower, humming to himself. He enjoyed

a good long, hot shower first thing in the morning. He'd have to cut it a bit short this time, though.

At first he honestly intended to take as little time as possible, but then the memory of her performance made him pause. She had sneered at them all, and a very good sneer it had been. It deserved to be rewarded by being handcuffed to a radiator for a while. Instead he decided that he may as well take his time. He was going to get in to work late as it was. Arriving with a supposed French police captain in handcuffs would be a feather in his cap. Explaining how he had unmasked her – literally – was going to be somewhat of a problem. Apart from the wrath of Frieda, Gertie and Susan there was the question of how the media might portray things if it ever came to court. And the Chief Constable was unlikely to approve.

Scrub that, he wouldn't be alive by that stage. He wasn't likely to be alive by the end of the day. Making lunchtime would be a bonus.

The idea that he might be dallying, not only to put off the inevitable, but also to keep Jean with him a little longer he put right out of his head. He liked her, she was good fun, she had more than her fair share of gumption but that was it. Definitely.

But she was extremely attractive. Not only in the physical sense. He had only once before met a woman who had had such an instantaneous effect on him.

No. He couldn't go down that path, not again. Forget it, have fun, Jean Tromperie or whatever her real name is would understand. Just a laugh and a bit of a giggle. Think about something else.

Like Frieda, Gertie and Susan?

Mmmm, perhaps not.

Frank Summers, you do like getting into trouble, he told his reflection in the mirror as he shaved.

Not true, his reflection replied. I do my best to stay well away from trouble. It just seems to find me no matter how I try to hide.

'Not too uncomfortable, are we, love?' he called as he came out of the bathroom. 'Just a few minutes more while I get dressed.'

He popped his head around the kitchen door.

'Oh, shit!' he muttered. The handcuffs lay on the table, on top of a scrap of paper. He picked it up.

"Thanks for the memories, Frank. Don't worry, you won't see me again. Tell them I've been recalled to the Sûreté urgently. The case of the performing pom-poms, or something. Thanks for the pizza. And the rest. I really wish I could have stayed around for something more long-term – I meant that bit. I could have taken you fishing. Long, peaceful afternoons on the riverbank. Oh, well, story of my life. Still, at least I know I'm leaving you in good hands – three pairs of them. I'd go with Gertie if I were you. Or maybe Susan. Or even Frieda. Hell, keep all three to yourself, you lucky bastard. Look after yourself. All my love, Jean.

Oh, and P.S., while we're on the subject, which we aren't, but pretend we are, you're a bloody liar, you are, one of the best I've met. If I talked in my sleep it wouldn't be Rodean. You'd be listening to the bleeding Bow Bells, you would. I might be good with accents, but I doubt I could, as you said, keep it up while I'm sleeping next to you.

Take care me old mucker

xxxxxx

(And no-one has ever got six of those. Bastard.)"

'Bugger!' Frank swore. He looked at the clock on the wall. 'And another bugger!'

He was now late for work and without an excuse. He could hardly walk in, wave his handcuffs around and say 'I had a fake French police woman tied up in these not so long ago.'

Still, he thought as he hurriedly dressed, maybe it was just as well. If Jean kept her word about disappearing people might wonder what had become of her, but eventually they would probably forget about her.

Hopefully.

Whether he would be able to ever forget about her was another question.

Of course he would. It had merely been a whirlwind infatuation, even he wasn't immune to such things, especially when he was getting so much grief from Frieda and Susan, not to mention Gertie's confession of how they had been sharing him.

He hurried to his bedroom to dress. She was an enigma. A wonderful, exciting, passionate, lovely, heart-breaking enigma. Just as well she had walked out of his life, he thought as he chose his smartest suit on the grounds that the sight might make the others pause before ripping him to pieces.

Just as well, he repeated to himself.

Definitely. He had checked in to Heartbreak Hotel once. He had no intention of repeating the mistake.

It was the Hotel California you could never leave. At least you could run from the Heartbreak Hotel, even if dressed only in panic.

He rushed down to his car, switched his police radio on and placed it on the passenger seat, planning to let the station know he was running late as he drove in. As he switched the ignition on voices came over the air.

'Alpha One to Control, Alpha One to Control.'

'Control here, over.'

'Alpha One. We're in position on the North Road. All traffic stopped as per orders. Over.'

'Control, Roger Alpha One. Control to Alpha Three, come in Alpha Three.'

'Alpha Three to Control. We've blocked the London Road. Traffic's backing up a bit. Over.'

'It's going to back up a lot more before we're finished,' commented Control.

Bloody hell! thought Frank as more cars reported their positions. The whole of Wellbury was being sealed off. Something big was happening. He fumbled for the police light under his seat, put it on the roof, switched the siren on and pressed the accelerator down.

The front of the police station was in pandemonium as he arrived, officers running to and fro, an ambulance loading a body on a stretcher, police vans coming out from the rear parking lot, sirens blaring. Frank ran into reception to find Frieda holding a radio, snapping out orders.

'Where the hell have you been?' she demanded as she saw him.

'I, er, overslept. What's going on?'

'Overslept?' Frieda asked, almost mechanically, as if she had heard the word but wasn't paying attention, alerting Frank to the fact she was both furious and fuming.

'I'll tell you what's going on,' she continued in a voice that Frank had not heard her use before, not even when she was in a temper to kill him. 'The result of that bloody useless Percy's negligence, that's what! Campbell and Hovis weren't at their hotel when Percy went to arrest them. They must have guessed we were on to them. Then they walk in here first thing this morning, bold as brass, along with someone they claim is Matisse's lawyer, hoping, I can only presume, that the early shift wouldn't know they were fakes. Keith Bute was still on duty. He reached for the panic button, but they must have realised what he was about to do. Before he could press it one of them took out a gun and pistol-whipped him. Hovis, I think, Campbell wouldn't be that stupid.'

'What?' asked Frank in disbelief.

'They tried to get into Matisse's cell without the keys. That didn't work. Hovis apparently injured himself in his leg using a chisel or something. Stupidity! Trying to break into one of our cells with a chisel! Just a pity it didn't kill him. They must have realised they were running out of time so they made a break for it. Gertie was just coming in. They hit her over the head and threw her into their car.'

For a moment Frank could not speak.

'What? They've got Gertie?'

'Precisely. We have a kidnapped police officer and two armed thugs on the loose.' She looked at him in fury. 'Those London sons of bitches are going to regret this, Frank. I've got every exit sealed off tight. No-one enters or leaves town until their cars are thoroughly searched. At the same time every hotel, boarding house, hostel, whatever, is going to be searched. Every bloody private home as well, if it comes to that. And anyone who mentions search warrants will regret it.'

They looked at each other for a few moments as the awful reality sunk into Frank's mind. He had become used to the almost civilised, if it could be called that, crime Wellbury was used to. Now something foreign and nasty had slipped into their lives.

And they had Gertie. His Gertie. His little sister.

'What do you want me do?' he asked finally, grimly.

'You're a trained marksman, aren't you, Frank? Get yourself a weapon. Sign one out for me. A pistol.'

Frank nodded and rushed along the corridor and down the steps leading to the armoury, passing a line of armed police officers coming up. He had thoroughly enjoyed his firearms training. What he didn't like was the concept of what firearms were designed to do. It went against his notion of what a policeman should be. Intellectually he understood that it might one day be called for, but mentally he had presumed that that day would never come. Now it had and it was Gertie's life at stake. If they couldn't find Campbell and Hovis and talk them into surrendering it would be someone's duty to take the men out with as little danger to a fellow police officer as possible. He might well turn out to be that someone. Right at that moment he wanted to avoid the thought as far as possible.

'Hi, Frank,' said John Stevens when he got to the counter. 'What will it be?'

'That FN serviceable?' he asked. John Stevens looked at him

aghast.

'Jesus, Frank, you can't take that out.'

'Why not?' Frank asked in a tone that brooked no opposition. 'And I'll need two twenty-round magazines and ammo. And a pistol for the Inspector, and another for me. 9 mill pistols, Berettas if you have.'

John Stevens looked at him as if he were crazy. If he was thinking of saying something he quickly changed his mind.

'Two pistols, a rifle, empty magazines and ammunition. Sign here, please,' he said uncomfortably. 'You know, you mustn't —'

'Load the full twenty, I know,' replied Frank. 'Maximum eighteen rounds to prevent the spring wearing out.'

John Stevens raised his eyebrows in mild surprise. Frank gave him a wry grin.

'I told you Jack Gilly had been my instructor. It was one of his favourite maxims. I think he would have preferred not to have magazines. Just single shot loading every time.'

'True enough,' replied John Stevens.

Frank checked the weapons and signed the log. He loaded the pistols, shoved the two rifle magazines into one jacket pocket, rammed a pistol in each trouser pocket, scooped the bullets for the rifle into the other jacket pocket and slung the rifle strap over his shoulder.

'Vest?' asked John Stevens, holding up a bullet-proof vest. 'I'd say a medium should fit.'

'No thanks,' said Frank, 'I want to be able to move quickly. I'll borrow one if I need one.'

'Don't be bloody stupid, Frank,' insisted John Stevens.

'I'll pick one up if I go out,' Frank replied as he began to leave. 'If I take one now I'll just lose it.'

'Frank,' John Stevens said softly, 'that FN – just remember I set the sights for my eyes, not yours. And that thing – you know how powerful it is. Don't take any chances, Frank, that's all I'm saying.'

Frank nodded.

'I know, John. Don't worry, I know the drill. I'm not going to use it unless it's absolutely necessary, and I'm not going to forget that the bullet will carry on travelling a long way.'

John Stevens watched him leave, a look of worry on his face. He liked Frank Summers. But he wasn't sure that Frank knew just how much damage the FN could do. Nor was he sure that the young officer was prepared for what he might have to do.

Frank raced back up the steps and back into reception, feeding bullets into one of the rifle magazines. In reception he handed one of the pistols to Frieda.

'Thanks, Frank,' she said, pushing it into the waistband at the back of her skirt. 'Let's hope we don't need these things.' Then her eyebrows rose at the sight of him as he pushed the almost full magazine into the rifle, slung it once again over his shoulder, and began feeding the other magazine, one jacket pocket bulging with a pistol, the other showing the bullets Frank was feeding into the magazine. 'I hope you haven't any ideas about imitating Rambo, Frank.'

'If people are going to start playing with guns I like to make sure I have more than them, and more firepower. A 7.62 bullet will go nicely through a brick wall at the right range. Just in case they think we aren't being serious.'

'Don't forget they have Gertie, Frank,' she said softly, concern on her face.

'That's exactly what I was thinking of. What's the latest?'

Frieda frowned at him, as if uncertain of whether she could trust his self-control.

'We've got everyone in place,' she said. 'No-one can get out now. Every roadblock has at least two armed officers standing guard while the others search the vehicles. Let's go to the ops room, I'm going to run this one from there. Hopkins, Small, you know what to do?'

'Yes, ma'am,' said one of two armed officers standing either side of the entrance doors, their backs to the wall so that anyone entering would be unaware of their presence until they were inside. A white-faced Eric Johns manned the reception desk.

'All neighbouring forces have been alerted – most of the men and women you saw are from their armed response units,' Frieda said as they walked down the corridor to the ops room. A large map of Wellbury lined the far wall. 'The media have been asked to broadcast descriptions of those two thugs, and warn people not to go anywhere near them. We have a helicopter overhead, with two more on their way. They're processing photographs of the so-called Campbell and Hovis from our CCTV cameras. Hopefully Scotland Yard will have some information on them. If they are Londoners.'

Frank was impressed.

'Remind me to apologise to the Chief Constable afterwards,' Frieda said thoughtfully. 'I might have been a little brusque with him.'

'Do we know how badly Gertie was hurt?'

'Keith was too badly beaten to see properly, but the CCTV images suggest it was a glancing blow Gertie got, hopefully nothing too serious.' She shook her head grimly. 'I don't know what those two think they're doing. If they think we're just a bunch of small-town plods they're going to get a lesson.' She turned and looked at Frank. 'I've issued a press release stating that Campbell and Hovis must give themselves up immediately. Any resistance will be met with maximum force. Anyone interfering with this operation will receive the same response. That's a polite way of telling the population that this is not a joke.'

Frank nodded. Had someone suggested that he would one day agree with such a heavy-handed response he would have laughed at the idea. But this was different. Somewhere out there Gertie was in the hands of those two thugs. The man who called himself Hovis was especially dangerous, even more so if he was wounded. Campbell you could talk to. Reason with. At least convince him to give Gertie up. Hovis wouldn't listen. He just hoped Campbell could control him.

'We're hoping to track Gertie's mobile,' Frieda said. 'Nobody knows exactly which company she's with, so we've contacted all of them. One of them should come through soon. Let's hope it's not too late.'

'So now we wait,' he said.

'Now we wait,' Frieda agreed. 'Patience, Frank, this is going to take all the patience we have. You know the score. We can't move too soon, and we can't move too late. But when we do we are going to hit them so hard … If they so much as touch Gertie, I'll kill them. I swear I will kill them.'

Frank nodded. His sentiments exactly. He looked at the map.

'Do we have any spare officers?' he asked.

'I wouldn't call them spare. We have a reserve. And, for a change, we can get as many as we want from neighbouring divisions. The Chief Constable has promised us anything we want. Why do you ask?'

Frank tapped the map.

'They can't get out of Wellbury – presuming that they haven't already done so. But they can move around inside the cordon, and sooner or later they will have to move. I think it might be an idea to have a team moving around, creating snap roadblocks every so often. Let the media know, that way Hovis and Campbell will also know. It will give us a little advantage and keep them off balance. They won't know where the next roadblock will suddenly turn up.'

Frieda frowned doubtfully.

'They've probably gone to ground and intend to stay there,' she said. 'But at least it's doing something. We'll need people who know Wellbury inside out. I'll get Allison Hardbury and Harry Wheatley on to it. They can take four armed officers with them.'

'Isn't Allison also firearms-trained?'

'Yes. Much as I dislike it, she's already kitted up. I don't like seeing our officers with firearms. But we have no alternative.'

Frank nodded.

'In the meantime I'm going down to see Matisse,' he said. 'Maybe he can shed some light on why those two were so eager to get at him.'

A white-faced Matisse sat on his bed in his cell. His face

blanched even further as the door opened and Frank walked in, rifle slung from his shoulder.

'Time to start talking,' he told the frightened man. 'And forget any bullshit about lawyers. I'm not waiting for Jadbhur or his partner to roll up. Please believe me when I say I'm prepared to beat the truth out of you. Let's start with your real name.'

The man looked down and held his hands together to stop them shaking.

'Park,' he said finally, with a gasp, 'Cecil Park.' All trace of a French accent had disappeared. He looked up at Frank. 'I didn't mean any of this to happen. None of it. It wasn't supposed to happen. You must believe me.'

'Of course not. But it has. Two gunmen are on the loose, and one of our officers has been kidnapped. The question is, why? What is so special about you that they're prepared to come into a police station with guns to get at you?'

'I told you, they think I have a painting by Matisse called The Blue Studio.'

'But you said it's not even a fake. Matisse never painted anything like that.'

Park sighed.

'Yes, Sergeant, but they don't know that. They think I've got a Matisse worth millions – about fifty million, in fact. I tried to tell them it isn't true, but they just won't believe me, they just won't believe me.' He groaned. 'I should never have started this, never.'

'A little too late now, Mr Park. Why don't you start at the beginning? Tell me all about it. And be quick. I'm in a hurry.'

Park looked at him, shook his head in resignation and looked down at the floor.

'I used to be an accountant,' he said slowly. 'In Bognor Regis, of all places. I hated the job. The only thing that kept me sane was my painting. I had to do it in my garden shed, the wife wouldn't tolerate the smell of the oil paints in the house. She also thought I was no good. Maybe I wasn't, in those days. And then she died. I took early retirement and converted one of the bedrooms into a studio. Perhaps it was better light, though I really believe that it was because I was free to do what I wanted. I think my wife's nagging and criticism had stunted my abilities. I discovered I was actually pretty good.'

'Pretty good at forgeries?'

'No, Sergeant Summers, not at first. The trouble was that I was painting in the style of people like Matisse, but that's gone out of fashion now. Only dead artists of that school sell these days. No-one was interested in buying my work. I used to sell at car boot sales, you know. If I had one sale it was a good day. Most days I couldn't give my work away. Then, one day, just for a laugh, or out of frustration, I signed one of my works Degas.'

He smiled bleakly at Frank.

'You won't believe the avarice of the average human being, Sergeant. People looking at the painting, pretending they weren't interested, even trying to haggle to prove their lack of interest, but I could see they were desperate to buy. In the end I was quite worried, and told them that it wasn't a real Degas, just something I had found somewhere.'

He paused and shook his head sadly.

'I don't know why I didn't admit that it was actually my work. Perhaps I rather suspected what was coming. Because, you see, and this is the remarkable thing; after I had laughed and assured them it couldn't possibly be a real Degas they wanted it even more. Imagine that!'

'They convinced themselves that they had stumbled across a painting worth a fortune,' Frank commented. 'That you hadn't realised the true value of what you had. You were some old duffer who couldn't recognise a work of genius.'

'I'm afraid so,' Park said, shaking his head at such stupidity. 'And from then on – well, it became almost an addiction, really. I would spend a few weeks creating paintings apparently signed by one of the famous painters, put them in my car along with my others, and then go on a driving holiday, stopping at a different town each day. I could have sold a dozen a day if I wanted. I told them that the works weren't masterpieces, but that didn't stop them. I even signed one as Shakespeare, and some idiot bought it.'

'The perfect con,' noted Frank.

'I didn't think of it as conning anyone, Sergeant. Not really. After all, it was their own greed leading them on. And I never asked for a fortune, just a few hundred pounds per picture. A few hundred pounds is not that much if you really have to learn that sort of lesson.' He looked up at Frank. 'And it wasn't even the money, you know. It was the excitement, the thrill, I suppose. Well, it was exciting to me, anyway, after all those years as an accountant. You don't know how much trouble I had as an accountant. It should be a very straightforward job, no scope for trickery, but no, it's one of the most devious practices you could think of. I was forever being asked to shift figures from their proper place to make them look more attractive. I spent my whole life arguing against it. Then suddenly I was the devious one. But the point is, I was the one telling the truth and it was the others lying to themselves.'

He sighed and looked at the floor.

'And there was the disbelief,' he said. 'I suppose I wanted to see just how credulous the average person is. Take it a little further each time. I believe I might have ended up selling paintings of Mickey Mouse signed by Goya or Van Gogh.'

'And then we come to The Blue Studio,' Frank said, prompting him to continue with his story.

'Yes, The Blue Studio. I still cannot understand how that happened. I was in a pub in London close to the National Gallery, celebrating selling the Shakespeare painting. I was wondering whether I could get away with selling a painting signed by Henry VIII, or even Elvis Presley. I'm afraid I let my sense of humour get the better of me. I got into conversation with the landlord, explaining that I'd picked up a painting signed by Matisse called The Blue Studio. How amusing it was, since Matisse only ever painted The Red Studio, even a first-year art student wouldn't fall for that one. And then I could not resist embellishing an already tall tale. Before I knew it I had acquired a French accent, and I told him that I should know, since I was Henri Matisse, grandson of the great painter.'

'I thought it was supposed to be Guillaume Matisse?'

Cecil Park waved a hand to indicate that it was of no matter.

'That was later. I'm afraid my memory for names isn't very good. Especially when I had invented it on the spot.'

'So, back to The Blue Studio. You wanted to see if the landlord would fall for it?'

'Precisely, Sergeant, precisely. I'm afraid he didn't, even when

I mentioned that, had it been real and not an obvious fake, it would be worth about fifty million pounds. Of course it wouldn't have been worth anything near that, but it was the first figure that came in to my head. I can only presume that the landlord was used to hearing tall stories.'

'How much would such a painting be worth if it really existed?'

Cecil Park shrugged.

'Quite a few hundred thousand, I suppose. You'd have to look it up. As with names, so with figures, I often read of paintings being sold for small fortunes, but the figures never interest me. When I was an accountant I could remember certain figures for weeks, months, even, but never the price of a painting. In fact the idea that a painting which some starving artist sold for a few francs a hundred years ago is now bought and sold as an investment for millions of pounds frankly appals me. The painting has no more nor less the beauty it had all those years ago, but now it is considered a treasure purely because enough people believe it is a treasure. It is like gold, Sergeant Summers, do you understand what I mean by that?'

'As valuable as gold?'

'No, no. What I mean is, what is the intrinsic value of gold? You cannot eat it. It will not keep you warm. It will not give you shelter. At heart it is nothing but a shiny pebble which can be turned into pretty trinkets. Yet men have lived and died for the stuff. Precious metal! What is so precious about it? And the same with paintings. Rich, avaricious men turn something of beauty into a possession, they put a value on something that is beyond price.'

'I'm sure you're right, Mr Park, but for the moment let's get back to your little story. If the landlord didn't fall for it, what did happen?'

'Unfortunately two thugs sitting nearby overheard. They did fall for it. They found out where I lived – followed me home, I can only suppose – and came to suggest a sale. That's a polite way of putting it. I was given the option, though not in those precise words, of either selling it to them or having my arms and legs broken. I pretended to be quite willing – after all, I told them, it's just a worthless fake. I promised them I would get it from my lockup garage, but instead disappeared as fast as I could. I'd been through Wellbury a few times. Knowing it to be a quiet town I thought I would be safe here for a while.'

'Until I nicked you,' noted Frank.

'Indeed, Sergeant.'

'But if what you say is true, why is it that so many European police forces are after you?' asked Frank. 'Or, to be more accurate, why are they after someone called Guillaume Matisse?'

Cecil Park looked somewhat shamefaced. A look of dawning shock suddenly passed over Frank's face.

'That Interpol poster!' he exclaimed. 'You made that bloody Interpol poster, didn't you?'

'Ah, er, yes, Sergeant, I have to confess that was a fake. A real fake. I was in the bakery section of the supermarket for fifteen minutes before you recognised my photograph, though I had passed you three times. I was wondering if I would ever attract your attention.'

'How the hell ...?'

'Oh, it was quite easy, really. I slipped into your reception during a busy period and left it on the desk. I'd been watching the police station, and I recognised you leaving, and followed you. Who would have thought it would be so difficult to get arrested these days?'

'But why?'

'Because those two thugs had found out where I was. I needed somewhere quiet for a few days, somewhere they'd never think of looking for me. A cell in a police station was the last place they'd look – and it appealed to my sense of humour, I must confess. I calculated that it would take a few days for you to establish that I wasn't really on an Interpol wanted list, that somehow there'd been a terrible mistake. The Italians, Spanish or French would be blamed, and I would be set free with many apologies, by which time those two thugs would have given up and left town. I just hadn't banked on having my photograph shown on local television. It was only this morning that I found out that the Scotland Yard officers I had been expecting to effect my release were in fact the same two thugs.'

'There you are, Frank,' Frieda said, entering the cell. 'We've got another problem. Captain Tromperie appears to have disappeared. She checked out of her hotel room early this morning and hasn't been seen since.'

Both men looked guilty. Fortunately for Frank Frieda only noticed Cecil Park's look.

'Something you wish to tell us, M Matisse?' she asked.

'Er, Park's the name, Cecil Park,' the man said. 'I'm afraid, um, well, from the description of this French captain, I rather think it might be my partner.'

'Your partner in crime you mean?' asked Frieda.

'No, my partner. Girlfriend. She's an actress. I think she likes older men. Some of them do, you know.'

There was a stunned silence, though Frieda and Frank were probably stunned for different reasons.

So that's why she wouldn't tell me the truth, thought Frank. Telling someone you've just slept with that the bloke in the nick is their boyfriend ... He could only guess that Jean had been experiencing the same pricks of conscience that he had been.

Cecil Park looked from Frieda to Frank in concern.

'I'm sure she didn't mean any harm,' he said. 'She knew about those thugs and The Blue Studio, and that I was staying in Wellbury for a few months. She must have caught the news broadcast about my arrest and wanted to do something. She's a bit – what's the word? Adventurous? She does the most dreadful things on a whim. It's her sense of humour, I'm afraid.'

'I'll give her adventure when I get my hands on her,' said Frieda. 'If we ever do. No doubt she's halfway to France.'

'Oh, she's not French, just good with accents. Born in Bermondsey, I think. If what she says is true.'

'So what's her real name?' asked Frank.

'Her stage name is Samantha Stark. Her real name is Jean Candour. But I'm sure she meant no harm, Inspector, she probably just wanted to see me and thought up an unusual way of doing it.'

'Candour?' asked Frank.

'That's what she told me,' Park said miserably. 'Sometimes

you just have to believe what people tell you, especially if it doesn't make any difference whether or not it's true.'

'We'll deal with her later,' Frieda said ominously. 'Frank, more importantly, we've had a phone call from those two thugs – or, rather, from the sounds of it, from the one calling himself Campbell. He left a message with Tricia. He wants to do a trade. Gertie for a painting called The Blue Studio by Matisse.'

Frank smiled grimly and turned to Cecil Park.

'There you go, Mr Park, your chance to redeem yourself. I think you can hand over The Blue Studio to our safe keeping.'

'You must be joking, Frank!' Frieda exclaimed. 'Hand over a Matisse worth millions to a pair of hoodlums? The Chief Constable will never agree to it.'

She paused for less than a second.

'Then again, you're right. It's Gertie's life at stake. That's worth more than any painting. If they want it they can have it. The Chief Constable can fire me afterwards. We'll give it to them as long as they can guarantee Gertie won't be harmed.'

'Oh, I doubt if The Blue Studio is worth anything,' Frank said easily. 'It's not even a fake of something real, isn't that correct, Mr Park?'

Cecil Park looked at them in turn, embarrassed.

'It's worse than that,' he said slowly. He looked at Frank. 'You might have wondered why I just didn't hand it over to those two thugs in the first place. Well, you know that saying about a verbal contract not being worth the paper it's printed on? The truth is ... I haven't painted The Blue Studio yet.'

Gertie sat on the floor of the main bar in the Blue Bliss,

hands and feet bound, a thin rivulet of dried blood on her cheek. The headache she had from being hit with the butt of a pistol was ameliorated by her anger, anger both at herself for not reacting as fast as her training should have led her to, and with the two men who had kidnapped her. And behind that was the fear of what the two men might be planning.

Sitting on the floor to her left were the dancing girls, looking fearfully at a leering Hovis, a kitchen towel strapped around his bloodied calf. On Gertie's right sat Phil Walthers, also tied hands and feet. Mrs Blower was strapped to a chair, a gag in her mouth.

'Never had a copper before,' Hovis said. 'Got nice tits as well.'

'And you aren't about to have one now,' Campbell said sternly. 'Once we've got the five million for the painting you can have as many dolly birds as you want. They'll come running to you.' He turned to the group. 'Allow me to assure you, that so long as everybody does what they are told they don't get hurt. We merely want a painting that has been promised to us. You have nothing to fear.'

'You don't think they're just going to hand over a painting worth five million to you?' asked Gertie. 'If I were you I'd give myself in now before you really get into trouble. As it is you're facing about twenty years inside.'

Campbell smiled at her.

'Your Inspector won't,' he said agreeably, 'but your boyfriend will. Sergeant Summers will be getting a personal phone call. He won't take any risks if his girlfriend is in danger, risks such as mentioning such a call to any of his colleagues. He'll come quietly, all on his own, to hand it over. And the painting's worth fifty million, not five. But we're not greedy.'

Gertie looked at him.

'What makes you think Sergeant Summers is my boyfriend?' she asked.

Campbell paused before replying.

'A difficult question. Almost philosophical, really. A husband is a husband by virtue of being married, that we can prove by a simple test. But a boyfriend or girlfriend? When does one become a boyfriend or a girlfriend? Is it a look? A declaration? A number of times you share dinner or other such treats? Such a pity we don't have the time to go into it right now.' He turned to Hovis. 'Mugsy, go find a room where we can lock this lot up. One with strong doors and no windows, got it?'

'Got it, boss,' said Mugsy, limping away.

'Mugsy?' asked Gertie in disbelief.

'His name's Malone,' said Campbell with a touch of refined distaste. 'He likes being called Mugsy. I have to humour him. He's not the brightest of stars in the night sky.'

'You won't get away with it, you know that,' Gertie said.

'Ah, Constable Gregson, please, no clichés. We know there are roadblocks all around Wellbury. We even know your delightful Inspector Garold has set up a roving roadblock to catch us. So sad she couldn't trust the media to keep their mouths shut, isn't it? But the thing is, my dear, I hold all the cards at the moment. I know exactly what I'm doing and what I'm going to do. Your colleagues can only chase their tails around wondering what my next step is.'

He turned to the girls and smiled.

'However, since we have a little time on our hands, which one of you feels like being pregnant?'

An ambulance weaved its way through the stalled traffic to the road block, lights flashing and siren wailing. Harry Wheatley held up a hand. The ambulance driver didn't appear to think that this referred to him until a shouted voice made him turn to find himself facing the barrel of a police firearm. The fact that it was held by Allison Hardbury was of little comfort. There were three other armed policemen behind her.

'Out!' said Harry Wheatley. 'Now!'

'I've got an emergency in the back, an old bloke,' the ambulance driver protested.

'You'll be joining him if you don't get out and open the back doors,' Harry growled. 'And keep your hands where I can see them.'

'Anything happens to him, it'll be your fault,' the driver grumbled fearfully, getting out with his hands in view, his wide-open eyes fixed on the rifle barrel pointing at him. He moved slowly and carefully to the back and opened the doors. 'See?' he said, gesturing at a figure on a stretcher, 'One old bloke. Now, mind if I get on?'

'After we've checked all these boxes and cupboards,' Harry said, climbing into the back of the ambulance.

'You've got to be joking!' protested the driver. 'This is an emergency!'

'What's your name?' asked Allison Hardbury.

'Jeff Hadley. Why?'

'So I can put it on the charge sheet when we arrest you for interfering in a police operation, that's why. That is to say, if something worse doesn't happen. We aren't carrying these things to look pretty, Mr Hadley.'

The ambulance driver looked at her in disbelief, his eyes wider.

'Okay, all clear,' said Harry, dropping down from the back of the ambulance. 'You can get off now.'

The driver closed the back doors and returned to the front, his fearful eyes never straying from Allison.

'If this bloke dies it'll be your fault,' he said in disgust.

'You don't watch out you'll be dead before him,' Allison threatened.

'Maybe we were too hard on him,' said Harry as the vehicle left in a hurry. 'It was an ambulance after all.'

'Now,' said Campbell to Gertie, 'I'll need your boyfriend's mobile phone number.'

'He doesn't have a mobile phone.'

Campbell smiled.

'A nice try, my dear, but I'm not that stupid. Now I don't want to hurt you, but I do need his number. I'll get it in the end, so you might as well hand it over now. I don't like rough stuff, but Mugsy quite enjoys it.'

'I told you, he doesn't have a mobile phone. He hates the things.'

Campbell smiled again and leaned over her, feeling in her pockets.

'Here we go,' he said, pulling out Gertie's mobile. 'Now, let's see, what would you keep his number under?' he asked himself as he pressed buttons on the phone. 'Sergeant? Sarge? Frank? Ah, here we go – Frank, home. No, Frank, work, that's more like it.'

He looked puzzled at the number that came up on the mobile telephone's little screen.

'This is a land-line number,' he noted.

'It's his office number. I told you, he doesn't have a mobile.'

Campbell thought for a moment.

'Well, you're just going to have to pray he's in his office then, aren't you?' he said. He smiled, took the battery out of her mobile and dropped both into his pocket.

'Frank, have you gone quite mad?' Frieda asked.

An easel had been set up in Cecil Park's cell. He had a book next to him, from which he was copying Matisse's Red Studio, only this one was in blue and was being done with a cheap set of children's watercolours and a thin brush of the sort that would last an eight-year-old a morning if the child used it sparingly.

'We need to have something to give them if it comes to that,' Frank said, frowning at the work. 'I doubt whether those two know anything about art. They probably have a vague idea of what it should look like, but I'm banking on their not knowing the difference between oil and watercolour. You need more greeny-blue over there,' he told Cecil Park.

'You're not related to my wife, by any chance, are you Sergeant Summers?' asked Park irritably. 'Or is it a case of everybody being a critic? I know what I'm doing.'

Frank frowned at him, torn between the urge to belt him one for Gertie's sake and the fact that Cecil Park was quite correct in what he said. He turned to Frieda.

'Any news on Gertie's mobile?' he asked.

'It was switched off about half an hour ago. The last signal they could trace apparently came from somewhere between Lords Acres and the Blue Bliss, though the person Tricia spoke to sounded less than confident. I've got a team searching the area, but I think we can presume it's probably been thrown away by now.'

'No further contact from Campbell and Hovis?'

'No. My guess is that they're trying to work out how to get The Blue Studio and get out without being caught. I don't think they've planned for this. Probably only thought as far as getting hold of Matisse – Mr Park here – and forcing him to tell them where the painting was.' She looked at Cecil Park. 'Can't you paint faster?' she asked.

'I'm working as fast as I can,' he said, scowling at his work. 'These watercolours are not very good quality, and it takes time to dry before I can go on with the next bit. Anyway, I'm used to painting in oils, not watercolours.'

'We'll leave you to it, then,' said Frank.

They had just come up from the cells into reception when Ed Watts and Bobby Stang came through the door, Ed holding a handcuffed but struggling Jean Tromperie alias Samantha Stark alias Jean Candour, Bobby Stang carrying a suitcase. Jean had abandoned her uniform for a navy-blue skirt-suit and light-blue silk blouse. Her hair was straight, her face adorned with thick glasses.

'Look what we found booking into the Old Railway Hotel,' Ed Watts said with a smile. The Old Railway Hotel was a small hotel situated, not surprisingly, near Wellbury's main railway station.

'Well, well, if it isn't our Captain Tromperie,' said Frieda. 'Or is it Samantha Stark? Or perhaps even Jean Candour? Or have you acquired a brand new name for the occasion?'

'She was calling herself Mrs Summers, would you believe,' Ed replied. 'Cheeky little thing, isn't she? I reckon she spotted our blokes on the platform of the railway station and decided to book into a hotel and lie low for a few days. Thought she could fool Wellbury's finest, didn't she? Now she's decided she's Sam Stark.'

The ex-French woman gave him a look of contempt.

'I did fool you,' she said. 'I would have got away with it if it wasn't for him,' she added, nodding at Frank. 'He's the only one of you with any brains in his head. The rest of him isn't bad either.'

'Oh?' asked Frieda, turning to Frank. 'And what exactly does she mean by that?'

There was a pause as Frank and Jean looked at each other. Frieda and the two constables looked at Frank.

'I could see that he didn't believe my act,' Jean said finally. 'I knew he was about to check up on me, so I legged it. Just bad luck these two plods turned up at the hotel as I was booking in.'

'Calling yourself Mrs Summers,' Frieda noted. Jean smiled at Frank.

'I thought I'd pay him a compliment. He is quite cute, isn't he?'

'I'll give you cute, young lady,' Frieda said angrily.

'Enough,' Frank said. 'We've got more important things to worry about.' He looked at Jean. 'Do you have a hairdryer in that suitcase?'

'Yes, a small portable one, why? Need a haircut?'

'Take her down to Park's cell,' he told the two constables. 'Take the cuffs off. She can help him paint a masterpiece. A hairdryer will solve Park's problem with slow-drying paint.'

'Go on, do it,' Frieda said peremptorily, as the constables paused uncertainly. Jean blew Frank a kiss as she was led away.

'You can't have him,' she called to Frieda, 'he's mine, all mine. I've always wanted a man I could call my own. You know, like pets. Not just for Christmas, that sort of thing.'

'Is there something between you and her I should know about?' Frieda asked, looking Frank in the eye.

'She's just trying to wind you up,' Frank said, checking his watch. 'I don't know what she's like as an actress, but that's one thing she really is good at.'

'True,' said Frieda after a pause to contemplate the discrepancy between the logic of Frank's statement and the outrageous behaviour of the other woman. 'What made you realise that she was a fake?'

'I couldn't believe that the French would send someone like that over. She was a bit too much of a cartoon character.' He patted his jacket pocket. 'Damn, I've left my radio in my office. I'll just pop there quickly and get it.'

Frieda watched him leave, a thoughtful look on her face. She couldn't help but feel that it was Frank who had been acting just then, and that obnoxious French girl who had been telling the truth.

But the girl wasn't even French. And Frank was far too innocent to tell a lie and get away with it. His straightforwardness and occasional naiveté were part of his appeal.

She closed her mind to the question. They would deal with Frank later. The crucial thing at the moment was to rescue Gertie.

Campbell and Hovis, or whatever their real names were, were either going to surrender or die. Tricia Leigh had taken the message from Campbell offering the exchange of Frank's girlfriend for The Blue Studio. She hadn't used the word "girlfriend" when passing the message on to Frank, but the meaning had been clear. Gertie might be competition, but she was also Frieda's responsibility. And also her friend, in a younger-sister way. Campbell and Hovis, Hovis especially, reminded her of her ex-husband, the wife-beater, when he had been in his cups and lost the veneer of a respectable police officer. She had often dreamed at one stage of killing him. The idea had never left her completely, despite intensive sessions with a psychoanalyst. Campbell and Hovis were going to serve as proxies for her ex-husband.

She touched the pistol tucked into the waistband at the back of her skirt. Had the psychoanalyst been right she would have been dreaming of stepping up to a cowering Hovis and pulling the trigger. But she wasn't.

She wanted Frank to put the pistol against Hovis's forehead and pull the trigger while she watched. No doubt there was something Freudian about that. But the idea was appealing.

The ambulance drove up to the entrance to the Blue Bliss. Two paramedics got out and one knocked on the door.

'A bit ironic,' said the one to the other, 'someone going into labour here. Last place you'd expect to find a pregnant woman, a nightclub. You'd think it would put the punters off.'

'I like a bit of irony in the morning,' agreed the other. 'Makes the day a bit more interesting.'

'Today's been a little too interesting so far. Coppers with guns all over the place. Ain't natural.'

'Well, at least we're well out of it. Give me pregnant mothers-to-be over guns any day.'

The other man considered this statement while they waited.

'That's a bit of a tautology, innit?' he asked.

'A tore – what?'

'You repeated yourself. Pregnant mother-to-be. Means the same thing, dunnit?'

'No it doesn't. And since when have you been learning big words like tore-wotsit?'

'Look, there's no need to start an argument just cause I know a few words you don't. And it is a repetition.'

'No it ain't.'

'Look, think about it. If a woman's a mother-to-be, she's got to be pregnant, ain't she? And if she's pregnant, she's a mother-to-be, in't she? It's the same thing.'

The door opened, ending this discussion. Campbell looked out at them.

'You called for an ambulance, mate?' asked the first paramedic. 'Woman going into labour?'

'Pregnant mother-to-be,' said the second. Ironically.

'Yes, indeed, come in.'

They followed him to an office. Inside one of the dancing girls sat on a chair, at first glance heavily pregnant. A closer look revealed two cushions stuffed underneath her dress.

'Ere, what's going on?' asked a puzzled paramedic. The two of them turned around to find Campbell holding a gun in his hand, a grinning Hovis behind him.

'I think it would be a good idea if both of you took your clothes off,' he said. 'Think of it as an emergency. We have plenty of aspirin of you suddenly find you have a headache. Which you will have if you don't do exactly as you're told.'

Frank sat down behind his desk. He needed time to think. They were pulling out all the stops to find Gertie and the two Londoners, but it was all automatic reaction, straight out of the training manuals, a plan designed to handle the first few hours of an unexpected and unknown threat. It was effectively a pre-planned knee-jerk reaction.

None of the roadblocks had come up with anything. No hotels or boarding houses had reported two men booking in recently. Their car had disappeared off the face of the earth. But Campbell and Hovis had to be still in the town somewhere. With Gertie. They wouldn't leave without The Blue Studio. So where could they be hiding?

They had rented a hotel room when they first turned up in Wellbury. Had they also rented a house or a flat somewhere?

Pretty unlikely, they weren't planning on a long stay. They had come to force Cecil Park to hand over The Blue Studio. Get in, get the painting, and get out. They couldn't know Wellbury very well. So where, finding themselves being hunted by every single policeman in Wellbury, plus units from outside, would they have gone to ground? On their own they could probably find somewhere to hide out, there were plenty of potential hiding places in Wellbury's many parks, or amidst the clumps of trees along the river or canal. But not with Gertie to keep an eye on. They couldn't take the risk of her managing to break out into the open. So they had to be indoors somewhere. But where?

'You've been a while, Frank,' Frieda said. He looked up. She was standing in the doorway. 'The Metropolitan Police have come through. Campbell and Hovis are a pair of petty criminals. The type always dreaming of the big one, the heist that will earn them a fortune, which explains why they're after The Blue Studio. Campbell's apparently reasonably intelligent, though they say he always falls for overcomplicated schemes which go nowhere – a bit of a Walther Mitty character. Hovis is basically a thug.'

'And their real names aren't Campbell or Hovis, no doubt.'

'Hovis's real name is Malone, Freddy Malone, calls himself Mugsy. Campbell is Charles, or Charlie, Sanders. But I think for the moment we will keep referring to them as Campbell and Hovis, things would become too confused otherwise.' She paused. 'But the interesting bit is that the latest London has on them is that they were last heard of trying to pick up a couple of replica pistols.'

'Fakes?'

'Just so. The impression the Met have is that Campbell

normally avoids firearms. Presumably this time he wanted something to frighten Matisse – Cecil Park – with, but nothing that would actually go bang. Apart from knowing what sort of sentence he would get if he were caught with an illegal firearm, they say he thinks firearms are somewhat vulgar.'

'Vulgar?'

'I got the impression that Campbell considers himself to be a refined sort of criminal – a modern Raffles presumably.'

'Well, thank god for that,' Frank said. 'That the guns are fakes, I mean.'

'Yes, indeed. I've alerted all the teams. They know that the weapons Campbell and Hovis have probably aren't real, but we're still not going to take any chances. The order stands: if they don't surrender they get taken out.'

'No,' said Frank, 'you never know.'

He stood up impatiently.

'Anything else happening? I suppose the Chief Constable is blowing his top.'

'He's been very supportive, actually. Anything we want we get. He's trying to locate the Chief Inspector.'

'Who has gone fishing. Fat lot of bloody good he is.'

'Now, Frank, don't be too harsh. The Chief Inspector has his reasons for not being here. I'll tell you about them sometime.'

Frank grunted, as if ill-disposed to excuse the Chief Inspector. He sat down again and drummed his fingers on his desk.

'Where the hell are they?' he demanded angrily. 'They can't have just disappeared. They've got Gertie, for Christ's sake!'

'Campbell and Hovis?'

'Of course Campbell and Hovis. Where could they have gone to ground? I'm sure they don't know Wellbury that well. So where do they know where they can hide out? It has to be indoors somewhere, it has to be!'

He paused.

'Of course!' he almost shouted. 'It's bloody obvious!'

'What's obvious?'

Frank took a breath and looked at her.

'You said that the last signal from Gertie's mobile came from somewhere between Lords Acres and the Blue Bliss?'

'Yes, but they couldn't be exact. The feeling I had was that they didn't know what they were looking for. That they were waiting for one of their engineers to come in to confirm it.'

'There are two places Campbell and Hovis know of in Wellbury. The two places we took them. The Blue Bliss and the house in Lords Acres Cecil Park was renting – 70 Glenbourne Avenue. People wouldn't notice if the Blue Bliss was closed most of the day, it only opens in early evening anyway. But there are too many people there, it would be too risky. But they know that Park's house is empty, and it has a garage where they could hide their car quite nicely. I think that's where they are. It's the only place that makes sense. Big house, large grounds, neighbours who keep to themselves. It has to be!'

Frieda looked at him. She was about to reply when his telephone rang.

'A little more green on the side,' Jean said, playing the air from the hairdryer on the painting. Cecil Park leaned back and wiped his sweating brow.

'In future I will stick to making copies of existing paintings,' he said. 'Inventing new ones is just too dangerous.'

Jean looked around, noting the open cell door. They seemed to have been forgotten.

'Why don't we make a run for it?' she suggested. 'I reckon we could slip out without anyone noticing. What do you think? Fun, or what?'

'I must finish this first. I feel I owe it to Sergeant Summers. Especially if it helps him get that young constable back.'

'Don't be silly, Cecil, you don't owe him anything. He was the one who arrested you. Come on, let's slip out now while no-one's watching. Anyway, I owe him one, and not the way you mean.'

'He arrested me because I wanted him to,' Cecil Park said with not a little pride. Then he paused as her words sunk in. 'You owe him one? Whatever on earth for? What do you mean, you owe him one?'

'Don't ask questions, Cecil, please. Come on, let's do a runner. If he's so bloody marvellous he can finish the painting himself, the bastard.'

Cecil Park knew enough about the ways of the world to know that, when a woman like Jean called a man like Frank Summers a bastard, it was not out of hatred, but exactly the other emotion. If they stayed in the police station, even just in Wellbury, he would end up losing the young woman to the Sergeant. There could be no doubt about that. He was not naive enough to believe that Jean would be around forever. Sooner or later she would get bored and leave him. But he intended to do all he could to make sure it was later than sooner.

'Sergeant Summers?' asked the voice.

'Yes, this is Summers here,' Frank replied, holding up a hand to Frieda to indicate he needed silence. 'That's Campbell, isn't it? Or shall I call you Charlie Sanders?'

The voice chuckled.

'So you know my real name, well done Sergeant Summers. But it makes no matter, I had always planned to disappear after this and find somewhere more salubrious under a new name – the south of France, I rather think. Or perhaps, thinking of that truly awful Captain Tromperie, Spain.'

'Give it up, Sanders, you won't find a hiding place anywhere in Europe. You won't even get out of Wellbury. Unless it's in a coffin.'

'You will have to forgive me if I try, Sergeant. And as far as Europe goes, perhaps you're right. Somehow I wouldn't like to have to settle down in a continent that produces police officers of the calibre of Captain Tromperie. No doubt the Spanish will be just as bad, if not worse. But you'll have to excuse me if I don't stay on the line too long, just in case you are tracing calls to your police station. We have something you want, and I am certain that by now you have convinced M Matisse to tell you where The Blue Studio is. I will call you in one hour to let you know where to leave it. Do not inform your colleagues about this conversation or you will not see your girlfriend alive again, understood?'

'We're still working on it,' Frank replied, thinking of words to say to keep Campbell talking. 'Matisse hasn't agreed to hand it over yet. He's still refusing to say where it is. We need more time.'

'You have one hour, Sergeant.'

'I don't believe your threats, Campbell,' Frank said. 'We know your record. You've never tried anything this big before. And you must know we have armed officers looking for you. The best thing you can do is to give yourself up. Otherwise you'll be lucky to end up in jail. You're far more likely to be on the end of a police sniper's bullet.'

'We only get a shot at the big one once in our lives, Sergeant Summers – if you'll pardon the unintended pun. And you'd be surprised at what I'd do for five million pounds. One hour. Be at your desk.'

Frank looked at Frieda as the line went dead. He replaced the handset.

'Campbell is going to call back in one hour to let me know where to hand over The Blue Studio. He told me not to tell anyone else. If he believes I'd keep quiet about this he must be mad. Still,' he added, 'we might as well play along. It should help to flush them out.'

'You are not going to take unnecessary risks, Frank,' Frieda replied. 'It's bad enough that Gertie's in danger.'

'You have another plan?'

Frieda looked at him.

'We've still got an hour,' she said. 'I'll send a team to Park's house in Lords Acres. And another to the Blue Bliss, just to be on the safe side.'

'I'll check on Park. See how his masterpiece is getting on. He'd better have it ready within an hour, criticism or no criticism.'

'I'm sorry to have to leave you, ladies and gentlemen,' Campbell said to the group sitting on the kitchen floor in the Blue Bliss, augmented by the addition of two paramedics in underwear, their uniforms now adorning, at a pinch, Campbell and Hovis. 'I'm sure you won't go hungry or thirsty in here. But please don't try to escape. We have left explosives in several parts of the building. Opening the wrong door might cost you your lives. Come, young Sonia, your performance in pregnancy might still be needed, and you have done so brilliantly up to now I would hate to see it spoilt.'

He motioned a frightened Sonia towards the door, paused and turned back to Gertie.

'No doubt you are wondering why we are leaving you here, Constable. Well, when I said Sergeant Summers would do anything for his girlfriend, I meant it. Only the girlfriend I was referring to was not yourself. No, the thing is that you're a police officer. They might take chances if it were you. His other girlfriend isn't a police officer.'

'His other girlfriend?'

'Not, of course, your delightful and ambitious Inspector Garold, who obviously has a soft spot for her Sergeant. No, I'm referring to Doctor Pleadle. I overheard them talking yesterday, and they weren't discussing fingerprints. I don't think he's going to try anything when he finds out that it's her he's swapping The Blue Studio for.' He paused. 'You know, I do wish I could stay around to find out the outcome of Sergeant Summers' many relationships. I find them absolutely fascinating. I must confess to having something of the romantic in me. Sadly that cannot be. Such is life. Perhaps, in a few years, I might give him a call to find out how the story ends. For the sake of auld lang syne, you could say.' He nodded at the group. 'Good day, ladies and gentlemen.'

He closed the door, and they heard the sounds of bolts being driven home, followed by footsteps moving away.

'Untie these,' Gertie ordered the girl nearest to her, holding out her bound wrists. The girl looked fearfully at her. 'Get a bloody move on! And you,' she told a second, 'untie Mrs Blower.' To a third: 'You, look after Mr Walthers. Jump to it!'

The three nominated girls rushed nervously to their tasks. Once untied Gertie stood up and hurried over to Mrs Blower where the second girl was failing to achieve anything, her fingers shaking too much to untie the knots. Gertie took over, undoing the gag around Mrs Blower's mouth.

'Thank you, Gertie, that was most uncomfortable, not to say distasteful,' Mrs Blower said, breathing deeply as Gertie began attacking the ropes around her wrists. 'When you have those two safely in a cell I would like a word with them. Possibly something more than just a word.'

'It will be my pleasure,' said Gertie. 'Just as soon as I've finished with them. But for the moment we need to find a way out of here.'

'What about the explosives?' asked one of the paramedics.

'They haven't left explosives anywhere,' Gertie replied. 'They were bluffing. It was just a trick to keep us here.'

'How do you know?'

'I don't. But I'm ninety-nine percent certain.'

'Oh, great!' replied the paramedic sardonically. 'What about the one percent, then?'

Gertie looked at him.

'Sometimes you just have to take a chance,' she said.

'It could be much, much better, Sergeant,' Cecil Park said, surveying the finished Blue Studio critically. Jean watched, an annoyed look on her face, like a child refused a treat.

'Just so long as it's good enough to con those two,' Frank replied. 'At least, long enough to get Gertie out safely.'

'We'll need to unpick it from its frame,' Cecil continued. 'And a cup of cold tea would be rather nice.'

'Cold tea?'

'To age it with. It is supposed to be a hundred years old, after all. And in lieu of any better alternative being available. Black, no sugar. We don't want to end up with sticky fingers, now do we?'

'You should have been on stage, Mr Park. I'll get someone to bring some. Right now I'm expecting a phone call.'

'Can we go now?' Jean asked Cecil when Frank had left. 'Though it isn't really as much fun as it would have been to see his face when he came back to find half a painting.'

'No, my dear, I intend to stay for the duration. I feel I owe it, somehow. You can slip off if you want.'

'What, and leave you here? Amongst all these dolly-bird coppers? No, Cecil Park, I am staying where I can keep an eye on you.'

'And keep an eye on Sergeant Summers, no doubt.'

'What?' she asked in simulated surprise. 'Why would I want to keep an eye on him for?'

'Because you're falling in love with him, that's why. I know you too well, Jean. I've seen the look in your eyes when his name is mentioned.'

'I hate the bastard,' she said, turning her face away.

On his way back from the cells Frank took a detour to the armoury.

'I'll take that vest now, John,' he told John Stevens. 'Looks like I might be going out soon.'

'Glad to hear you're being sensible, Frank,' the other man replied, handing over the vest. He watched as Frank took his jacket off and slipped the vest on.

'You know the irony of it all, John?' Frank asked, putting his jacket back on. 'We now know that the weapons the two bastards we're after are carrying are replicas.'

'So, why the jacket all of a sudden?'

'Frieda wouldn't let me go out without it.'

He paused as he noticed the grenade sitting on the counter, the pin back where it should be.

'Mind if I borrow that for a while, John?' he asked. John Stevens' brow furrowed.

'I don't suppose you'd like to tell me what you intend doing with it?'

'They have dummy guns,' Frank said, picking up the grenade and putting it in his jacket pocket. 'No reason why we shouldn't have dummy grenades. I don't know if I'll get the chance to use it, but if I do I'm going to scare the shit out of those two. It might reduce the urge I have to kick their guts into next year.' He smiled. 'What would you do if you were in a room and a grenade came flying through the window?'

'Get out as fast as possible, of course.'

'Precisely. If the chance arises it should flush them out quite nicely. They won't stop to look after Gertie, and she knows it's a dummy. We'll be able to pick them off as they try to escape, before they start wondering why it hasn't exploded.'

'I bloody well hope Gertie remembers,' noted John Stevens.

'It's no good, we need something heavier,' Gertie said, her hair loose, sweat pouring down her cheeks. They had loaded a trolley with the heaviest objects they could find, and were using it as a battering ram against the doors. So far they had been in more danger from heavy pots falling from the trolley than from breaking the doors open.

'Push or pull?' asked Phil Walters thoughtfully, his own face covered in sweat, his breathing heavy.

'Push or pull?' asked Gertie.

'We're trying to break it down. Perhaps we should be trying to pull it down. For a start we're pushing against the doorframe, and that's rather too solidly constructed.' He looked around. His gaze rested on a steel table. 'Now that's nice and heavy,' he commented.

Gertie nodded.

'Pull it to the door, tie some ropes to the doors, plenty of slack, and then push it away as fast as possible away,' she said. 'The sudden force as the rope gives up slack could do the trick.'

'Exactly, my dear. I think it has something to do with the word inertia. And with a tea towel under each leg and all of us pushing it should slide rather nicely.'

'Be a sod to lift,' Gertie noted.

'We only need to lift one leg an inch at a time for the tea towels,' Mrs Blower said. 'Come on, girls, showtime!'

'Did you hear that?' asked Inspector Percy Hanson.

'Someone's making a hell of a racket,' agreed Detective Sergeant Pete Phillips. They lay in the undergrowth outside of the Blue Bliss. The nightclub was surrounded by armed officers.

Percy held a pair of binoculars to his eyes, scanning the front and side of the nightclub. Unbeknownst to him he was also being observed. Under a nearby bush lay Nelson, a not very happy dog. Percy and Pete Phillips had unknowingly taken over Nelson's favourite hiding place. Nelson was not only unhappy. He was becoming increasingly angry. That hiding place was all in had in life and now it had been stolen from him.

A loud crashing noise came from within the night-club.

Percy Hanson switched the transmit button on his radio.

'Something's happening,' he whispered to the armed officers surrounding the nightclub. 'Remember, if it's them, they've got Gertie with them. Don't take any chances.'

'Constable Stang to Inspector Hanson,' a soft voice replied.

'Go ahead, Bobby.'

'I've just seen some movement. Looks like a woman being dragged through a doorway. Could be Gertie. Blonde hair, the size looks about right.'

'Sons of bitches! Right, any bloke – I repeat, bloke – who

comes out with a weapon in his hands gets taken out, understood? No ifs or buts. We're going to show these bastards we mean business. Just make sure Gertie's not in the line of fire.'

He turned to Pete Phillips.

'You sure you know how to use that?' he asked. Pete patted his rifle fondly, smiling. It wasn't a happy smile.

'I used to be able to get six out of six in a four inch circle from this distance,' he said.

'Used to?' asked Percy.

'Aye, it's been a while, but you never forget. Like riding a bicycle, it is.'

Percy looked at him, worried. He didn't like that "used to" bit. And Pete was using a rifle drawn from the armoury, not one he had personally trained with and zeroed the sights in himself. The Armed Response Units all had weapons allocated to them personally. Percy Hanson wasn't a trained marksman, but he did know you couldn't pick up any old rifle and take out a sixpence with your first shot.

And he had this nasty feeling that the rifle Pete Phillips was holding wasn't standard issue.

'Just don't pull that bloody trigger until I tell you to,' he said.

Phil Walthers stood just outside of the broken kitchen doorway, holding Gertie's arms, trying to restrain her.

'No, my dear, I insist,' he said. 'It's far too dangerous for a young woman like you. I shall make sure there are no explosives myself.'

'Mr Walthers, I am a trained police officer. You are a civilian.

I am ordering you to go back into the kitchen and stay there. Anyway, you wouldn't know how to check for explosives.'

Phil Walters smiled, bent down and picked up a piece of piping that had previously served as a door handle which had come adrift when the kitchen doors were pulled down.

'I shall open doors at a distance,' he said. 'And if we're lucky, and those two thugs are still around, they might mistake this for the barrel of a rifle. I often had to do with less when I was training to be a thespian.'

'But you never became an actor,' Gertie pointed out.

'Yes, but I still dream of having my one great moment in the limelight. Just one great moment. This may well be it.'

'Doctor Pleadle?'

Susan looked up. She had been trying to concentrate on a file in front of her while listening to the radio, following the updates about the police operation in progress. A police constable had been abducted, that much they had revealed. She locked on to this thought, the idea that it had been a constable, knowing that that meant it could not be Frank. She tried to ignore the obvious possibility that they had got the rank wrong, breaking news was invariably unreliable in terms of facts. Even then, if they had got the rank right, believing that it wasn't Frank was only marginally comforting. He would be in the thick of it, and the two abductors were armed. She could only pray that he would look after himself.

To her surprise the voice which had disturbed her belonged to a paramedic standing at the door, with an extremely pregnant and frightened woman next to him. A second glance told her that there was something strange about the woman's pregnancy, and the paramedic's uniform was too small for him. And she had seen this man before somewhere.

A third glance revealed a gun in his hand, pointing at the woman next to him.

'Now I'm sure you don't want the young lady to get hurt, Doctor Pleadle,' Campbell said. 'So if you'll just come with us? We have an ambulance waiting.'

Frank stood in his office, looking out of the window. His radio was on the windowsill, voices crackling through occasionally. Normally, were volunteers asked for, he would be sitting underneath his desk with an innocent look on his face, making sure no one found him. This time it was different. He wanted to be where the action was.

He had put the rifle against his desk, realising that, apart from making him feel somewhat foolish, it was just a dead weight to carry around.

Out there, however, it would have a purpose. And he did not want to find his fingers trembling, however slightly, from having carried a dead weight around for no purpose but show.

The rolled up canvas of The Blue Studio sat on his desk next to the barrel of the firearm. One or the other, he thought. The fake or the FN.

Somewhere downstairs an engineer was monitoring incoming phone calls, hoping to trace a specific one. Frank checked his watch. Two minutes to go.

'All clear, here,' came a voice on the radio.

'The house in Glenbourne Avenue is clear, Control,'

confirmed another voice. 'Do you want us to hang on here or return to base?'

'Return to base,' Control ordered.

Frank switched to the frequency the Blue Bliss team were using.

'Confirmed, Inspector,' said a voice. 'It's their car alright. They must be inside.'

Right! thought Frank, that's it. Campbell and Hovis were in the Blue Bliss. He wasn't going to hang around here. He grabbed the rifle and made for the door. The question of whether he would train a rifle on another man and pull the trigger he had answered during his waiting.

That answer was yes.

The telephone rang.

He paused. Sod Campbell. He was surrounded. He would hear the sound of a police megaphone soon enough. No need for a telephone.

'Don't you think you'd better answer it?' asked Frieda, entering his office, a radio in her hand.

Frank looked at the telephone.

At least it would confirm that Campbell and Hovis were in the Blue Bliss.

'Detective Sergeant Summers,' he said in as calm a voice as he could muster.

'Frank? Frank, it's Susan. They've got guns and they're threatening to kill Sonia to prove they mean business. And they say I'm next if you don't do what they say.'

'You know, Jean,' Cecil Park said thoughtfully, 'I would like to do something more to help. After all, it is really my fault. I just never expected anything like this to happen. What sort of idiot believes they've found a fifty-million pound painting at a car-boot sale?'

'You mean apart from the couple of hundred idiots you've already sold fake paintings to?' asked Jean.

'Yes, but fifty million? I might have well as said fifty billion.'

'Performance,' Jean replied moodily, 'it's all in the performance. When I'm Cleopatra people really believe I'm Cleopatra, even though they should know I'm not. With you it's being the innocent old duffer who can't recognise a valuable work of art in front of his nose.'

Cecil Park was a sensitive man. He knew it would be thoughtless to point out that Jean's last performance, indeed as Cleopatra, had been some eight months ago, and that had only been in a dog-food commercial. It hadn't even been a very good commercial. Why the advertisers had thought anyone would associate Cleopatra with dog-food was anyone's guess.

And he did wish she would stop referring to him as an "old duffer". The same phrase Sergeant Summers had used. Even though that was exactly the part he had played. And he had been good at it. He had more than a sneaking suspicion that the relationship between himself and the young Jean was reaching its inevitable end, and that "old duffer" was a phrase heralding that end. Still, it had been good while it had lasted.

'There must be something we can do,' he said, sighing.

'Ain't half dangerous around here, innit?' said a voice from the open cell door. They turned to find a small man looking at them, a piece of paper in his hand and a pencil behind his ear. 'I was looking for Mister Summers, Sergeant Summers. They told me he was down here.' He peered behind himself nervously. 'Almost got shot three times already, and it's hardly lunchtime.'

'I'm afraid Sergeant Summers is quite busy at the moment,' Cecil Park replied. 'They have an emergency on.'

'Wish they'd have their bleeding emergency somewhere else,' the man said, turning back to them. He looked thoughtfully at the empty easel. 'Vic Brown's the name,' he introduced himself. 'And if there's anything in the way of artwork you're looking for, reckon I could find it dead cheap. No questions asked.'

'No, thank you, Mr Brown,' Cecil Park said civilly, 'I think we've had more than enough art for the moment.'

'Wot about a nice Cezanne?' suggested Vic. 'Fake, obviously, but done to a charm. I promise you, you couldn't tell the difference, not if they was hung in the National Gallery alongside each other. Bloke I know does them on the side. Discount for any orders over half a dozen. Tell you what, you look like an honest, decent bloke, I'll give you ten percent off straight away, wotcha say?'

Cecil sighed again and looked at the floor.

'No, Mr Brown, definitely no Cézannes. No Goyas, Van Goghs or any other noted artists.'

'What about a Volkswagen?' asked Jean.

'Volkswagen?' asked Vic Brown, surprised. 'Not much call for him, but I'm sure I could find one dead cheap. Know his first name, do you?'

'Two litre Turbo,' said Jean, smiling.

'Jean, stop it,' said Cecil.

'You said you wanted to help out,' she pointed out. 'We both know what they look like, Campbell and Hovis. We could drive around and see if we could spot them. Wellbury's not that big. And it will be doing something, I'm tired of sitting here.' She turned to Vic Brown. 'You do have a car, I take it?'

'Well, yeah, a Renault Kangoo, French thing, right little beauty, lots of storage space, never know when you'll need it in my line of work, but –'

'Good, we're going for a drive.'

'Now, Jean,' protested Cecil.

'You're having a Steffi,' Vic Brown added, to no avail. She was already pushing them out of the cell.

'Steffi?' asked Cecil.

'A laugh,' Jean translated. 'Steffi Graf is rhyming slang for laugh. Now let's get moving. I want to find those two before Frank does. That'll show him.'

'Door's opening,' noted Pete Phillips, watching the Blue Bliss.

'Get ready, everyone,' Percy Hanson called softly into his radio. 'Someone's standing just inside. If it's one of our two London friends and you can see the chance, take him out. Just make sure Gertie's clear.'

Both men tried to flatten themselves further into the undergrowth. Pete Phillips checked that the safety catch of his rifle was off and lined the cross-hairs of his telescopic sight on the slowly-opening door.

Behind them Nelson let out a low growl. No-one heard it apart from Nelson. He found himself in a dilemma. He wanted to bite these humans who had stolen his hiding place, but at the same time he wasn't sure he wanted anyone to notice him.

Phil Walthers stretched his arm out, slowly pushed the front doors to the Blue Bliss a quarter open, and, keeping back, carefully tapped the steps to the entrance with the iron piping he had picked up. Logic made him suspect that no-one could have planted explosives underneath the tiled steps without it being apparent, but he wasn't in a mind to trust even solid concrete. Or what had the appearance of being solid concrete.

In the office Gertie was desperately trying to get through to the station. Frank's direct number was busy, so she had dialled the switchboard. There was someone new on the switchboard who didn't appear to realise that "Gertie" equalled Detective Constable Samantha Gregson, despite Gertie having explained it twice.

'Just put me through to Sergeant Summer's office, for crying out loud,' she insisted.

'I'm afraid that line is still busy at the moment, caller,' came the calm reply. 'Would you like to hold or try again later?'

'Try Inspector Garold, then.'

'Inspector Garold is very busy at the moment, I'm afraid she's unable to take any calls.'

'I know she's fucking busy, you moron!' swore Gertie. 'Just tell her that Gertie's on the phone. Do it! Now!'

'Caller, this is a police station you are speaking to. You could be arrested for using such language. If you have a personal problem I suggest you try the Samaritans.'

The line went dead.

'You're right it was a police station I was talking to,' Gertie muttered. 'I think I got the biggest bloody concrete blockhead in it.'

Feverishly she tried Frank's direct number again.

'Jesus! He's got a rifle!' Pete Phillips exclaimed, and involuntarily pulled the trigger on his own firearm.

He was obviously out of practice. And the weapon was also obviously not standard issue. He hadn't realised that it was switched to automatic. The magazine emptied in seconds as the barrel lifted up with the kick.

Cecil Park was amazed at the ease which they had left the police station. Vic Brown had lead them with nonchalance out towards the back, making loud statements whenever a police officer had appeared.

'Typical of these old places,' he had said at one stage as a constable hurried past. 'Plaster's going. Look up there. Make a note of that, Miss Johnson. We'll have to replace all the cupolas.'

'Yes, Mr Braithwaite,' Jean replied, the thick-rimmed glasses back on her face, Vic Brown's pencil and piece of paper in her hands.

'Cupola?' asked Cecil Park after the constable had gone. 'There aren't any cupolas around here. A cupola is a domed ceiling or roof.'

'Ah, but they don't know that, do they,' said Vic Brown with a grin. He paused for a moment. 'So that's what one of them is, is it?' he asked. 'A domed ceiling or roof. Well, there you go. I've always wondered about that.'

'Susan? Susan? Are you okay?' Frank screamed down the telephone.

'Now, now, compose yourself, Sergeant,' Campbell said, coming on the line. 'Doctor Pleadle is quite safe at the moment, as is the young Sonia from the Blue Bliss. You can collect Sonia from Doctor Pleadle's office. Doctor Pleadle herself is, however unwillingly, accompanying us at the moment. However, If you do not co-operate I might have to let Mugsy have his way with her.'

'You harm a single hair on her head and I'll rip you to pieces, Campbell!'

'Tsk, tsk, Sergeant Summers, temper, temper. However, it is obvious that you value Doctor Pleadle's life. Enough to part with The Blue Studio, I would say.'

'Don't be a fool, Campbell. We've got the Blue Bliss surrounded. You can't get away.'

There was a pause, followed by a quiet chuckle.

'We left the Blue Bliss quite some time ago, Sergeant. We're two steps ahead of you and counting. Now listen, this is what you are going to do if you wish to see Doctor Pleadle alive again.'

'That's not a car, it's a van,' protested Jean. 'A box with windows.'

'You'll hurt her feelings,' Vic Brown sniffed. 'She's a lovely car, just right for my entrepreneurial enterprises. Sometimes I don't know what size of shipment I might be required to transport at a moment's notice.'

'Yeah, but it won't do above sixty, I'll bet,' Jean replied.

'I've had her at seventy, once, easy,' Vic Brown said proudly. 'And anyway, why would you want to do more than the speed limit?'

'Because we might have to chase some London gangsters,' Jean pointed out.

'I quite like the idea,' Cecil said, rubbing his hands with enthusiasm. 'It's about time we started chasing them instead of the other way around. I've had enough of running away.'

Vic Brown stared at them.

'You're mad, the pair of you! Chasing London gangsters? No way! No way! You don't know what them bastards are like!'

Jean smiled evilly at him.

'Vic, baby, Either you drive, or we drive and you walk,' she said.

'Please, do not alarm yourself Doctor Pleadle,' Campbell said as Hovis tied a rope around Susan's ankles in the back of the ambulance. 'So long as Sergeant Summers does exactly what he is told I promise you we will not harm a hair on your pretty little head.'

'You're mad!' exclaimed Susan. 'It doesn't matter what Frank thinks. You're up against an entire police force. More than that, from what I heard on the radio. There isn't a single place in the country you'll be able to hide.'

'Now, now, my dear. I understand you're suffering from a little shock, and believe me I wish it could be otherwise. Trust me, I know exactly what I'm doing. Within a very short time, less than a few hours, you will be free and we will be gone.'

He gave her an apologetic, almost wry, smile.

'We should, ideally, be having this conversation over a glass of champagne, you know. In a civilised fashion. You would toast the failure of my mission, and I would toast its success. In the end Sergeant Summers would come galloping on his white steed to rescue you, but I would be gone, a laughing cavalier with the ill-gotten gains. Do you not agree?'

'I think you should see a psychoanalyst,' Susan replied. Campbell's smile disappeared.

'You had better pray that I don't have to hand you over to Mugsy here, Doctor Pleadle. He is, I am afraid to say, much less refined than I am in his treatment of ladies.'

'Just give the word, boss,' Hovis replied. 'She ain't exactly my type, but I'm not proud.'

'Fucking hellfire! Brimstone! God's holy waters and Mother Mary!' Phil Walthers exclaimed as he launched himself backwards, the bullets from Pete Phillips' firearm ricocheting around the reception. Hearing the noise Gertie came rushing out.

'What the hell's happening?'

'Get down! They're still out there! Tried to shoot me with a sub-machine gun or something.'

'Bugger!' said Gertie. She paused to think. 'They'll be coming in very soon. Keep them busy. All I need is five minutes.'

'Keep them busy?' asked Phil Walthers. 'With bloody what? They've got machine guns out there. Bloody rocket launchers,

Bill Dughaille

for all I know. What am I supposed to do, throw bloody beer mats at them?'

But Gertie had gone.

He looked at the miserable piece of piping in his hands.

'Is this a rifle I see before me, the butt towards my hand?' he asked.

Try as he could to reply in the affirmative, the answer was an emphatic no, however much he might pretend otherwise. Suspension of belief did not enter into it. Only someone extremely short-sighted or gullible would fall for that one.

He thought of taking a quick peek out of the window to see what was happening.

'How now, you secret, black, and midnight hags,' he quoted to himself softly. Not quite accurate, but appropriate. More or less.

'I don't think you got him, Pete,' Percy Hanson said, his face white, his ears ringing.

'I'll get the bastard next time around, though,' Pete Phillips said, ramming a fresh magazine into the rifle. 'Just let him show his face at a window and he's history.'

'For Christ's sake, Sergeant! Gertie's still in there. And god knows who else.' He took a deep breath to compose himself. 'I'm sure you've made our point for us, Sergeant. I don't doubt they now know we're serious about this business. But I think it's time we made contact with them. Dialogue, as the training manuals say.'

He winced as Pete Philips let off another few rounds.

'Jesus Christ! Stop bloody shooting, Sergeant! And put that

weapon on to single shot! Not even the army run around with their guns on automatic the whole time. In fact put the fucking safety catch on! And don't pull the trigger until I give you written authorisation. In fucking triplicate!'

'Sorry, sir, I thought I saw one of them looking out of the window.'

Percy buried his head in his hands. No-one could deny that Detective Sergeant Pete Phillips was a good, honest, decent, stolid copper. But give him two weeks' holiday and put a firearm in his hands and he was a bloody health hazard.

Detective Percival Hanson felt like weeping. Here he was, in charge of armed officers, in a critical situation, a testing ground which he had long thought would never appear, one in which he could show the mettle he was made of, the fact that he could command a large body of men in a successful operation. And what was happening? It was turning into a version of the Keystone Kops. Where the hell had he gone wrong?

'Sergeant Phillips,' he said slowly and calmly, raising his head, 'give me your rifle.'

'But you aren't licensed to use it,' Pete Phillips protested.

'Sergeant Phillips, give me your rifle or you will find yourself trying to retrieve it from your duodenum. Understand?'

Pete Phillips didn't know what a duodenum was, but he understood the concept perfectly. He handed the rifle over. Percy put it firmly to one side, out of Pete Phillips' reach.

Phil Walthers crouched beneath the window sill. He had tried peeking out and almost received a new parting in his hair. His whole body was shaking. Being tied up by those hoodlums had been an unnerving experience, but he had found confidence by reminding himself that he was a journalist and as such should stay remote and concentrate on the story. That, and the fact that those two London thugs were obviously only interested in some painting, not in hurting anyone in the Blue Bliss. Hovis might have been a threat, but Campbell was in control. You could negotiate with such people, reason with them.

But now real bullets were flying past his ears, and they weren't stopping for a chat. Someone was going to get killed this way, and it looked increasingly as if it might be him. This was no longer a joke.

He looked back to see Mrs Blower on hands and knees, crawling towards him with a carving knife between her teeth.

Oh, dear god, that's all I need now, he thought. Boadicea with a butcher's knife.

'You are going to leave The Blue Studio in the kitchen of the house that Matisse was renting,' Campbell said. 'In the middle of the floor, somewhere obvious. Hovis will collect it. He will bring it to me. You will not follow him. If you try anything – well, you know what the result will be. Once I am happy that it's the genuine article we will release Doctor Pleadle. Somewhere far from civilisation, but not too far that she won't be able to walk to safety within an hour or two. Got that?'

'How do I know I can trust you?' asked Frank.

Campbell laughed.

'You don't. But you don't have any choice. One hour,

Sergeant Summers. One hour and we shall be out of your life forever. And you will have the delectable Doctor Pleadle back in safety, unharmed and in one piece, in your arms and holding on tightly as if she never wanted to let you go. Keep that lovely image in your thoughts.'

'I'm going to kill you, Campbell,' Frank said in, to himself, a surprisingly even and calm voice. 'You know that, don't you?'

It was too late. Campbell had already switched his phone off.

'Look, you ever heard of the phrase a needle in a bleeding haystack? The bloody proverbial?' asked Vic Brown through gritted teeth. He had accepted the offer of being chauffeur as the alternative was to lose his car.

'I know, Vic, sweetie,' Jean said next to him. 'But it's better than sitting in a police cell doing nothing, isn't it?'

'I've often enjoyed doing nothing in a police cell,' Vic muttered. 'Some of me best memories are of sitting in a police cell doing nothing.'

'I've been putting a great deal of thought to this,' Cecil Park said calmly from the back.

'Oh, great,' Vic said sarcastically. 'That's all we need. Thinking. It rots the brain, you know. And doesn't half get you into trouble. Trust me, I know.'

'These London thugs,' Cecil continued, unfazed, 'they probably don't know Wellbury very well. Jean, you were with Sergeant Summers. Did he tell you where they took those two?'

'The house you rented and the nightclub called the Blue Bliss, same places they took me. Why?'

'Well, I rather suspect that that is where we will find them. In one or either place. We'll try the house first. Mr Brown, do you need directions?'

'Yeah,' muttered Vic Brown, 'back to frigging London, for a start. I might even take in a play. A comedy, I reckon.'

To the amazement of both men Jean suddenly burst into song.

'Something appealing, something appalling,' she sang.

Frank and Frieda looked at each other.

'They'll be watching from somewhere,' he said. He looked at the rolled up canvas. He picked it up. Then he slung the rifle over his shoulder.

'Frank, Hovis might be already waiting in the kitchen,' Frieda said gently.

'In which case he dies,' he replied grimly.

'Campbell still has Susan.'

'I'll go after Campbell after I've sorted out Hovis. Maybe if we show Hovis' body strung upside down from a lamppost Campbell will realise what he's up against. It worked with Mussolini.'

'Frank,' said Frieda softly, blocking his exit. 'I'll take the painting. They can't be stupid enough not to realise that we all know what's going on. You're too emotionally involved. You'll start shooting at the wrong moment.'

He looked at her, his face showing implacable determination.

'Frank, Susan's life is in danger. I'll take the painting. You can act as backup. Please.'

'No. If you go your life will be in danger too. Campbell might have a veneer of civilisation, but Hovis is the kind of man who likes to hurt women.'

'That's a risk I'll have to take, Frank. Give me the painting.'

'I said, no.'

His phone rang.

Harry Wheatley held his hand up as the ambulance came towards them. It stopped and the paramedic driving put his head out of the window.

'What's the problem, officer?' asked Hovis.

'Couple of blokes on the run, armed,' Harry replied. 'What's in the back?'

'One pregnant woman, went into labour early. Her waters broke a few hours ago. Got to get her to hospital as soon as poss. Might die otherwise. Looks dodgy for the kid as it is.'

'Why haven't you got your siren on?'

The question seemed to stump Hovis.

'Out of the question, officer,' Campbell said, leaning over Hovis. 'Loud noises are the last thing the poor woman needs right now. How would you feel if you were giving birth and someone switched on a siren over your head?'

Harry contemplated the question for a few moments before deciding that he didn't like the idea.

'Right, get on then.'

'Cheers, mate.'

Harry and Allison Hardbury watched the ambulance slowly gather speed as it went down the road.

'Why didn't you search that one?' asked Allison.

'A pregnant woman in labour? I'm in enough trouble over a dying old man. Imagine what the papers would say if we held up a pregnant woman in labour while we searched the ambulance. And I'm sure I recognised those paramedics. Must have seen them on a shout before sometime. Traffic accident or something.'

He grimaced.

'Anyway, can you imagine what it looks like in the back of that thing?' he asked.

Bullet-proof jacketed and carrying a firearm, Allison Hardbury too grimaced at the thought.

'Yuk!' she said succinctly.

For a moment they looked at each other. They were not formally engaged, but it was only a matter of time. And then there would be a wedding, and then ... One day it might be Allison in an ambulance like that, pregnant and in labour.

They turned their attention back to the road, to an approaching car. There would be time for such thoughts. At the moment they had a job to do.

'Fancy getting married sometime?' Harry asked suddenly.

Allison considered this.

'Is that a proposal?' she asked.

'Sort of, I suppose,' Harry admitted. 'Only I've been worried about asking you proper-like, you know, on bended knee and with the ring and everything. Just in case you said no.'

'Bout bloody time you asked,' commented Allison.

'Well, we haven't really been going out that long, have we?'

'Long enough. You know right away, anyway, whether you're

in love with someone. That's if you're serious, and not just trying to get me into bed with you.'

'Course I'm serious,' protested Harry, trying to reconcile the fact that they had worked together for years before going out with her latest statement on instantaneous love. In fact she had only fallen in love with him after she had belted him with her handbag, and he wasn't sure that such a start was a good omen or not.

They stood in silence for a while.

'So you'll say yes, then,' asked Harry, to nail the subject down.

Again Allison seemed to consider the idea.

'Tell you what,' she said slowly, 'we get Gertie out safely, lock up those London shits, then when we're having a drink tonight in the Sergeants Arms to celebrate you can announce that I've said yes. Okay?'

'Okay,' replied Harry with little enthusiasm. All he had wanted was a simple one word answer, yes or no. Not a bleeding conditional one, which he wasn't sure he understood.

He had grown up in poverty in London. He had grown up understanding very simple things. Like when you said the wrong thing your mam belted you one. Or your dad. There was a right and a wrong. Do the wrong and you got belted. Simple. What he had never been able to understand was women. But not even that bloke Eisenstein probably understood women, and he had come up with that theory of relatives, hadn't he?

Sergeant Summers would know, he thought to himself. He understood women. He had enough of them after all, didn't he?

'What, precisely, do you think you're doing, Mrs Blower?' asked Phil Walthers primly, keeping his head down.

Mrs Blower made it to the wall next to him, leaned a shoulder against it and took the knife from her mouth, breathing out heavily.

'Gertie said she needed five minutes, Mr Walthers,' she pointed out. 'It might not be much, but those thugs won't come rushing in here if they know we're armed. The first one to cross that doorway is dead meat.'

Walthers shook his head sadly. Just when he thought things couldn't get worse God had sent him Rambo in tweed. With a large bosom.

What exactly did Mrs Blower intend to do? Yell out that she was armed with a knife? That, if anyone tried to enter, they would regret it?

'I warn you, I'm armed,' Mrs Blower called out in a very dignified call. 'I have a knife. Anyone trying to enter will regret it.'

She smiled at Phil Walthers. It was a satisfied smile.

'That ought to do it, don't you think?' she asked. 'For five minutes, anyway.'

'Undoubtedly,' Phil Walthers replied bitterly. 'Such a pity you weren't at Stalingrad, Mrs Blower. The Germans would have surrendered much earlier.'

'Now, now, Mr Walthers, courage. No need for sarcasm. It was pluck and daring that got us through the Blitz, and that's what we need now.'

'Mrs Blower, I rather think I'd exchange pluck and daring for a couple of hand-grenades at the moment.'

'Hand-grenades, Mr Walthers? Be serious. I'm sure you wouldn't even know what to do with a hand-grenade. I certainly wouldn't.'

'No, Mrs Blower, but I dare say we would learn very quickly.'

Mrs Blower considered the point. Then they smiled at each other.

'I believe it was the Finns who first invented the Molotov cocktail,' Phil Walthers noted.

'And we do have some kerosene in the kitchen,' said Mrs Blower, now smiling broadly. 'Or maybe it's paraffin. Anyway, whatever it is, it burns very nicely.'

'I don't think they'll stop to ask for the recipe.'

'Allow me to say, Mr Walthers, that if I was able to choose anyone with whom to spend the last hours of my life in a furious and desperate battle, it would be your gallant self. You understand style and etiquette. And the notion of *je ne sais quoi*. So few do, sadly, these days. The Bulldog spirit appears to have quite gone out of fashion.'

'Allow me to reciprocate, Mrs Blower, by saying that I could wish for no better company in the face of an unquestionable end than your own, my dear lady. I'm afraid these youngsters today have no idea whatsoever. So we shall teach them by example, what say?'

They smiled at each other. One hand reached for another and both squeezed.

'I could not agree more, Mr Walthers. What do you say to the idea that we teach these upstarts outside how Wellburians die?'

'I agree with you wholeheartedly, Mrs Blower,' Phil Walthers said. 'However, perhaps General Eisenhower's words are more apposite. That you do not win a war by dying for your country, but rather by making the other son of a bitch die for his. I quote, naturally.'

'Either way, Mr Walthers, either way. Allow me to say I wouldn't have missed this for the world. I don't think I've felt this young even when I was young.'

'But we are young, Mrs Blower. We are young.'

'Let us then, to recipes ourselves devote, Mr Walthers. I seem to recall that soap was part of the recipe of a Molotov cocktail, though the reason quite escapes me.' She paused. 'I wonder whether that should be biological or automatic?' she asked herself. 'Biological,' she decided, 'it's better for the environment.'

Frank looked at his ringing phone. After a pause he lifted the handset.

'Yes?' he asked.

'Frank? Thank god! It's Gertie. Are you there, Frank?'

'Yes, Gertie! Gertie, are you okay? Where are you? Are you okay? Gertie speak to me!'

'I'm in the Blue Bliss, Frank. I'm okay, I'm fine, really I am. But those two thugs are outside and shooting at us. Phil Walthers almost copped it.'

There was a silence.

'Frank? Are you still there? Hello, Frank? Speak to me Frank.'

'I'm here, Gertie. That's not Campbell and Hovis shooting at you, Gertie, that's Percy and his prats.'

'What?'

'Listen, Gertie, stay away from the windows. I'll get in touch with Percy and explain the situation. Okay?'

'Shit!' said Gertie. 'I've just remembered. They said they were going after Susan to hold as a hostage.'

'Too late now, Gertie, they've already got her.'

Gertie paused.

'Frank, get Percy and his prats off us. I want to go after those two thugs. They'll wish they were dead by the time I've finished with them.'

'They will be dead if I get to them first,' Frank promised.

'Park over by that tree,' Cecil Park said. 'There's a back way in. It's probably better they don't see us.'

'They wouldn't see us if we weren't here at all,' Vic pointed out.

'Stop whinging, Vic,' Jean said. 'Where's your sense of adventure?'

'Sense of adventure? Are you mad? If those two are like some of the others I've met – well, they aren't going to take nicely to us turning up. You don't know them. They don't have any sense of humour, those people.'

'Don't worry, Mr Brown,' Cecil said reassuringly, 'they won't see us. All we're going to do is ascertain whether they are in the house. If so we will call Sergeant Summers and leave the rest up to him.'

'You know what's cute about you, Vic?' asked Jean.

'No.'

'You lose your cockney accent when you get excited.'

There was a pause.

'Apples and pears,' Vic Brown said bitterly. 'Plates of meat.'

'Trouble and strife?' asked Jean.

'That as bloody well,' replied a morose Vic Brown.

'You what?' asked Percy Hanson in a stunned voice. 'Control, repeat that.'

'Campbell and Hovis are no longer in the Blue Bliss. I repeat, Campbell and Hovis are no longer in the Blue Bliss. I don't know who you've been firing on, Inspector, but it isn't them, and Gertie's inside with innocent civilians.'

'Shit!' said Percy. 'Shit! Shit! Shit!'

'Quite so, Inspector,' Control replied.

Percy and Pete Phillips stood up slowly.

In the Blue Bliss Mrs Blower peeked over the windowsill before dropping down again.

'They're coming, Mr Walthers,' she said.

Phil Walthers looked at the rod in his hand.

'Well, I suppose I could do someone some damage with this,' he said. 'If I catch them as they cross the threshold. It should slow them down if I can whip it across one of their faces.'

'Such a pity,' said Mrs Blower. 'I was looking forward to those Molotov cocktails. I suppose we shall have to rely on cold steel.'

'Yes, I suppose so. Still, they don't like it up them, do they? Or so I'm told.'

'Pass me the megaphone, Sergeant,' Percy told a chastened

Pete Phillips. Pete picked it up and handed it over. Percy switched it on and raised it to his mouth.

Just then a furious Nelson launched himself at Percy, burying his fangs in Percy's buttocks.

'Did you catch what they said, Mr Walthers?' asked Mrs Blower.

'Sounded like a scream, Mrs Blower. A war cry, perhaps.'

'I'll give them a war cry.' She looked at the knife in her hands. 'I don't suppose you know, Mr Walthers, but does one cut from the right or the left? I'm not sure there's an etiquette about this type of thing.'

'I very much doubt that they'll be bothered about that. No standards, these modern London thugs. No tradition, I'm afraid.'

'Ah, they might not have standards, Mr Walthers, but I do. There is always a proper way to do things. My cousin Samuel once disgraced himself when he was eight by using a steak knife during the fish course.'

Phil Walthers considered this for a moment.

'That is bad,' he commented.

Frank was about to leave for the house in Glenbourne Avenue when his phone rang again. Frowning, he returned to his desk and picked it up.

'Frank? Gertie again. Listen, there was something I forgot to tell you. Campbell and Malone have hijacked an ambulance. That's how they got away from here.'

'An ambulance? Right, thanks for that, Gertie, they won't be able to hide that very easily. How are things at the Blue Bliss?'

'Percy and Pete are walking towards us now. Very slowly. Percy's limping for some reason. I'm not sure whether they're worried that Campbell and Hovis are still here, or worried about the reception they're going to get when I get my hands on them. If I get to them before Mrs Blower and Mr Walthers, that is. They weren't very amused when I explained what had happened.'

'Forget them, Gerts my sweet. Get back here as fast as you can.'

'Okay, Frank. I'll sort those two out later.'

Frank turned to Frieda.

'Campbell and Hovis have got their hands on an ambulance,' he said. 'That's how they made their getaway from the Blue Bliss.'

'I'll alert everyone, we'll get the number of the missing ambulance,' Frieda said. She paused. 'Okay, Frank, you get that painting to Glenbourne Avenue. I'm going to pack Lords Acres with unmarked cars to back you up.'

'They mustn't do anything until we're sure Susan's safe.'

'Don't worry, Frank, they won't, I'll make sure of that.'

Frank looked at the rifle. He took the pistol out of his pocket and put it on his desk.

'Better not,' he said.

'No, Frank, better not.'

'Just in case they surprise me. We don't want to hand over real guns to them, after all.'

'I can't see anyone inside,' Cecil Park said, peering at the back of the house in Glenbourne Avenue from behind a bush.

'No, obviously empty, waste of time, let's get out of here,' said Vic Brown.

'Shush, Vic,' Jean reproved him. 'I thought I saw a movement then. In the kitchen.'

'Probably just a burglar, nothing to do with us.'

'No, I think it's one of them,' Cecil said.

They peered through the bush for a while without seeing or hearing anything else. Jean was just about to say something when a voice spoke behind them.

'Well, well. M Matisse and Captain Tromperie. Would you care to introduce your friend?' They turned around slowly to find Campbell pointing a gun at them.

'Miserable, incompetent, bloody useless excuses for police officers!' Gertie greeted Percy and Pete Phillips as they walked carefully into the reception of the Blue Bliss.

'Look, love –'

'Don't you bloody look love me, Inspector Hanson. I'll have you for sexism as well as the rest. I need a car. Now.'

'We're all going back to the station, Gertie.'

'What about the explosives?' asked Phil Walthers.

'Explosives?'

'Campbell said they'd booby-trapped this place,' Gertie explained. 'I'll leave you to look after that. I'm going back to the station. I hope they blow you up, you mindless, cretinous, moronic ... morons!'

She swept past them.

'And someone is going to have to clear this mess up,' Mrs Blower said indignantly.

The only happy party seemed to be Nelson, lying in his reclaimed hiding place, chewing on a piece of trouser.

'Control to all teams,' crackled Harry Wheatley's radio. 'Campbell and Malone have hijacked an ambulance. They are dressed as paramedics. They have Doctor Pleadle and a woman from the Blue Bliss hostage. They are pretending that the woman is in labour. Report immediately any ambulances in your area.'

Harry's face went pale.

'It – it couldn't have been,' whispered Allison.

Harry tried to find support for this statement but failed.

'No. It was. It was those bastards. Oh my god. Oh my god.'

Control's mistaken assertion that Sonia was in the ambulance was at that moment being disproved by Susan's boss, Doctor Woods. The mild mannered man had walked into Susan's office for a reason he immediately forgot when he discovered a young woman in Susan's chair, gagged and bound hand and foot, a terrified look in her eyes.

He stopped abruptly, his face a picture of incredulity.

'I do apologise,' he said politely, gathering himself together and moving behind Susan's desk to remove the gag from the young woman's mouth. 'I'm not used to finding beautiful young women tied up, waiting to be rescued. Much as I might have dreamed of the occasion when I was a youngster.'

He looked at Sonia who was breathing deeply, sucking clean air into her lungs.

'I'm not often given to the use of epithets,' he said, 'so I do hope you will excuse me when I ask you a little question. Just what the hell is going on?'

'I'm Sonia,' Sonia said huskily, 'and you are the sexiest man I have ever met.'

Doctor Woods nodded understandingly.

'You're suffering from shock, my dear. I think a strong cup of tea is called for.'

'I'm just turning into Glenbourne Avenue now,' Frank said into his radio.

'Could you go around the block once, Sarge?' requested Control. 'The backup-up units aren't in place.'

'Sod the back-up units, I'm going in.'

'Sarge –'

Frank switched his radio off and put it into his jacket pocket. It met with resistance.

Damn, thought Frank, that blasted dummy grenade.

He took the grenade out and tucked it into a pocket under the bullet-proof vest. It might still prove useful, and the thickness of the vest would prevent it from being noticeable.

'I think I'll have the French bint,' Malone said, looking down at Jean who was sitting on the kitchen floor between Cecil Park and Vic Brown. Their legs were tied, their arms bound behind their backs.

'I told you, stop thinking about birds,' Campbell said irritably. 'It's going to be difficult enough to pull this off without you thinking about totty the whole time.'

'I owe her one,' Malone insisted. 'She needs a lesson in respect.'

'You will not get away with this,' Jean said in her French accent, re-adopting the guise of Captain Tromperie. 'The French police will hunt you down wherever you choose to hide. And you will find out that we are not so civilised as the British with scum like you. I would advise you to surrender to your own police while you still have the chance. We still send people like you to Devil's Island. From there you will never escape alive.'

'And you're going to find out how civilised I am with rude little French bitches,' Hovis said angrily. 'Probably enjoy it as well, you little tart.'

'Shut it!' said Campbell. 'Summers is coming up the drive. Get into place.'

Frank paused at the front door. It was ajar. He pushed it open carefully. He walked slowly along the passage until he came to the kitchen. Stepping inside he was confronted with the sight of the three sitting tied up, against the wall, Hovis leaning against a work surface, a sneer of victory on his face.

'Looks like we're going to have a party. You got that picture, copper?'

Frank nodded. He held up the rolled canvas in his hand.

'Where's Doctor Pleadle?' he asked.

'Safe,' said Campbell behind him, pointing his gun at Frank.

'Mugsy, check him for a gun. Take his radio away.'

Mugsy searched Frank's jacket, taking his radio from his pocket.

'No gun, boss,' he told Campbell. 'Not in his jacket, anyway.'

'No gun?' asked Campbell smiling. 'And there I was, thinking that all the plods – sorry, police officers – in Wellbury were running around armed to the teeth, ready to shoot on sight. Can't believe a word you're told these days, can you?'

Hovis bent down, patting Frank's trouser legs, searching for a weapon.

'Do stop that, Mugsy,' said Campbell. 'Sergeant Summers is a British police officer, not Dirty Harry. He is hardly likely to have a Derringer strapped to his ankle. It isn't his style, is it, Sergeant?'

'Here's The Blue Studio. Where's Doctor Pleadle?' Frank asked.

'Let's have a look at that painting first. Put it on the counter there. Unroll it and move away from it.'

Frank did as bid. Campbell and Hovis stepped up to look at the canvas.

'Doesn't look like much,' Hovis said, 'a two year old kid could do that.'

'You don't understand art, Mugsy,' Campbell replied with the air of one who does. 'What you are looking at is a masterpiece painted by Matisse about a hundred years ago. Fifty million quid's worth.' He cocked his head while looking at the painting. 'Mind you, I wouldn't pay fifty pence for this. Still, each to his own. If some rich art collector thinks it's worth fifty million, then it's worth fifty million. Don't you agree,

Sergeant Summers?'

'Where's Doctor Pleadle?'

'Safe and sound, Sergeant, safe and sound. And she will remain so, so long as you do as you're told.'

'We agreed a deal, Campbell, the painting for Doctor Pleadle.'

'And so it shall be. But you don't think we have Doctor Pleadle here, do you? Oh, no, Sergeant, so long as you do what I say she will be returned to you unharmed. Try something funny and you'll get her back in bits and pieces.'

Frank did not reply. The dead hatred in his eyes told Campbell all he needed to know.

'Now,' Campbell continued, looking away, 'I have no doubt that everyone knows you're here. I am quite sure that you told your Inspector exactly what was going on. And by now she will know about the ambulance. So we're going to give her an ambulance. It's parked in the garage. You are going to drive it around for an hour. Not too fast, not too slow. But no stopping. Ambulances have transponders, devices which send a radio signal to let their base know where they are. We've just changed the frequency on the one you are going to be driving. It's a frequency which we will be tracking instead. If we see that the ambulance stops moving so does Doctor Pleadle. Permanently. Understand?'

'You're mad,' Frank said. 'I can't drive through stop signs and traffic lights.'

'It's an ambulance, Sergeant. It has flashing lights and a siren. No need to stop for other traffic.' He tossed Frank a set of keys. 'One hour, Sergeant. By then we will be out of your life forever and you will have Doctor Pleadle back in your arms.' He smiled. 'And don't bother warning me about roadblocks or asking how we're going to get out of here. When you figure it out no doubt you'll kick yourself. It really is very simple when you think about it. Now go. I'm sure we both wish to get this over as soon as possible.'

Frank backed out of the kitchen and then ran down the passage and to the garage. He pulled open the doors, jumped into the ambulance, reversed out of the garage and drove it down the driveway. He wasn't sure whether Campbell had been lying about a tracking device, but he knew he wasn't going to take the chance. But how was he to warn Frieda that Campbell and Hovis would be in his car and he was in the ambulance? If he couldn't manage that, everybody would be gaily chasing him in the ambulance while Campbell and Hovis made their getaway in his car.

Back in the kitchen Campbell smiled at the three sitting against the wall.

'I'm afraid you three will just have to wait until someone comes to rescue you. It shouldn't be too long.' He waved the canvas at Cecil Park. 'To think of all the trouble you could have avoided, M Matisse. And you a Frenchman, you should have known better than to upset the English. Captain Tromperie, I would like to be able to say it's been a pleasure, but I'd be lying. Come, Mugsy, time to transfer Doctor Pleadle from the garden shed to the boot of Sergeant Summers' car.'

'We just going to leave these three here? Like this?'

Campbell paused.

'You know, I think not. A small change of plan. But first gag them. And untie their legs.'

'Chopper One to Control, Chopper One to Control.'

'Control here, Chopper One, go ahead.'

'We've got your ambulance for you. Number on the roof is confirmed. It's heading towards the Old Town.'

'Roger, Chopper One. Keep it in sight. We're going to give these boys the biggest surprise they'll ever have. They aren't going to get away this time. They either stop or we are going to stop them. By the time we've finished with them they will need an ambulance. Or a hearse more likely.'

Frank looked at the ambulance radio in his hand. It must have been Campbell's sense of humour. Whoever had cut the wires had carefully replaced them to look as if they were undamaged. Until he picked the radio up.

For a moment he wished he had joined the almost universal urge to own a mobile phone. The thought didn't last long. Campbell would have taken that from him as well.

So how the hell was he going to keep the ambulance moving and still alert Frieda to the current situation? And where were they holding Susan? And was she okay?

He took the grenade from underneath the bullet-proof vest and put it back in his pocket. It had started chafing. It had become just another irritant that he could do without.

'I didn't know we were tracking that ambulance,' Hovis said as he drove Frank's car.

'We aren't, Mugsy. But will Sergeant Summers take that chance?'

'A bit like the explosives we didn't put in that nightclub,' laughed Hovis.

'Just so, Mugsy, just so. People will believe the most impossible things if you say them the right way.'

'So what's this plan, boss? How're we going to get out of this place?'

'Ah, yes. A plan,' Campbell said thoughtfully.

'You do have a plan, don't you, boss? You told that copper it was so simple he'd kick himself when he found out.'

'Well, that was rather to get him to chase himself in circles looking for something that doesn't exist, Mugsy.'

'But we gotta have a plan, boss, otherwise how are we going to get out of here?'

Campbell considered this for a moment. Mugsy was the sort of person who would trust any plan, no matter how unbelievable. Like a child believing in the tooth fairy.

'Okay, Mugsy, let's say there's Plan A and Plan B. Plan A is that, if we can't find an unguarded exit, we wait until we get close to one of the roadblocks, put the siren on and drive like hell – I presume there will be a siren in this car. Do it right and they'll let us through without checking, especially if they recognise Sergeant Summers' car. By the time they realise what's happened we'll be far away and have dumped the car.'

'And Plan B?'

'Plan B? We dump the car in Wellbury and find somewhere to hole up for a few days.'

'Where, boss?'

'The last place they'd look, that's where.'

'Good one, boss,' Hovis chuckled. 'That'll fool them.'

Campbell sighed inwardly. He still had to work out where the "last place they'd look" was. What should have been a very simple and lucrative job had gone badly, badly wrong, and it looked as if it was going to get a lot worse. Mugsy had proved useful in the past, but the basic truth was that he was now worse than an encumbrance. He wished that he had the ruthless streak to do what he knew to be the common sense thing to do – dump Mugsy and move on his own. He could move and think faster on his own, and the police were looking for two men together, as a singleton he would stand a better chance of slipping through the net.

The problem was, how could he get rid of Mugsy? The man was as thick as they came, but he'd soon smell something fishy if he suggested they should split up. And his reaction would be that of the Neanderthal he was.

Still, it was a chance worth taking. Especially if he could do it so that Mugsy ended up in the arms of the law. The coppers would be too busy concentrating on Mugsy to spot himself slipping away quietly.

He smiled to himself. It was an ingenious plan. But then he was an ingenious man.

'Control to Chopper One, I've got three cars on an interception course. Is the ambulance still headed for the Old Town?'

'Chopper One to Control, there's something strange going on.'

'Control to Chopper One, repeat please.'

'I said there was something strange going on, Control.'

'Explain yourself, Chopper One. What is the location of the

ambulance?'

'If you look out of your window you'll see it, Control. It's circling the police station. I think they're showing you the finger.'

Frieda looked at the radio in front of her with eyes that widened in surprise and then narrowed in fury. She took the pistol from her waistband and ran from the ops room down the corridor, into reception and then outside onto the entrance steps. Two uniformed officers had got there first. They were gaping at the sight of the back of an ambulance disappearing around the corner at about fifteen miles an hour.

'What the hell do those bastards think they're playing at?' she asked rhetorically. She pumped a bullet into the breech of the pistol. 'I know what they're going to get, though. Ed, get two armed officers out here now. Steve, get someone to block off that ambulance's path.'

'Er, Inspector, there's something you should know,' Ed Watts said.

'Not now, Constable, not now, just do as you're ordered.'

'Er, Inspector, it's Sergeant Summers driving the ambulance.'

Frieda paused before exploding.

'What?'

'Sergeant Summers is driving the ambulance, Inspector. He was trying to shout something to us, but we couldn't hear what he was saying. Look, here he comes again.'

Frieda watched in amazement as the ambulance reappeared, travelling slowly, with Frank Summers' head out the window shouting something about Susan.

'Well, don't just bloody well stand there,' she said as the

ambulance disappeared around the corner again, 'Ed, get some uniforms out to keep the roads clear.'

'Sorry, Inspector, I thought you just said –'

'Not now, constable, not now, just do as you're told. Steve, run as fast as you can the other way around, shout to Frank that he's to open the passenger door on his next pass.'

As Steve Right disappeared on his mission Frieda kicked her shoes off and put the pistol back into her waistband.

'If I'd known that this was going to happen I would have worn trainers, not high heels,' she muttered as she crossed the road.

She waited until the ambulance was about twenty feet away before starting to run, trying to look in front of her and at the approaching ambulance behind at the same time. She was doing about eight miles an hour when the open passenger door came alongside. She moved into a sprint, grabbed on to the frame and hauled herself inside.

'I'm impressed,' Frank said with a smile. Frieda smiled back breathlessly, a lock of hair hanging loosely over one eye.

'Me too, I haven't done that sort of thing for ages,' she said.

Their smiles lingered, and then disappeared as they remembered what they were doing. Frank explained the situation quickly as he continued to circle the police station.

'Your car?' she asked, puzzled. 'I don't see how that's going to help much, even if they did get an hour's grace.'

'That's what I can't work out. Campbell's obviously got some plan or other, and he's confident it's going to work. The only thing I can think of is that they're going to try to get through one of the roadblocks with light flashing and siren going. But they can't do that without being recognised. It doesn't make sense. Not unless Campbell is stupid, and he hasn't come across that way to me. Delusional, perhaps, but not stupid.'

'We'll have to worry about that later. Drop me off on the next pass. I'll have someone get you a radio so that we can stay in contact.'

Frank slowed down as much as he dared, and Frieda stepped out, hitting the road running. She slowed down and limped back to the entrance. Gertie was waiting on the steps.

'Gertie, thank god you're safe,' she said, giving her a hug.

'I would have got back sooner, but we were diverted to chase that ambulance. What's happening?'

'Come on, I'll tell you inside,' Frieda replied, 'after I've sorted something out.'

Frieda opened the door to the Control room.

'Sid, alert all officers that Campbell and Hovis have taken Frank's car. The details will be on the computer. If they don't stop they're to open fire, tyres first. Tell them not to hit the petrol tank, whatever they do. Oh, and they have Frank's radio as well. Send out a message warning everyone to change frequencies.'

'Petrol tank?' asked Gertie.

'They might well have Susan with them, quite possibly in the boot. I don't want to take chances.'

'Not to hit the petrol tank whatever we do?' queried Harry Wheatley. 'Why does that sound like one of those orders which means the opposite of what it says? Why tell us not to do something we wouldn't have done anyway? Reminds me of a sergeant I once knew who would say "don't be too heavy on the suspect" when he meant beat the crap out of him.'

'Accidents happen with these things,' Allison Harding replied. 'And I don't intend to take any chances with a pair of armed thugs. If we hit the petrol tank by mistake and it blows up, well ... tough.'

'But what about Doctor Pleadle? Couldn't she be in the car?'

'Obviously Inspector Garold knows more than we do. She must know that Doctor Pleadle isn't in the car.'

Harry Wheatley sighed.

'Sometimes I wish our so-called senior officers could just say what they mean,' he said. 'I don't like these half-hints and innuendo things.'

'I need to get a radio to Frank,' Frieda said as she slowly and painfully put on a pair of trainers Tricia had brought down from her office. She winced. 'That tarmac is not good for the feet. And my stockings are ruined.'

'I'll take one to him,' offered Gertie. Frieda looked at her.

'You mean you'll try the same trick and jump in alongside him?' she asked.

Gertie shrugged.

'If they are tracking the ambulance it won't be long until they work out where he is, and why he's driving in circles. Instead of doing that we could be out going after Campbell and Hovis in the ambulance.'

Frieda thought about this.

'Very well, but no taking chances, Gertie. We've already been scared to death about you once today.'

'I owe those two thugs. And Susan's still out there somewhere.'

'Frank's firearms are still in his office. Take them with you.'

Gertie went to the office they shared. Inside she quickly swapped her shoes for an old pair of running shoes she had once brought to work in the overly-optimistic idea that she would use her lunch hours to get some fitness training in. She slipped them on, picked up the pistol and put it into her handbag. She looked at the rifle, decided against taking it, and ran down to collect a radio.

'Got everything?' asked Frieda as Gertie passed her in reception.

'Yup. I left the rifle behind, don't fancy trying to jump into a moving ambulance with that thing on my back.'

'I'll get someone to retrieve it from Frank's office. I don't like having firearms littering the place. You've got a firearm yourself?'

'I've got Frank's pistol,' Gertie said, patting her handbag.

'Here, take mine for yourself, Gertie,' Frieda replied, pulling the weapon from her waistband. 'I don't know why I asked for one in the first place. Hardly likely to need one inside the station. Panic reaction, I suppose. Be careful, there's already a bullet in the breech.'

'Thanks. I know just what I'll do with this if it comes to that.'

They looked at each for a few seconds.

'Take care of yourself, Gertie.'

'Will do.' She paused. 'Suppose I'd better go join that silly sod out there before he gets dizzy driving in circles.'

She turned and ran outside. The ambulance was just passing

as she came out. She waved at Frank, put two fingers in her mouth and whistled.

'Taxi!' she shouted exuberantly. She ran across the road to wait for the next circuit. When Frank reappeared she emulated Frieda's method of boarding a moving ambulance with the minor modification of diving in, almost landing head-first in his lap. Once she had sorted herself out she turned to him, beaming.

'Where to, Sarge?' she asked. He smiled back at her.

'It's good to see you, Gerts, I was a little worried for a moment.'

'Only a little, Sarge?'

He laughed and ruffled her hair.

'Watch the road, Sarge, you'll get us killed.'

'Only two people I want killed today,' he said grimly, paying attention to the road. 'Tell Control we're on our way back to Lords Acres. The hour will be up by the time we get there. There are three people who need untying, to start with.'

'Campbell and Hovis might still be there,' Gertie pointed out.

'I know it's a possibility, but I doubt it. Campbell's obviously got some plan. I just wish I knew what it was. But I tell you something. When I catch up with those two I'm going to beat the merry shit out of them and shove their fake firearms somewhere the sun doesn't shine.'

'Leave one of them for me, Sarge.'

Control informed them that two patrol cars would be joining them soon as backup.

'Here they come,' Harry Wheatley said grimly as the sound of a siren reached them. 'The bastards must think we were born yesterday.'

Allison Harding and three other officers checked their weapons and pointed them in the direction of the oncoming vehicle. Two police cars formed a roadblock that would leave no innocent driver in doubt that stopping might be a good idea.

'They're about two hundred yards away, Control,' Harry said into his radio.

'Roger. Other units are coming your way to cut them off. Do not let them through whatever happens.'

'Don't worry about that, Control,' Harry whispered, his throat tightening as the vehicle came towards them without losing any speed.

Two police cars pulled up behind the ambulance parked at the end of Glenbourne Avenue. Four officers got out and joined Frank.

'This is the plan,' he said after introductions had been made. 'You two take the road behind this one. Park at the back of number 70. Make sure you can be seen without it being obvious. Pretend to be using your radio every so often. If they are in there we want them to think that we're not actually coming in, just hanging around. That way they won't move until we're ready. You two,' he said, turning to the other pair, 'wait until we're inside the grounds. There should be enough cover for us to get to the house without being seen. Give us five minutes, and then drive halfway up the drive. Just wait there. We'll radio if we need you.'

'What are you going to do?'

'Find out if Campbell and Hovis are hiding in there somewhere. If they are we'll slip out and arrange for reinforcements before trying to take them. Okay, Gertie, radio off. We don't want to give ourselves away accidentally.'

Only Gertie amongst them knew that Frank had no intention of doing any such thing. If Campbell and Hovis were in there he was going to found out where Susan was by any method necessary.

'Shit!' swore Campbell. 'They aren't going to break!'

'What shall I do, boss?'

'Do? Make the fastest bloody u-turn you've ever done and get the fuck out of here! Those bastards with the guns look like they intend to use them.'

Hovis pulled on the handbrake and swung the wheel over.

'They're trying to get away!' called Harry Wheatley. Allison Harding raised her gun.

'No they don't,' she said and squeezed the trigger. The three alongside did the same.

'Jesus! They're fucking firing at us!' exclaimed Campbell, trying to keep his head down.

'Well, fire back!'

'With what? Replica guns? Fakes?'

'They ain't fakes, boss,' Hovis said, a small smile on his face as he pushed the accelerator as far as it would go. 'They wanted too much for the fakes, so I bought real ones instead. They were loads cheaper.'

'Real ones?' asked Campbell in disbelief. 'Are you out of your tiny fucking mind? Do you know what we'll get if we're caught with real guns?'

'Well, we're getting shot at right now, aren't we, boss?' Hovis pointed out with the happiness of someone not intellectually equipped to understand the import of the situation.

Campbell had his head stuck beneath the dashboard. He tried to turn it to look at Hovis. It was a look of disbelief. He wanted to say something, but was unsure of what.

'Where to now, boss?' Hovis asked happily.

Campbell considered this request for directions. He was still trying to come to terms with the idea that, instead of the gentleman's game of bluff and guile he had thought he was controlling, he was now an armed criminal with more heavily armed police after him, and no-one was in control.

'Boss?' prompted Hovis.

Campbell gritted his teeth.

'Take the first turning you can,' he said slowly, 'slow down, find some back streets where we can dump the car. We'll have to nick another one, and quick.'

'But what about –'

'Never mind what about! Just do it!'

What really worried him was the smell of petrol coming from the back.

'Control, they're getting away,' Harry Wheatley said. 'One of our cars is about to go after them.'

'Hold that car,' Control replied. 'All road blocks to stay in place. They might double back.'

'They won't get far,' Allison noted. 'I'm pretty sure at least two bullets hit the boot. They're probably leaking petrol all over the place.'

'Control, suspects' car has received several hits,' Harry said over the radio. 'No indication that any of the tyres were hit, but damage may include hits to the boot and petrol tank.'

There was a pause. A long pause.

'Repeat that last statement, constable,' Control requested slowly.

Frieda stood in the ops room studying the map of Wellbury when Percy Hanson walked in.

'Looks like we've got them now,' he remarked.

'How do you mean?' asked Frieda absentmindedly.

'Didn't you catch that last report?'

'What last report?' asked Frieda, looking at her radio and realising that it was silent, and had been for some while.

She shook it, but it remained stubbornly mute.

'Of all the times to go on the blink,' she growled. 'Bloody useless thing!' She hurled the offending radio at the wall, where it shattered into several pieces.

'I'll get you another,' offered Percy, nervously.

'Make it two, just in case,' she said as he left. She turned back to the map. She wondered idly what she had missed, presuming, from Percy's lack of emotion that it could not have been anything important.

Frank and Gertie slipped quickly and quietly through the

garden of the house in Glenbourne Avenue, pistols at the ready. They could see no sign of movement at any of the windows. When they reached the door Frank gestured to Gertie to take one side, while he gripped the handle firmly and slowly pushed the door inwards. He leaned forward slowly and peered down the hallway. Nothing moved. The house seemed silent.

He entered the hallway, carefully avoiding stepping on any shards from the broken vases, followed by Gertie. Slowly and silently they made their way along the passage, pausing at each doorway before suddenly whipping in, crouched, pistols pointing, looking for a target just as they had been trained to do. Frank could not help but feel a certain foolishness. After all, the men they were going after were armed with nothing more than fakes, and here they were imitating some B-grade American cop movie.

Ten minutes later it was apparent that no-one was concealed on the ground floor. They came to the stairway and Frank gestured towards the ceiling with a thumb. Gertie nodded and they began to ascend the stairs slowly and softly. If Campbell and Hovis were still around they would most probably have taken the high ground, not only as a better observation post, but because it would be easier to hold. And they would have the other three with them, Cecil Park, Jean and Vic Brown.

Once upstairs they moved swiftly from open door to open door, covering each other. Five minutes were sufficient to confirm that all the rooms were all empty.

'Looks like –' Gertie began. Frank held a finger to his lips.

There was a slight knock from the ceiling, as if someone had accidentally kicked something.

'Attic,' Frank mouthed at Gertie.

'Control, Inspector Garold here,' Frieda said into the radio Percy had returned with. 'I've been off air for a few minutes. What's the latest?'

As she listened an increasing look of disbelief and horror crept over her face.

'Oh my god, no,' she whispered, 'not Susan. Please not Susan.'

Frank and Gertie looked up. In the middle of the passage ceiling they could see a trapdoor. Frank motioned Gertie to one doorway while he took another, their guns pointed at the trapdoor. Slowly someone began to open it, clumsily.

Frank held up a finger to Gertie, pointing upwards. Then he made walking movements with two fingers, pointed towards the ground, held up two fingers together, and then pulled a finger across his neck. Gertie nodded and gave him a thumbs up. Wait until they're on the ground, both of them. And then take them out.

The trapdoor scraped open. Muffled voices came from beyond it, raised in anger. Slowly a pair of legs appeared.

Bare legs.

Then a skirt.

A body plummeted down, hitting the floor and rolling over, swearing what would have been imprecations at the ceiling had Jean not been gagged, with her arms tied behind her back. Still swearing she eased herself up until she was sitting against a wall and tried to stretch a bruised shoulder. It was some seconds before she turned to see the amazed eyes of Frank and Gertie on her.

She swore at them too.

Frank held a finger to his lips for the third time, desperately gesturing for her to shut up and come towards them. After some more muffled oaths she struggled to her feet and staggered towards them.

'Who else is up there?' he whispered into her ear. 'Campbell? Hovis?'

She turned her head around so fast it hit Frank's. A spurt of invective suggested that the answer was no.

Frank untied the gag. She breathed deeply and then spat.

'God! That rag was revolting,' she said. 'I do not want to know what it was last used to clean. The drains, by the taste of it.'

'Who is up there?' Frank demanded softly.

'Who do you think? Laurel and fucking Hardy, that's who,' she replied. 'Go on, look at them.'

Gertie and Frank turned back towards the trapdoor. Cecil Park's and Vic Brown's gagged faces looked down at them.

'We'll let you down, they said,' continued Jean bitterly. 'You won't get hurt, they said. Forgot to mention the bit about dropping me. Or maybe they'll claim they did mention it, only it got lost in their gags. I should have wondered how they were planning to let me down gently with their arms tied behind their backs and them looking the wrong way.'

'You seem to have lost something,' Gertie noted without much affection. 'A French accent, for a start.'

'Not now, Gertie,' Frank said. He turned back to Jean. 'Where are Campbell and Hovis?'

'Long gone, I would say. Made us climb up there with our hands tied behind our backs, and told us not to move because they'd be downstairs. Finally we realised they must have gone and those two came up with the wonderful idea of dropping me out of the bloody sky.'

'Gertie,' said Frank, 'see if you can find a ladder and get those two down.' He turned back to Jean. 'Did they say where Susan was? Doctor Pleadle?'

Her face dropped.

'They –'

'Yes? Come on, what did they do?'

'They said they were going to put her in the boot of your car. They had her in the garden shed. Frank, I'm sorry, I couldn't warn you. They only said it when you'd left.'

Frank didn't answer. He took out his radio and switched it on.

'Summers to Control,' he called. 'Come in Control.'

'Control here, Sergeant, go ahead.'

'Those bastards have got Susan – Doctor Pleadle – in the boot of my car. Make sure everyone knows that.'

There was a pause before Control replied.

'Will do, Sergeant,' he said softly.

Jean looked up at Frank's furious face.

'I know you feel like punching someone,' she said gently, 'but if it has to be me, could you untie my arms afterwards please?'

At a roadblock on the outskirts of Wellbury five officers

stood, having overheard the exchange, unable to look at each other.

'We probably didn't hit the petrol tank,' Allison said finally.

No-one replied. They knew that that was exactly what they had done.

'Control to Foxtrot Seven, come in Foxtrot Seven.'

'Foxtrot Seven here, Control, over.'

'Foxtrot Seven, report your current operation.'

'We're just sitting here at the moment, Control.'

'Foxtrot Seven you're to drive to the Blue Bliss. Alpha Three are already there. They'll explain the situation.'

The two constables were sitting in the car watching the back of 70 Glenbourne Avenue. The driver shrugged.

'They know what they're doing,' he said.

'Roger, Control, on our way,' the other told his radio.

'They'll have the description of this car pretty shortly,' Campbell said as they drove in an old fashioned mini that Hovis had broken into.

'This old thing?' asked Hovis in surprise. 'Nobody's going to miss this thing in a hurry.'

'This is just the sort of thing people will miss,' Campbell said. 'Probably someone's pride and joy. And even if they don't nobody's going to ignore the sight of two big blokes crammed into a mini. Take the next right. We'll dump it and walk a few blocks before nicking another.'

'And then, boss?'

'Then we drive to their bloody Lords Acres, stop a few streets away, and hole up in the one place they'll never think of. Matisse's place. That attic will come in very handy.'

'But won't the coppers be there?'

'They can't be everywhere, can they? They don't know we put those other three in the attic. That Sergeant Summers has probably been back, had a look and left, presuming we've taken the others with us. Most they'll have is one or two uniforms standing outside looking bored. We'll slip in the back way. So long as we keep dead quiet they'll never suspect a thing.'

Any average person would have recognised it as a mixture of desperation and wishful thinking.

'I'll be able to carry on where I left off with that French totty,' Hovis said happily.

Campbell closed his eyes. He no longer cared. All he wanted to do was get out. Not even The Blue Studio mattered any more. He had never intended to hurt Doctor Pleadle, and he had definitely never intended to end up being shot at. It had all been a huge bluff.

Unfortunately they had believed him.

'Control, we've recovered that car,' Bobby Stang said. 'The one, er, that was leaking petrol. The fire brigade say it's too dangerous to approach. They want to smother it with foam first. They don't think anyone could be alive in it.'

'Negative, Control,' Frieda's voice said. 'Tell them to hold on. I'll be there in twenty minutes. Half an hour at most.'

'Negative, Inspector,' Allison said. 'I'm ten minutes away. I'll do it. It's my responsibility.'

'Control, is that my car we're talking about?' asked a voice.

There was a long pause.

'I'm sorry, Frank,' Control said.

Harry Wheatley turned to Allison.

'I'll go,' he said. 'You stay here. Someone has to man the roadblock.'

'I pulled the trigger, Harry. I have to do it.'

'I won't let you, Allison. You stay here.'

'We'll go together,' she said finally and almost firmly.

'We'll get you lot off to hospital,' Frank said in the kitchen of number 70 Glenbourne Avenue, a grim look on his face, his eyes looking nowhere blankly. 'Routine check-up, just in case.'

He and Gertie had pocketed their firearms and untied Cecil Park and Vic Brown before leading them down to the kitchen. Cecil Park seemed to have aged twenty years since he had last been in his cell.

'I don't need a hospital,' Jean said firmly. 'I'm fine. And we've caused this. So we might as well do our bit to help clear it up. Plus there's something I'd like to do to that Hovis thing.'

'The ambulance is already on its way,' Frank said tiredly, irritated. 'Anyway, there's nothing you can do. It doesn't matter any more. It just doesn't bloody matter any more, okay?'

Jean looked at him in concern. Gertie noticed the look.

'I like ambulances,' said a voice from the door.

They turned to find Hovis pointing his gun at them.

'Hovis,' said Frank, his eyes brightening. 'Just the bastard I've been looking for.'

'Don't go for your gun, Summers. I can drop you before you can blink,' Hovis said, moving into the kitchen

'I'm not worried about your fake little replica, Hovis, but it does give me the excuse to give you what's coming to you.'

'It's not fake, Sergeant,' Campbell said, leaning against the doorway. 'I'm sorry, he bought real ones. He wasn't supposed to do that.'

Frank gave a bitter smile.

'Doesn't make much difference, now. I'm not worried about dying. I haven't anything left to live for. But I'll take the son of a bitch with me.'

'I'm sorry, we can't let you go further,' the fire chief said to Harry and Allison.

'You think you're going to stop us?' asked Allison. He looked at the firearm in her hands.

'Guess not,' he said.

Harry nodded and they continued walking towards the car. The keys were in the ignition. He took them out and walked to the boot. It took several pulls to open it.

'Fuck me,' whispered Harry Wheatley.

Allison turned and threw up.

'I warn you, copper,' Hovis said as Frank put his hand in his trouser pocket. 'I'm going to pull the trigger.'

'I'm not reaching for my gun, Hovis. It's in my jacket pocket.

Would you like me to take it out and throw it down in front of you?'

'You do that, copper,' Hovis snarled, sweat forming on his brow.

Frank took his hand from his trouser pocket, put a thumb and a finger into his jacket pocket, withdrew his pistol carefully and tossed it down in front of Hovis.

Hovis looked down at it, and then back at Frank with a triumphant sneer.

'Not so brave after all, are you, Summers?' he began. Then his eyes screamed open with fear at the thing Frank had taken from his other pocket while Hovis' attention had been diverted.

'Recognise it, Hovis?' In his left hand he held the dummy grenade. The pin was swinging between the thumb and first finger of his right.

He dropped the pin slowly.

'It's a grenade, Hovis. The pin's out. It has a three second fuse. Three seconds after I let the clip open, Hovis. Three seconds. No chance of you getting away before it goes bang. You pull the trigger and you're dead. You can drop your gun or take the consequences. Your choice.'

He took a pace towards the other man, whose eyes were riveted on the grenade. Hovis stepped back.

'You're mad! You'll kill us all!'

'I don't have anything to live for, Hovis. Doesn't bother me too much.'

'Non!' cried Jean, stepping forward in front of Frank. 'This is not the way to do this. You, Hovis, you will put that gun down. Now! As a French police officer I am ordering you to.'

'Shove your orders,' responded Hovis, almost whispering, his attention still on the grenade in Frank's hand. 'You aren't going to take me in, I know what your jails are like, you French bitch. I'm not ending up in bloody Devil's Island. Not me.'

Behind Hovis a weary Campbell lifted his pistol and aimed it at Hovis's back.

'Get out of the way, Jean!' shouted Frank, trying to push Jean to one side. She shook him off and lunged at Hovis. Hovis's pistol went off.

So did Campbell's.

The grenade fell to the floor, bounced, and the clip sprang open.

'It's empty!' breathed Harry Wheatley. 'It's fucking empty! It's fucking, fucking empty!'

'Allison Hardbury to Control,' Allison called over the radio, trying to steady her nerves, her heart beating out of control as Harry did a jig.

'Come in Allison.'

'The boot of Sergeant Summers' car is empty. I repeat, the boot of Sergeant Summers' car is empty. Over. The boot's empty, over, over.'

'Well thank fucking Christ for that,' whispered Control.

In the ops room Frieda sat down suddenly on the nearest seat available, her knees weak. Percy Hanson and Pete Phillips immediately did the same.

'Thank fuck for that,' murmured Pete Phillips.

It took Frieda a few seconds to respond. She stood up again.

'But we still don't know where Susan and those two London bastards are,' she said. 'We're not out of the woods yet.'

'They're on the run,' Percy noted, also standing up. 'They'll probably try to nick another car – probably have, already.'

'Yes, but then what? They either have to try to ram through a roadblock or go to cover somewhere.'

Percy stepped up the map of Wellbury. He tapped it.

'Plenty of hiding places along the river,' he said. 'I could take a unit and flush them out if they're hiding somewhere there.'

'They're townies, Percy,' Frieda pointed out, tired. 'Their first instinct will be to get indoors somewhere. If they hadn't already used the Blue Bliss I might think they would be stupid enough to try there again.'

'We've got the Blue Bliss covered. I ordered Foxtrot Seven to back up the other unit there.'

Frieda paused and turned to look at him.

'Foxtrot Seven? But that was supposed to be with Frank.'

Percy looked stunned.

'I told Control only to use a unit that wasn't already in action,' he protested.

Frieda grabbed her radio.

'Control, has Sergeant Summers reported in yet?'

'No, ma'am, his radio's still not answering. Nor is Constable Gregson's. Last contact was from the house in Glenbourne Avenue.'

'Glenbourne Avenue? Control, get Foxtrot Seven back there at once! And radio the other unit that's supposed to be with

Frank. Find out what the hell is happening there.'

'We ain't fashion models, you know,' said the driver of Foxtrot Seven as he stood next to his patrol car while Phil Walthers took photographs.

'Of course not, constable,' Phil Walthers assured him in the manner of a journalist agreeing entirely with what the other said, whatever the truth. 'But this is a most newsworthy event. One cannot argue but that there is a public interest. It is my duty to inform my readers of such events.'

'Well, since you put it that way,' the driver of Foxtrot Seven said, pulling in his stomach and pulling back his shoulders, unaware that Phil Walthers was carefully making sure that the Blue Bliss was strongly shown in the background.

After all, what he had said was true, but a little innocent advertising was hardly against the ethics of journalistic reportage, was it?

'Foxtrot Seven, Foxtrot Seven,' crackled the radio on the driver's seat. 'Return immediately to Glenbourne Avenue. Proceed with caution. There have been reports of gunfire.'

'Oh, shit,' muttered the driver of Foxtrot Seven as he scrambled towards the driver's door, his partner rushing from the doors of the Blue Bliss.

Phil Walthers caught several shots of the action.

'I saved him, didn't I?' gasped Jean, a trickle of blood dripping down from her mouth along her chin. 'I did save him, didn't I? He's okay, isn't he? Frank?'

Her eyes were glowing, her head feverish, shivering as she lay in Cecil Park's lap and looked up at him, pleading, her little hands clutching at his shirt, a red stain spreading across her blouse.

'Of course you did, my love, of course you did,' Cecil said, smoothing her hair gently, his eyes wet, trying not to look at a softly crying Gertie, Frank's white face in her lap, his eyes closed, the white contrasting with the bright red of the blood that was slowly ceasing to run down the side of his face. Her pistol lay alongside. She didn't need it after she had shot Hovis.

'I did it,' repeated Jean. 'I walked on water, didn't I, dad? Dad? Dad, are you there?'

'Be still my love,' Cecil begged her. 'The ambulance will be here soon. You need to keep your strength up.'

'I walked on water, Dad,' Jean whispered, her eyes turning towards the ceiling and beyond that towards the heavens.

'I didn't mean it,' Campbell whispered, kneeling at the doorway. 'I was trying to stop him. Mugsy. I was trying to stop Mugsy. I didn't know they were real. Honest, I didn't know they were real.'

At the police station Percy Hanson answered his phone to find a perplexed Eric Johns on the other end.

'I've got two Frenchies in reception,' he said. 'From some place called the Loire Valley, wherever that is. Their English isn't very good, but from what I can understand they're saying you ordered an enema?'

A few miles away at the Blue Bliss Phil Walthers looked at the open back of his camera in disbelief. He could only presume that, because of the excitement, he had made the most elemental mistake a journalist-photographer could make. It was a disaster.

He had forgotten to load his beloved pre-digital camera with film.

They found Susan several hours later. Frieda had come to 70 Glenbourne Avenue to take personal charge. The ambulances had come and gone. Nobody had thought of searching the garage or garden shed until then. Susan was faint from fear and shock. She managed to rally her spirits one last time.

'Bloody Frank, eh,' she whispered to Frieda as she helped her around the house to a waiting ambulance. 'Typical man, never there when you want him to be.'

Frieda tried to smile at her, concealing her tears. But she couldn't speak.

The Funeral

It was on a Wednesday two weeks later that the new and young choir of St Mary's Junior School in Old Merrick gathered together in the church from which the school had originally gained its name. An enthusiastic new music teacher had decided that the cherubic youngsters should learn the more traditional hymns of their culture in the little time left before they became unruly teenagers with time only for the latest manufactured boy or girl band, and music that sounded like a mental retard repetitively banging a brick against a tin sheet.

The teacher hadn't planned on their singing at this service, but when it had turned out that their practice was likely to overlap with the service it seemed only sensible to combine the two events.

The children were dressed in red cassocks and white surplices, angelic faces eager to prove that the hard practice they had undertaken over the past few months was now about to provide results which they could be proud of. They understood it would be a funeral they would be singing at, but only at a very superficial level. To their minds this was a dress rehearsal for Sunday evening service when they would first publicly reveal their prowess. Someone had said that there might even be television cameras from a television programme from the BBC.

They took little notice of the main mourners, two ancient men, two women surely almost as old, and a somewhat younger one, all dressed in black. Some of the girls noted that the younger woman needed recourse to a handkerchief during the more emotive hymns, and concluded that these tears were a result of a passionate and tragic love affair with whoever it was in the coffin. This happy thought engaged their minds for all of a few seconds before their attention returned to their own pre-occupations.

Gertie, in her early twenties, was already over the hill in the minds of ten and eleven year-olds.

At another time the two "older" women, Frieda and Susan, might have reacted with dismayed incredulity at this notion of their advanced years, but on this day and occasion they would have struggled to show more than mild surprise and little interest.

Their mien was totally alien to that of the bright-eyed and glowing children. They had adopted the stance of those for whom the church and service were something they had once grown up with, and wished to pay the proper respect they felt due, but at the same time not quite sure that they could remember how things were supposed to go and not wishing to embarrass themselves, their responses read automatically and tonelessly from the missals in front of them, joining in the hymns with the quiet and understated reverence of people who fear their voices might, if raised too loud, make somewhat of a mockery of the solemn event.

They stood. They knelt. They sat. They sang. They murmured the prayers and responses. The vicar preached a short sermon praising the life of someone he had never known, but whose positive character and traits were exalted to the small congregation. Then they stood again. Knelt. Sang. Murmured low responses. And came towards the end of the brief service to commemorate the end of a life.

The two parties, those of mourners and choir, shared a common emotion when the vicar announced the final hymn prior to the procession to the newly dug grave, that of relief. Relief, for the mourners, of a necessary but painful service, relief for the choir of approaching the end without having made any major or obvious mistakes. And thus it was that they took up their oral cudgels to do justice to this last task, and the words flowed through the old church with a gentle power and emotion which the young voices could feel if not understand.

"Abide with me ... fast falls the eventide,

The darkness deepens... Lord with me abide

When other helpers fail and comforts flee,

Help of the helpless, oh, abide with me ..."

Gertie's handkerchief was pressed into more use by the time they reached the seventh stanza.

"I fear no foe, with Thee at hand to bless,

Ills have no weight and tears no bitterness.

Where is death's sting? Where, grave, thy victory?

I triumph still if Thou abide with me."

As the hymn came to its end the vicar stepped down from the pulpit and the pall bearers stepped from the pews to bear the coffin to its resting place. The choir stayed behind as the small procession of mourners moved out of the front doors of the church, down the side, past a mausoleum and ancient tombstones, the cemetery almost perversely celebrating summer in its greenery, and the occasional colour of fresh flowers on a neatly tended grave.

'Ashes to ashes,' intoned the vicar as the coffin was lowered into the newly dug hole.

And dust to dust. Whether any of those there were really

listening and heard the rote would lie in their unspoken thoughts.

When the vicar had finished Cecil Park stepped up first to pick up a handful of soil and let it fall gently onto the coffin, the others following suit one by one as their proximity prompted. Once this ceremony of leave-taking was completed Cecil Park stopped for a polite word of thanks to the vicar, who then hurried away to his other duties.

Cecil Park turned to Frieda.

'It was very good of you to come, Inspector,' he said. 'Especially since ... well, it was all my fault, really. Everything. Everything.'

'No, Mr Park, it wasn't your fault,' Frieda replied in her firm Inspector's voice. 'You never planned it or wanted it. Ultimately it came down to the two men calling themselves Campbell and Hovis. But it's over now.' She paused. 'We're going for a drink at the Hangmans, if you'd like to come along.'

Cecil Park almost flinched at the name of the pub off Heading Square.

'No, thank you. Mr Brown has kindly offered me a lift to the railway station. I'm packed, I have my ticket. But thank you all the same. It is very kind of you.'

They nodded goodbyes and the three black-clad women watched the two "ancient" men walk away.

'Frank would have loved the singing,' Susan said wistfully, 'especially Abide With Me, that was beautifully done.'

'I was thinking of that when they sang Guide me, O Thou Great Jehovah', Frieda said. 'Football supporters use much the same tune when they taunt the opposition fans, when their team is losing and they've gone quiet. They use the words, "You aren't singing any more". I couldn't help but think that Frank would have found the temptation difficult to resist. Though perhaps not on this occasion.'

The thought silenced them for a while. Finally Frieda broke the silence.

'Come on. It's been ages since I was in a pub this early in the day.'

Gertie sipped at her gin and tonic in the Hangmans in Heading Square. Susan sat next to her, Frieda opposite.

'I hate funerals,' commented Frieda as lightly as she could. It came out as a dirge.

The others did not reply.

'All for nothing,' Gertie finally said. 'All for a fake.'

'I'm surprised Cecil wanted her buried in Wellbury,' Susan noted.

'Her best performance, he said,' Frieda added. 'It certainly had us fooled.'

She picked up her drink and took a sip.

'Have you been able to find out anything more about her?' asked Susan.

Frieda put her drink down.

'Orphaned at twelve,' she recited as if from an official document. 'Daughter of two actors, always on the road, apparently already a bit of a tearaway then. When they died she was taken in by an elderly great-aunt who could hardly handle her. Charged with several offences from shop-lifting to assaulting a police officer. The great-aunt died when she was seventeen. God knows how that affected Jean. She took to the road and, by all accounts, disappeared until a few years later when she appeared in a minor part in some play or other. I can only guess that she got in touch with friends of her parents, she had no family at all left by then. And no further criminal record until she turned up in Wellbury. And, if you think about it, you could argue that her impersonation of a French police officer was not really a crime. More a prank.'

'A prank?' asked Susan, surprised.

Frieda grimaced.

'As Frank put it, she was a cartoon character. The sum of all our pre-conceptions. If we had tried to take her to court on a charge of impersonating a police officer the jury would kill themselves laughing at us.' She added softly: 'She was only twenty-four.'

'Was her name really Jean Candour?' asked Susan.

'Her name was Jean Candour, yes. Her father's name was Henry Smith. He changed it to Candour for some reason. Presumably he thought it a better stage name.'

There was another silence for a few seconds.

'I feel guilty –' Gertie started, and then suddenly stopped.

'For hating her?' prompted Frieda. 'Yes, I know, Gertie, I know. I feel the same way sometimes. I let my emotions get the better of me. All she really was was a child craving affection, in her own way.'

'Frank was the only one who saw through her.'

This brought on another protracted silence of introspection.

'Visiting time in forty-five minutes,' Frieda said finally. 'We've time for another quick one. I'll get them in.'

There was no opposition to this suggestion.

'I phoned the hospital before I left this morning,' Frieda said once she had returned with their drinks, showing no sign that she knew the others would have done exactly the same. 'They say Frank had a relatively good night last night. They're beginning to think he might make a full recovery, physically.'

Another pause.

'They said much the same to me,' Gertie said. 'What worries me is the way they stress the physical side, as if there's something else they don't want to mention.'

'Head wounds can be pretty unpredictable,' Susan pointed out. 'Some people recover without any problems, others, well … They can sometimes seem like a totally different person afterwards.'

'Maybe he'll say his first words today,' Gertie said. It was a suggestion that one of them had made each day for the past week.

'No doubt he'll appreciate the irony when he recovers,' Frieda said. 'The only reason we know that he can speak is because he shouts when he's having his nightmares.'

'He never used to have nightmares, did he?' asked Susan, addressing the question to Gertie, the only one of them who had shared a night with him, even though that had been on his sofa-bed as a guest for two weeks.

'I don't know,' Gertie admitted. 'A couple of times I noticed that his sheets and duvet were all over the place – when I passed his bedroom on the way to the kitchen. I never really thought about it at the time.'

They sipped their drinks and considered this information.

'When he recovers, you said,' Gertie quoted Frieda. She stopped, trying to find the words that could not be spoken. Eventually she settled for 'I wish the doctors were more confident.'

'Fuck the doctors,' said Susan, consuming a third of a gin and tonic in one go. 'I am one. They never know what they're talking about. We'll get him better. Won't we?'

'Course we will,' Gertie said, enthusiastically downing her drink. 'Course we will. We can do it. And it's Frank we're talking about. He's not going to let a silly little bullet get him down, is he?'

Only Frieda failed to agree. Perhaps her position as Detective Inspector with heavy responsibilities allowed her no easy optimism. Or perhaps, because staffing levels were important issues for her, she had to consider the possibility that she might be short of a detective sergeant for some time to come, and, in this case, he might not be coming back. Or perhaps she had just suffered too much the pain of loss in the past to clutch at hopes of the future.

October

There is an old-fashioned second-hand shop in the Old Village in Wellbury. It is the sort rarely seen these days, in these modern times when new goods are cheap and local rubbish dumps easily accessible. It is a shop which contains all the bric-a-brac of other people's lives, unwanted furniture and mementoes of people who have passed on. Wooden tennis rackets, black and white or sepia pictures of anonymous people, some stiffly posed, some smiling. A couple of old typewriters, one large which would once have been some secretary's badge of office, the other in a battered carry-case which might have been a travelling journalist's. Boxes of books, mostly leather-bound and covered in dust. A shop that stands as guardian to the memories of lives that relatives had no longer any use for.

The owner watched as a man studied the goods on offer outside. A youngish man, wearing a slouch hat. Strange, that, a hat on someone so young. It was true that the weather was turning cold, the first days of winter, but not really yet cold enough for a hat. The man moved awkwardly, as if moving was something he wasn't used to, or something he was no longer sure of.

At length he picked up a couple of items, stumbled slowly on the step into the shop and placed them awkwardly on the counter.

'Good choice,' said the owner. 'You don't often find old fishing rods like that these days. All carbon fibre and that sort of thing, these days, plastic looking, if you know what I mean. Those old wooden rods are the genuine thing.'

He paused as the man silently handed over a twenty-pound

note. He was about to ask if he had anything smaller, but decided against it. He handed the man his change.

'Good luck with the fishing,' he said. The man nodded slowly, as if it hurt his head to do so, and made his careful way out.

The fishing rod was as old as the hills. What the man wanted it for was anyone's guess. It could, probably, be still used as a fishing rod, but it would be better suited to a museum. As for the trophy entitled "Best Performance", well, he hadn't been able to get rid of that for years. Nobody wanted "Best Performance" these days.

Frank kneeled slowly, and carefully placed the trophy gently on the grave. It was not yet quite old enough for a gravestone. The earth had yet to settle some.

He remained there for a while, his hands in his lap, looking at the grave. Some anonymous benefactor had placed fresh flowers on the earth.

An elderly verger walking past a short distance away saw the young man in the hat, paused, thought of offering solace in his grief, decided against it, and continued walking.

Frank stood up slowly, as if unsure of his balance. He brought his hand up and took his hat off, standing as if in mute salute. The verger, about to negotiate a turnstile, turned around. It was at a distance, but he thought the young man seemed to have a strange hairstyle, as if part had been plucked out, and part had turned prematurely white.

The man's lips moved. At that distance the verger could not make out the words. He presumed it was a prayer.

'Comedy in tragedy, and tragedy in comedy.' Frank

whispered. 'Goodbye, Jean.'

He paused before adding:

'Rest in peace, my love.'

And then:

'Unless there really is a heaven above, in which case you're making the angels' lives hell. I'd like to think so.'

'I really would like to think so, Jean, my love,' he added, after a pause.

The verger watched as the young man replaced the hat on his head, as if it were an item of clothing he was both unfamiliar with, but also a new part of him, a necessary part of him. He watched as the young man turned and walked slowly in the direction of Wellbury river. For the first time he noticed the fishing rod in the man's hand, a bag slung over his back.

He could not help but feel that there was something slightly disrespectful about popping into a cemetery to visit the dearly departed while on the way to do a bit of fishing. It smacked of an afterthought. One might not hold a person in esteem during their life, but there was a right way and a wrong way to treat those who had passed on, if only for appearances' sake.

But that was the youth of today for you. They didn't understand these things.

Frank sat on an old folding stool he had picked up with the fishing rod. The riverbank was dry, the water in front of him flowing slowly past as if on its way to somewhere but quite happy to enjoy the scenery as it passed.

Alone. At peace. Far from the madding crowd.

Another man appeared, an older man, moving slowly and

easily, as if he too had all the time in the word. He paused, and then sat down some paces away from Frank, close enough to be almost a companion, not close enough to intrude. He said nothing, but placed his rod in a holder and sat looking at the water.

The tears began to pour down Frank's face, slowly, silently, unstoppable.

The other man nodded and continued looking at the water. Sometimes a man needed company, silent company.

With luck some of them recovered. Never fully, of course.

Never fully.

Winter

Christmas came and went. Frank spent it at his parents' house. He had officially returned to work, but Frieda had done her best to ensure that his duties were as light as possible. Even so, his face stayed grim, and he never smiled. It was obvious that he had much time to go before he could be termed as fully recovered.

Gertie was also given time off to visit her parents during the festive season. Susan, with her parents living in Wellbury, celebrated the holiday with her own family. Both families commented on the feeling they had that their daughters were not enjoying themselves, almost as if they wished this time to be over, that there was something missing that they hoped to return to once the celebrations were over.

Frieda was on duty for both Christmas and New Year. Had anyone asked why she would have pointed out that Percy Hanson had done the same the previous year, and this year was her turn. Pete Phillips offered to take on Frank's duties, but Frieda easily brushed this aside by pointing out that crime during the festive season was pretty much limited to domestics, and he didn't want a domestic of his own, did he? Not when the missus was four months' pregnant.

That pretty much removed Pete Phillips' argument. As he said to Eric Johns, 'Fabulous couldn't have put it more diplomatically, almost like Frank would have, you know.'

The statement had been made in the middle of Eric Johns' lunch. The implicit comparison between the twinkle-eyed Frank of old and the drawn, dead-eyed ghost which now roamed the corridors had killed his appetite.

Banquo, alive, but not alive, in the corridors of Wellbury

305

police station.

Frieda found her Christmas and New Year probably more enjoyable than Susan or Gertie. She wasn't plagued by relatives while she sat in her office trying to come to terms with a Frank who appeared to want nothing more than to sit in solitary seclusion on a river bank. The three of them, her, Susan and Gertie, had continued the rota once Frank was out of hospital, but whereas before it had had that tinge of excitement and mischievousness, now it was as if they were nursing a patient who knew about the rota and had no wish to recover.

Two things combined to snap her out of this mental murk.

The first was when she phoned Frank on Christmas morning to wish him a Happy Christmas. His mother answered. Like all mothers she was more than happy to discuss her son.

The second was a visit at Christmas lunchtime from Vic Brown. Christmas and the New Year were some of the few days that the police canteen was closed, officers expected to bring their own refreshments in. For some reason known only to himself, Vic Brown had ordered Christmas Fayre from one of the local Tandoori restaurants for all the officers on duty during this Holy Period.

Vic Brown never let a contradiction get in his way.

'I asked em to do summat special for you, Mrs Inspector,' he told Frieda when entering her eyrie with a box full of evil-smelling foodstuffs. 'Drumsticks, I told em, Mrs Inspector is on duty like, she can't sit down and enjoy a proper meal like as we can. Drumsticks like you can eat wif your and, I told em, and then a fork for the veggies and stuff, none of your bloody chopsticks ere, mate, the Mrs Inspector is a civilised lady, know what I mean?'

Frieda could not suppress a smile. Vic Brown, taken all in all, was totally bloody useless. But he had made her smile, and no doubt the officers below were celebrating his largesse, however much it might have been paid for by some windfall gained from less than legal entrepreneurship.

So perhaps Victor Brown was not totally useless after all.

'What I sez, Mrs Inspector,' Vic Brown said solemnly, which suggested that he was about to bring forth a diamond of philosophy or a lie, 'what I sez is, well, you've gotta ave a laugh, aven't you? Mr Summers, he was always good for a laugh. Nobody ain't had a sense of humour like him. Only he ain't got that sense of humour no more.'

Frieda couldn't disagree. Frank had lost his humour.

Peter Pan had not grown up. Peter Pan had grown old.

'I'll leave you now, Mrs Inspector,' Vic Brown said. 'I knows how busy you are.'

Frieda watched him leave. She picked up a drumstick and bit into it. She was surprised at how good it tasted. Perhaps lacking something of the Noël ambience, but tasty as hell. Nothing wrong with curry at Christmas.

As she slowly enjoyed the strange Yule-tide meal she came to a decision.

Two decisions.

Firstly Frank would just have to get back to being the old Frank they all knew and loved, even if she had to kick his backside every day until he agreed to do so.

Secondly the rota was out. It had been fun, but, and much as Frank might have enjoyed having three girlfriends at the same time, they couldn't go on forever like this. He was using it to avoid making a decision, any decision. She would have a word with the other two as soon as the New Year had settled in. There was just no other way.

Frank was going to have to choose. Susan, Gertie or herself.

Whether he liked it or not.

It would be for his own good.

End of Book Three

Other novels by Bill Dughaille:

The FFSG series (aka the Wellbury Chronics)

Summers

The first in the FFSG series.

Detective Sergeant Frank Summers is a man on a mission: to keep his head down, stay out of trouble and enjoy the relaxed atmosphere of the easy-going, genteel town of Wellbury, his new posting. It's a town just made for him, where, he believes, even the criminals take bank holidays off. But, while perceptive in his professional life, he tends to miss the subtleties in his private life. In this case he fails to realise that his own tranquillity is being threatened by three women and a philanderer. The fact that the women in question are his boss, his constable and the local pathologist adds just the touch of danger to his life that he had hoped to avoid. The philanderer has been dead several decades. The women are very much alive. And ticking.

The Eighty-five-percenters

The second in the FFSG series.

Detective Sergeant Frank Summers is faced with an unexpected crisis as the staid citizens of the genteel town of Wellbury rapidly descend into disorganised anarchy after a sociology professor announces on radio that eighty-five percent of the population will die in a coming cull. The prediction appears to be coming true as apparently total strangers are felled one by one according to a list of the ten-most-disliked Wellburians, from nagging neighbours to estate agents ... and the police, at a poorly performing number ten. But Frank fails to realise that there is a graver danger closer to home. Three women have decided that he is their responsibility: his boss, his constable and the local pathologist have agreed to become best of enemies. Now they intend to re-arrange his fate the way it should be. And they aren't asking anyone's permission.

Jokers

The fourth in the FFSG series.

The doctors have pronounced Detective Sergeant Frank Summers physically fit following recovery after his shooting, but his colleagues fear that his sense of humour was extracted along with the bullet. They are, as always, more than willing to interfere in his life in the pursuit of a good cause. If that wasn't enough, a bunch of criminals calling themselves the Joker Gang are laughing at him, the university students are creating mayhem during their rag week, and someone called The Shocker is trying to kill him. The only advantage is that it take his mind off of the ultimatum the three women in his life have given him, one that he has only until the Sunday to resolve. Or leave town.

Prophecies

The fifth in the FFSG series.

Detective Sergeant Summers is under a hex, otherwise known as his colleagues. First they don't want him to get married, then it is imperative it must happen. Then they decide that a prophecy has been made which threatens the wedding. They don't believe in prophecies, but aren't sure that prophecies understand that. So they'll have to Do Something About It. And if their bumbling efforts aren't enough to ensure he never makes it to the altar, he has to cope with visiting aliens and resident ghosts. He does have tiny Squishy to protect him, but what match can even this plucky little kitten be against a prospective mother-in-law?

Loonymoon

The sixth in the FFSG series.

The Inspectors Summers have tied the knot and embarked on their honeymoon in a small family-run hotel in Normandy. She has very definite ideas of what she wants out of a honeymoon: to set a seal on their love, and to form a foundation for life-long devotion. He just wants to nick a French police officer's kepi. He had a Bobby's helmet nicked from him once by a French girl while he was on crowd duty one New Year's Eve in London, and now he intends to return the favour. Neither is about to achieve their aim unless they can solve the mystery of the woman in the bath and the missing heroin. Which means pitting their minds against the French Inspectors Simenon. That's Mr and Mrs Simenon, whose marriage has gone beyond the rocks and is now beating itself to death against humdrum reality. One or either or both or neither could be the guilty crumpet. More importantly, is their marriage a portent of what could become of the Loonymooners? Ultimately the decisive question could well be: which side do the peas go?

Others:

The Window

Jim Allbright, ex-bobby and now easy-going window washer, innocently responds to an advert for window washing placed in the newspaper by the local council. The response is a torrent of paperwork, political correctness and a computer system doing exactly what it was told to do, but not quite what was intended. But if the system cannot be beaten, the interchange of letters can be used to have a little fun and get to know some of the people struggling behind it. There's Sandi, who signs herself as "(pp the Administrator)"; her four-year old little angel Helen; Graham, a shadowy computer programmer who definitely has too much time on his hands, and a slew of Project Managers and Senior Administrators eager to ensure standards are upheld no matter how many problems they create. Against a run of bad luck and circumstances Jim and Sandi aim to meet up one day, eventually. Hopefully. The window might even get washed. Maybe.

Diary of a Sane Man

In a cross between 'Last Of The Summer Wine' and 'One Flew Over The Cuckoo's Nest', set against a backdrop of the brave new world of New Labour's end of honeymoon, Fred is the Last Cynical Optimistic Realist.

Believing that he's found the perfect niche – three square meals a day plus all the newspapers he can read just for occasionally pretending to be mad – he's not going to be the one to rock the apple cart. Oh, no.

Safe from the wiles of women and the woes of the world, he's not going to rock the boat. Oh, no.

No, he's just going to sit and observe, and comment quietly on the insanity of life outside.

Well, maybe just little one tug of the loose strand of wool on life's jersey ...

Did you know they elected a monkey as mayor in Hartlepool?

The Weekend At Longwood

A whodunnit in the classic sense, set against the backdrop of World War II and the trials, tribulations and romances of nine suspects.

A group of friends get together during the last weekend of August 1939 at the rural retreat named Longwood, just a few miles from Portsmouth. They are there to celebrate the last time they will see Georgina Riley, famed American novelist and socialite, for some time, as she is scheduled to leave for her native New York in order to marry her childhood sweetheart. During the afternoon they good-humouredly assign to each other the most suitable names of the nine muses, the daughters of Zeus and Mnemosyne:

Calliope: the muse of epic poetry and rhetoric

Clio: history

Erato: love poems and mimicry

Euterpe: lyric poetry

Melpomene: tragedy

Polymnia: hymns to the gods and heroes

Terpsichore: dance

Thalia: comedy

Urania: astronomy, astrology and prophecy

The following morning Georgina is discovered in her bedroom covered in blood, her throat slit, barely alive. Her American maid is dead. A tiara Georgina had been flaunting the day before has disappeared.

Detective Inspector Rudman arrives to investigate. But with Georgina in a coma and no solid evidence there is little he can do apart from haunt their lives. With Germany's invasion of Poland a week later they disperse across the land, some to the air-force, some to the army, others to reserved civilian jobs.

But Rudman does not give up. Wherever they are he can be found. Whatever other duties he is tasked to, he will find time to keep tabs on them. Whatever the defeats and victories of the Allied cause, he has only one aim: to find the person responsible for the murder done that weekend in Longwood.

The war ends; some of the Muses have survived, some not. Some have prospered, some married, some matured, others have found despair. And then comes invitation to spend another weekend at Longwood. The message is that Rudman has found the evidence he has been looking for.

And so one of the surviving couples motor slowly down to Portsmouth, remembering the original weekend, the trials and the tribulations of the past years, and wonder: what will be revealed during the coming weekend at Longwood?

Firelight

A modern-day tale of an ordinary family gathering at Christmas; the good, the bad, the dysfunctional and the forgotten.

George Browne and his wife Winifred have retired to a large, run-down pile in the country. Rumour has it that it was once the abode of a mad aristocratic family with a penchant for Satanism, and that both they and their victims still haunt the corridors. Other rumours are that it was a lunatic asylum for much of the nineteenth and twentieth century, and bodies of the inhabitants are buried around the large gardens in unmarked graves.

The Brownes are an unremarkable retired couple who, depending on who you might ask, have bought it as an investment, or alternatively as somewhere with enough bedrooms to accommodate their children, grand-children, and the little baby great-grandchildren. Too often in the past excuses have been made at special times, the most common of which has been of the "I don't want to put you to any trouble" variety. That excuse can no longer hold water.

Now it is approaching Christmas. Winter has set in, but the house is snug with oil heaters and real fires. As the various relations arrive, or don't arrive, it becomes clearer why invitations might have been refused in the past. The men of the family believe in having their way. The women of the family are strong-willed in their own different ways, and have various means of getting what they want.

The guests of the family - friends, boyfriends, girlfriends, wives and husbands - discover that their partners have a totally different side to them as the explosive hatreds of long-nurtured fights and feuds simmer to the surface before quickly boiling over.

One evening Winifred Browne encourages them to each tell a story as they sit in the lounge with the large fire warming them, the television off, no access to broadband, computers or mobile connections. Reluctantly at first they begin. As each evening passes: with different members taking turns, they announce in stories the feelings and hopes they cannot voice in public.

Finally it's the turn of Winifred Browne. Her story will be the one that tells them who they are, where they come from, and maybe why they have turned out the way they have.

For further details on these visit:

www.dughaille.info

www.ingramcontent.com/pod-product-compliance
Lightning Source LLC
Chambersburg PA
CBHW071101250626
47159CB00002B/548